Tinsel, Texts and Temptation

By

Glyn Timmins

Tinsel, Texts and Temptation

Julia Carter disliked Christmas. She didn't hate it, she just disliked it.

For thirty-something Julia Christmas had begun to epitomise life, big on hype and expectation, low on delivery. She was ten years into a marriage that had begun to grind along like the wheel-rim of a burst tyre on the long, pot-holed road of marriage. The only glimmer of light on the horizon was Andy, the good-looking, glib-tongued young man who worked for a rival company. With Andy she was a few weeks into a blossoming relationship of snatched moments, steamy texts and breathless anticipation.

Julia felt bad … and good! Bad because her husband hadn't done anything particularly wrong, it was just that he had struggled to do anything particularly right over the past few months. Bad because she didn't feel the way she did when he had swept her off her feet more than a decade before. Bad because, her marriage was becoming like the Christmases of her childhood, a fading myth based on warm, long passed memories. She felt good because a new man had stepped in to massage her faltering ego and tickle her more or less redundant fancy.

Her titillating, text driven romance thrived as Christmas raced relentlessly into view. The tinsel and glitter of the season added sparkle and spice to her dangerous game. Every lingering meeting brought a decision about her future closer. Julia craved the happiness and light-headed thrill she had felt when love had first come to visit, and she was sure that Andy heralded its return … wasn't she? If only there was someone, somewhere she could take fully and completely into her confidence, someone who could share her joy and her pain, someone to show her the way … but she had no one close enough to take on that massive role in her life just now.

As Christmas week began it was as if a countdown timer had begun. With each passing second Julia was drawn towards the decision that would shape her life for the years that lay ahead of her. It was a strange and perplexing week, a sequence of days that seemed to have almost been taken out of her control. A series of messages on her 'phone began to take her places she didn't expect to go. It was a week that would flick open some of the pages in the book of life and invite to her to read what she would from it; but what, if any, lessons would she learn?

My thanks go to Christine and Christopher Burns for the cover design and photograph, to Natalie Timmins for proof reading and editing the story and to Julie Bishop Bailey for her unstinting and steadfast support for this project from the start and for discovering my abandoned draft of the story and making me do something with it.

Dedicated to the Memory of Louis Gamon

(1947-2013)

A quiet, unassuming, gentle family man, who liked to laugh and enjoy the simple pleasures of life. A great friend and brother-in-law. Sadly missed but never forgotten by those who loved him.

Table of Contents

MONDAY – Getting Ready 8

MONDAY – Christmas Party...16

MONDAY – Stepping Close to the Line 25

TUESDAY -Taxi Ride...39

TUESDAY - Special Delivery 57

TUESDAY - A Quick Drink After Work...69

TUESDAY – Diversions in Place...87

TUESDAY - Wake Up Call..107

WEDNESDAY - What's Love Got To Do With It? 124

THURSDAY - Thursday's Child 160

THURSDAY – With My Body I Thee Worship 181

FRIDAY – Freezers and Fairy Tales 189

FRIDAY – No Glass Slipper, No Coaches and No Balls 202

SATURDAY – Shopping Spree..223

SATURDAY - Jean and Ken..239

SUNDAY: Bloody Sunday...262

SUNDAY - The Nightmare Before Christmas.................................276

SUNDAY – Making a Statement...294

CHRISTMAS DAY – Opening the Present.....................................306

BOXING DAY: Stepping into the Future..321

Tinsel, Texts and Temptation

by

Glyn Timmins

MONDAY – Getting Ready

Julia Carter disliked Christmas. She didn't hate it, she just disliked it. It wasn't the result of some traumatic seasonal crisis in her life. It wasn't the time of year when mum and dad had discovered they simply couldn't live together any more. It wasn't that Santa had failed to deliver the much cosseted dolls house to an eager, wide-eyed five-year old girl. It wasn't the fact that every romantic film she had watched since adolescence promised snowfall on Christmas Eve and nature had folded her arms contemptuously and declined to deliver, year on year. It was none of that.

As she sat in front of the mirror on her dressing table she dabbed lotions and creams at her face, squinting to see if she had acquired any more crows feet, making the outcome of the exercise inevitable and her disappointment unavoidable. That in turn made her screw up her nose and frown and the effect was the opposite she had strived for. "Mirror, Mirror on the wall, who is the fairest of them all?" "Julia, Julia look away, Snow White you ain't, it's not your day."

With a grunt of disapproval Julia drew her head back from the mirror and continued to dab at her face with her armoury of youth endowing products; the same commodities that, ironically, caused her husband, Jim, to age prematurely, when he now and again came across the till receipts.

Christmas was hard work for a woman with a family, she reflected as she glared accusingly at a tiny but expensive tub of face-cream. There was the planning, the present buying, the arguments with Jim over the amount she was spending on relatives they rarely saw and who he invariably disliked in any case. Then there was the wrapping, the cooking and worst of all the office Christmas outing. It was Julia's heartfelt view that she had to spend a year socialising, chatting and sharing small talk with her 'friends' from the office, which made the enforced festivity of the staff do painful and tedious. To Julia it simply meant her wasting precious hours watching people she wasn't that keen on in the first place, getting pissed and obnoxious in an ever-ascending spiral of excess.

This year, however, Julia had stood firm. She had

declined the agony of the actual staff Christmas meal, avoiding the stilted conversation, forced merriment and worst of all the obligatory paper hats. In truth she had made some feeble excuse involving her daughter's school play, but she felt that the deception was at least emotionally, if not financially justified. She had no desire to squander thirty quid on a predictable menu of re-warmed, rubberised fodder that was, to the palate, the equivalent of gnawing on the corner of a low quality rug.

Nevertheless it was for her appearance at the after-party that she tugged mercilessly with the straighteners at her shoulder-length brown hair, pulling her head roughly towards her shoulder. It was equally fair to say that she liked this Christmas no better than any she had experienced since she had married Jim, ten years before.

She glared disapprovingly at her reflection, the beginnings of a snarl twitching on her upper lip. In truth, she was being very harsh on herself. Her hair shone, her skin was smooth and bore little evidence of the ravages of time that she so feared, and if she chose to smile her face was endearingly pretty. The 'smoky' eye shadow and 'lush curls' mascara she had so carefully and patiently applied had gently accentuated the deep blue of her eyes.

"Mirror mirror on the wall, will I be fairest at the ball?"

"Julia, Julia now you're done, out of ten, I'd give you one!"

(What a crude and brash looking glass it had turned out to

be.)

Julia stood up and turned to the full-length mirror on her wardrobe door. She cocked her head momentarily to one side as she examined herself up and down, standing fully made up and properly coiffeured, wearing only her under garments. Sucking in her tummy very slightly she looked at her trim figure, adorned in her new navy satin underwear and some sheer black stockings. The grimace faded slowly and shyly into a grin. A little sunshine poked out from behind the cloud that had sat above her shoulder, whilst she had simmered in front of the dressing table mirror. 'Looking good, girl,' she mused indulgently.

After a few seconds admiring herself she pulled on her 'party frock', a flattering dark navy, knee length dress, and stepped into her heels. The first few steps she took thereafter were a little lacking in grace, but it was a far, far better thing she was doing … than she actually wanted to. She emerged from the bedroom tottering like a newborn deer. Heels, particularly of this height, were not part of her usual attire, but as her calves stretched out sexily beneath her knees and she felt her bottom lift a little, her gait and confidence gained a simultaneous swagger, which manifested itself about the hips. She was lubricated, stretched, pulled, sprayed and flattened in all the right places and, despite her reservations about the party, she felt good about herself.

As she tottered down the hall her faltering steps continued to gather rhythm and pace. By the time she reached the living room door she was sashaying like a catwalk model. She stopped momentarily by the open door and popped her head into the living room, where Jim was watching TV.

"I'm ready to go," she said, unable to beat back a sultry smile which stretched vampishly across her sumptuously glossed lips. She readied herself for Jim's breathless reaction to her glamorous makeover.

"Right," he said airily, his eyes fixed on the TV screen, "I'll just put this on record and we can be off."

However, as he turned towards his wife he paused momentarily and his eyes briefly swept up and down the gorgeous, pouting sex kitten that stood before him in the hallway. There was an element of confusion and disorientation in his eyes as Julia blinked coyly at him. He raised his eyebrows briefly but chose not to waste words on articulating his thoughts, or complimenting his wife on her appearance. He simply pursed his lips and gave an approving nod as he brushed past her into the hall. He swept the car keys from the hall table into his hand and stopped, turning to Julia, who stood silently in the hallway, positively glowing. His lips parted as if to speak, Julia's heart beat a little faster in anticipation of the compliments that Jim seemed poised to bestow. She wondered tremulously whether he would reprove her for making too much effort for a pub full of lairy, drink-addled men.

"Do you think you need a coat Julia?" were the actual words that trickled innocuously from his mouth.

Julia shook her head disbelievingly, the twinkling smile fading to a resigned frown, like a single grey cloud passing over a sunny sky.

As she manoeuvred herself into the passenger seat of Jim's car she once again questioned why she had even agreed to go to the *drink* after the works Christmas meal. She knew that people, who ordinarily should know better, would be loud and lewd, in fact it felt as if it was expected behaviour. Julia was not a prude or a killjoy, she just had her boundaries, and trespassers weren't welcome. However, she harboured one dubious reason for going, and she was far from proud of it, although Jim's underwhelming response to her appearance did nothing to intensify the sensation.

In fact, now, as the car zipped through the dark and empty night-time streets she felt a tingle of expectation and nervousness tickle the lining of her stomach. She stared directly ahead avoiding any chance of eye contact with Jim. There was no idle conversation between Jim and Julia, such chatter was a rarity these days. Instead they let a bland radio station fill the air with its inane prattling and insipid muzak. Jim and Julia simply sat in a silent bubble filled with their own, separate thoughts.

Finally Jim swung the car into a busy car park, lit by a dazzling fluorescent light. He sat quietly, staring frontwards, the car's engine purring efficiently as Julia fumbled with her handbag, such as it was. She yanked the visor down and took one last critical look at herself in the dim light of courtesy mirror. She dabbed a finger at the corners of her mouth for no obvious reason.

"I'll get a taxi home," she said matter-of-factly, half glancing at her husband. "I've no idea when they'll call this shindig a night."

Jim nodded with an air of disinterest and dutifully turned towards Julia to offer her a kiss on the cheek. She pulled away, narrowing her eyes:

"Don't Jim, you'll smudge my make-up," she admonished.

Jim rolled his eyes and shrugged his shoulders but didn't protest. His eyes returned to their forward facing position and his hands took their place firmly on the steering wheel.

Julia carefully removed the seatbelt before extricating herself from the car, unfurling her body from the velour seat into the cold, grey car park of the pub. Her high heels lifted her above the roof of the vehicle and she had to bend her knees awkwardly to drop to a position where she could see through the passenger window.

"Have you got your 'phone?" asked Jim, eager to drive away, poised over the wheel like a racing driver in poll position watching for the green light.

"Yes, and don't forget to pick up Katie from mum's on the way home. Straight to bed when she gets in. No DVDs," ordered Julia.

"Yeah, ok," grunted Jim, his right foot hovering impatiently above the accelerator pedal.

"See you later," said Julia, with the faintest of smiles.

There was a crunching noise as the wheels of the car moved slowly across the gravelly surface of the car park towards the exit. Julia turned carefully and a little precariously towards the entrance the pub. Even as a liberated, confident woman she still didn't like walking into a pub on her own. There was something awkward and uncomfortable about it. Tonight that sense of slight discomfort was increased by a sense of the uncharted.

MONDAY – Christmas Party

There was so much noise as she walked in. Music blared; a thumping bass-line dwarfed a barely coherent melody. Competing, or rather attempting to compete with this and, in fact, each other, were the raised and raucous voices of as many people as could be corralled into a large, hot room without completely demolishing the fire regulations.

The atmosphere was friendly and vibrant in an overwhelming kind of way. The air smelt of a heady mix of of perfume, beer, cheap after-shave and festive hedonism; most of the revellers packed into the pulsating pub were inoffensively sliding towards some degree of sensory deprivation.

The music continued to blare in the background, a seasonal loop of Christmas classics, though little heed was being paid to the guttural throb of the sound system. The bar was situated in the centre of the pub and that was where Julia was headed as she twisted herself between the unmoving clumps of people oblivious to her presence. All she could hear now was a continuous clinking of glasses and bottles as drinks were passed across the bar to waiting punters, who stood three deep in the queue to be served, waving bank notes vainly at the beleaguered bar staff. Most of them were suitably adorned in some way to reflect this happiest time of the year, but there was a weariness etched into their sweaty faces that set them apart from the exhilarated partygoers on the other side of the counter.

Someone reached out and grabbed Julia's arm, pulling her into a tiny space occupied by a small group of females. Someone else thrust a glass of almost undrinkable *anti-freeze*, masquerading as white wine, into her hand. The girls from the office had rescued Julia from tidal flow of bodies dragging her to the safety of the island they had formed on this section of pub carpet.

In a short time Julia had settled into the small huddle of thirty-something women, who laughed and chattered, gossiped and sniped at the people outside their clique.

"Where have you been? We thought you weren't coming," said Alison as she drained her wine and seamlessly picked up a bottled vodka mix to replace it.

"I did have second thoughts about coming out," shouted Julia, adjusting her tone to the competition from the ambient din around her, "but I didn't want to let you girls down. How was the meal?"

"Dreadful," summarised Helena, "the food was rubbish, David made a crappy speech, and the crawlers made themselves look idiots laughing like hyenas at his pathetic jokes."

"Same every year, that's why I bailed out," said Julia plaintively.

"Think I'll do the same next year," interjected the fourth

member of the group, Dawn, a little drunkenly, "boring bunch of knob-heads, all of 'em".

"Your round Dawn," announced Helena, picking on the weakest member of the herd without conscience.

Dawn drew her head back a fraction as if to aid her to focus on the face from which the command had just been issued. She blinked and her eyes rotated slightly fixing at a point either side of her nose giving her the appearance of having ever so slightly crossed eyes. Slowly she nodded in acknowledgement.

"The young barman wearing the furry antlers fancies you," teased Helena, straight-faced, "you're in there."

"He won't know what's hit him," slurred Dawn, staggering determinedly to the bar, her slight frame bouncing off a couple of young men, minding their own business, on route.

"Fancy a fag?" said Julia to Helena conspiratorially.

As a secret smoker Julia had to pick her moments, and her friends, so as not to reveal this naughtily illicit vice to the wider world.

"OK, Dawn's going to be a while, we can sneak out to the smoking shelter for five minutes. Alison?"

"Filthy bloody habit," admonished Alison, " and I'm surprised at you Julia. You're such a goody two-shoes, I don't know what's got into you lately."

"I think we know *who* would like to get into her," sniped Helena, much to Julia's immediate chagrin.

"Shut up Helena," she snapped, " are we having a cigarette or not?"

Helena smiled broadly, raising her eyes knowingly at Alison. Julia rummaged in her tiny handbag, which was little more than a purse on steroids, for her pack of ten cigarettes that fitted so neatly and discreetly into the clutch. As she did so a tinkling message tone seeped into the surrounding racket.

"Is that your 'phone?" asked Helena.

Julia nodded as she deftly moved her keys aside using only her forefinger and retrieved the small, sleek, white smartphone that had beckoned her with such immediacy. The irresistible need to respond to the summons of a mobile phone is quite Pavlovian, and whilst Julia fell short of salivating at the sound of the little bell, she demonstrated an involuntary eagerness to feed on its content.

"Was it a message?" shouted Helena, keen for Julia to share the detail within.

"I think so," said Julia stabbing her finger at the icons on the screen.

Contained in a message bubble on the glass surface of the handset was the secret reason she had agreed to attend her company's night out, the reason she had preened and prettied herself, the reason she felt so guilty about going. She stared at the mobile 'phone that she held in her hand and felt herself tremble. A mobile 'phone is a collection of tiny circuits and chips encased in a hard plastic shell. It is a handheld computer, an advanced communication device available for the benefit of the masses. Occasionally it doubles as Pandora's box – Pandora's iBox!

Resistance was futile and obediently Julia responded to the flashing icon by tapping nervously on the screen, which rewarded her by revealing that the message was from Andy:

'*Where r u ?*' It asked simply.

The instantaneous need to react to a text message causes a bubble of oblivion to envelop the sender. For those few seconds while she negotiated her reply via the key pad, the music lowered in volume, the ambient babble around her dulled and her friends faded briefly from her immediate consciousness.

'*In the Lion. How long will you be?*'

Julia rescanned the message in the blink of an eye before jabbing the 'send' command with a trembling finger.

As the message swooshed successfully into the beery atmosphere Julia's real-time world began to magically fade back in. The incessant thumping music resumed its former tumult and the screeching volume of chatter intensified as her hearing returned. It took a split second for Julia to refocus on the conversation that was taking place around her, though it took a few seconds more for the words to form into coherent sentences in her distracted mind:

"Sorry, *H* What did you say?" she said straining her ear against the noise that had re-launched its attack on her auditory senses.

"I said was that Jim?"

There was a mischievous glint in Helena's eye as she asked the question, knowing full well that it was unlikely to be Julia's predictable and currently uninspiring husband.

"No," replied Julia honestly, pausing for just a second, caught somewhere between faint embarrassment and girlish thrill, "it was Andy. He wondered where we were, I think he's coming over to meet up with us."

Julia had added the communal aspect to her answer in a weak effort to dilute the relatively obvious implication that it was clearly she that he was coming to see. She experienced a tiny shiver of anticipation at the prospect of sharing time with Andy, a sensation that was quickly washed over with a wave of contrition. Julia over-rode the feeling with a shudder of annoyance. Andy was coming to see *her* and she felt a little dangerous and a little naughty.

Andy was a practiced and self-assured charmer. He looked good in a tousled, boyishly casual sort of way. His manner was confident and engaging, and that attracted its share female attention, but his own high estimate of his sex appeal was, in fact, a little beyond its actual net worth. He had known Julia and her small circle of friends for a number of years, and had even dated some of them, albeit briefly, as had been his way back then. It was only since Julia had moved to work in the same office complex that their casual acquaintanceship had taken a more intriguing turn. Julia was in turn the kind of woman who could be fiercely home loving in one setting but playfully flirtatious in another. Jim knew this about Julia, recognising it as a harmless and innocent aspect of his pretty wife's quirkiness.

Like many a young, married woman, Julia's ego drew occasional sustenance from the warm reassurances of her husband's appreciation and admiration. It was scant excuse for the situation in which Julia currently found herself, more of a mitigation, that this had become an ever less frequent occurrence as the marriage progressed through the years. As the primary source of her self-esteem became ever more barren she had sought nourishment for her self-image elsewhere. Occasionally this led her to take the exchange of flirtatious frippery to a marginally more precarious level. It seemed to get her noticed, and became all the more sweet if it scored her 'points' against someone she considered to be 'competition' or a rival for attention. However, it was in the case of 'randy Andy' that things had strayed significantly beyond the bounds of safety, with the dispassionate assistance of the mobile 'phone and the audacious secrecy of the text message.

For the last few weeks Julia and Andy had taken full advantage of the clandestine safety of the sneaked message, the delete command being the implacable guardian of their indiscretion. The digital revolution had outwitted the French Revolution; this was Dangerous Liaisons gone techno. No parchment scrolls hidden in secret recesses or carried by trusted messengers, no handwritten proclamations of love or lust waiting to be uncovered by jealous spouses or outraged lovers. For Julia and Andy their tryst was set on digitally encoded messages carried on the ether, bouncing unseen in the stratosphere, flowing through the air that everyone breathes, captured securely in a tiny box for which only the recipient holds domain.

Back in the room the 'phone tinkled once more and Julia flushed as Andy's name appeared on the screen. She tried to shield it from Helena's inquisitive stare but it was a hopeless effort.

'Be there in 10. Can't w8, hope ur keeping a space 4 me.'

"You might well blush," hissed Helena through a sneering smile.

"I haven't encouraged him," protested Julia, a little limply.

"Really?" challenged Helena, unconvinced, " we should examine the facts. Fag?"

With that Helena turned on her heel and headed to the side exit through the crowds, who seemed to swell and recede like the tide.

"Hey! Where you going?" called Alison who had been distracted by some unspoken communication with a dark haired man who sat on the edge of a loud group of men in suits and ties.

"Fag," replied Julia, disappearing into the throng in Helena's wake.

"Fag hags," she snarled bitterly, looking to see where Dawn had got to with their drinks.

MONDAY – Stepping Close to the Line

Andy sank the last of his beer from the glass with a self-satisfied gulp.

"Another?" asked a mate as Andy reached forward and placed his glass firmly on the bar.

"No, duty beckons," he replied, a swaggering smile turning the corner of one side of his mouth and raising the opposite eyebrow.

"Home to the *lady*? Waiting for you wearing a welcoming smile and not much else?" leered another member of the group.

"Oh no, she's just going to have to wait. I've been popping charm coins into a different fruit machine for the last couple of weeks, and I think she's about to pay out."

"You dog," said the first male approvingly.

"Not the married piece from the office?" sneered another member of the group, slurping at the green bottle of lager in his hairy hand.

"A gentleman doesn't kiss and tell," smiled Andy gathering his coat with a flourish from a nearby barstool.

"You're not a gentleman," grinned the lager drinker, " and I shouldn't think you've got a kiss out of iron-knickers yet."

"Gentleman or not, I cannot divulge the level of progress with that lady, but shall we just say I like a challenge … very much."

With that Andy swept out of the pub watched with a mixture of envy and admiration by three sets of half-cut eyes.

Despite the crass words exchanged with his cronies at the bar Andy was undeniably attracted to Julia and looked forward to the hastily convened assignation. Though for Julia the decision to step a little closer to the 'line' was a means to challenge the boredom and mundaneness of the daily grind of married life, for Andy it was a flirtation with someone 'out of bounds'. For both, and for their own reasons, it added spice to the recipe of life and kicked back against their sense of being taken for granted, and for the things they unconsciously took for granted themselves.

Andy slunk into the driver's seat of his company car and pulled the seat belt eagerly over his shoulder. He took his mobile from his inside pocket and poked the stand-by button so that the screen lit, reflecting a magnified image of its coloured icons in the windscreen of the otherwise darkened car. He tapped in a message that in a few seconds would bring a flush to Julia's face:

'Be there in 10. Can't w8, hope ur keeping a space 4 me.'

He pressed send with a silly grin etched on his boyish features; 'from text to sex' he thought salaciously as he turned the key. 'Christmas, drink and boredom, what a cocktail of lowered inhibitions that would be,' he mused, contemplating his impending encounter with the pretty, *good girl* from the other firm.

As Andy made the short journey to the 'Lion' the area between his ego and his loin flickered in anticipation. In that same time Julia stood in the smoking shelter with Helena clutching her guilty pleasure cigarette like a life preserver thrown to a drowning woman in a turbulent sea. She didn't speak much while they stood hunched against the cold, sucking the poisonous tar from its paper tube. Instead Julia stood smiling benignly like a happy simpleton. This irked the brash Helena:

"How long is the love muffin going to be?" she snarled, crushing the remnant of her cigarette with the sole of an expensive shoe.

Julia tried to throw her a withering look, but it emerged more like a surprise attack of stomach acid. Helena simply shook her head:

"I hope you know what you're doing," she chided, "shall we go back inside?"

Julia nodded sheepishly, but felt compelled to add:

"I haven't done anything," and as Helena charged back towards the side door of the pub, in a low, barely audible voice she added, "yet."

Julia returned to her cluster of friends to a series of knowing glances, wordless but explicit in the way borne of special female telepathy.

"He's not just coming to see me, he was looking for all of us," protested Julia feebly and red-faced as they stared at her in unison.

She felt a little embarrassed; this was schoolgirl stuff after all, except that the potential ramifications of 'Andy loves Julia' were much greater at this stage of her life. In a way she really didn't mind looking a little foolish. Tonight she stood centre-stage, taking the plaudits of the 'audience' who stood, applauding her re-discovered allure and attractiveness. Helena broke the impasse in the only way she knew how:

"My round, same again?" she asked rhetorically. Without waiting for affirmation she turned neatly on her heel, casting a knowing smile in Julia's direction, before striding purposefully towards the bar where a young barman wore furry reindeer antlers and a very cute smile.

There was a Captain Oates look in her eyes as she appraised the bar tender, they sent a message to her compatriots that said; 'I may be gone some time.'

That left Julia, Alison and Dawn temporarily closing the circle to keep the uninvited at bay. From time to time they had inevitably repelled incursions from a drink-imbued member of a group of male revellers with a mumbled, incoherent offer of drinks and introductions. Now and then they would be accompanied by cringe-worthy chat up lines, suggesting, for example, that the interloper had never had the pleasure of meeting four super-models on break from a photo-shoot. Each attempted infiltration was succinctly and successfully repelled, sending the *invader* skulking back to his eager-eyed, expectant friends, round shouldered and sulky, looking like a chastened schoolboy. In a morose huddle they would mutter darkly, by way of consolation, that they were probably tarts or lesbians anyway.

The three women continued to chat and laugh, but Julia was noticeably distracted, repeatedly checking her watch and looking towards the entrance door to the crowded, noisy pub. This was definitely a man's idea of ten minutes.

Helena returned to the fold clutching the drinks she had gone to collect from the young man in fur antlers. As she handed them round she giggled:

"I think that barman quite fancies me. He's asked what I'm doing when he finishes."

"He probably wants some help collecting the glasses," laughed Dawn.

"Cow," replied Helena simply. "I take it your slathering approach before scared him off."

"He must be all of 25, shame about his failing eyesight at such a young age," Alison remarked cuttingly, to curtail Helena's moment of triumph.

"Whereas you prefer IQ of 25 as opposed to age 25, based on your last boyfriend," countered Helena snidely.

They laughed and clinked their glasses in girlish

solidarity, except Julia who remained quiet and introspective. "He'll be here soon," said Alison condescendingly, complementing the remark with a bittersweet smile.

Julia made no comment but, handing her glass to Dawn, she headed to the *ladies*. Unusually this was a solo trip, no volunteers to make up the usually statutory brace. In the muted confines of the toilets she washed her hands and carefully splashed a little water on her face. She stared into the mirror and gazed intently at her reflection. The noise from outside was little more than a pulsing throb, and it was a little easier to think. Julia was thirty-three. She was a woman of medium height and though not sporty she had an athletically slim frame. She had grown her mid-brown hair long and worn it down for some months now, a neat fringe framing a pretty face, which was complemented by lovely, deep blue eyes. Maybe, and in spite of the assertions of drunken partygoers, Julia wasn't a supermodel but she was a 'nice model' by any standards, the sort of person people noticed, not always on first glance but she had the whiles to quickly merit a second or third glance. The only person who needed convincing of her attractiveness right now was Julia herself.

A slight sensation of guilt suddenly washed over her, sending a tingle down her back that made her her shudder. She shrugged off the sensation but wondered, fleetingly, if she should phone Jim to make sure he was OK. After all, home was generally where her heart was; it was just that occasionally it took a day off. Instinctively she ran her slender fingers over the outside of her clutch purse, the glint of her engagement and wedding ring catching her eye as she did so. The sight of them did nothing to soothe the raging torrent of emotions surging through her veins.

She could feel the square packet of cigarettes and the serrated edges of her keys but not the solid oblong outline of her phone. A mild fit of panic overtook her and she flicked open the bag and rummaged urgently through it. She stood aside as someone entered the toilet and passed anonymously into a cubicle as she frantically searched her bag. This was a micro-bag, no more than a purse with attitude really, and she was not Mary Poppins. There were no deep, magical recesses in which the sturdy, polycarbonate bodied phone could hide.

Returning to the bar Julia couldn't have felt more disoriented or bewildered. A mobile phone is so much more than a means of communication, it's a fashion accessory as vital as shoes or handbag, it's an extension of your personality, it's a friend, it's a vital organ. Without it Julia felt naked, and as she returned to her group of friends, oblivious to her surroundings she failed to notice Andy staring at her 'naked' body. Although he stood talking casually and confidently with Helena, Dawn and Alison, his eyes bored into her as she wriggled vacantly between the other women to create a space in which to stand. The way he stared through her she may as well have been naked. Luckily, at this point, Julia didn't even know Andy was in the room.

Helena was the first to notice Julia's obvious disquiet. "What's the matter? You OK?" she asked with genuine concern.

"Yes, I suppose so. Have you seen my phone?" said Julia fretfully.

"Well not since you last used it," replied Helena anxiously, "have you checked your bag?"

Julia returned the glance of a thousand icicles. The look quickly informed Helena that her well-meaning question ranked as one of the top ten most stupid questions being asked in any British pub at that particular moment. But her sense of pique did not prevent Julia having just one more glimpse into the diminutive clutch purse, just to make sure it hadn't been playing a little trick on her.

"Helena, ring my number on your phone, we might hear where I've put it then," said Julia in a moment of desperate inspiration, the frown temporarily easing from her brow.

"We'd be lucky to hear it in here," commented Alison less optimistically.

Alison had a point, the volume in the pub was far from diminishing, it was approaching ten o'clock and 'the Lion' was rocking.

Seeing the look of concern reform on her brow Andy

jumped in, sensing an opportunity to come valiantly to Julia's assistance and make his presence felt by the distracted young woman. As he dabbed her number into his handset Julia noticed that he was amongst the group for the first time and shot him a coy, girly smile of gratitude. She felt a sudden rush of excitement to see him smiling confidently at her. That brief meeting of their eyes was yet another tremulous stirring of the heart to add to the many that had preceded it, each individually meaning very little, but collectively adding up to a fragile relationship of snatched moments and furtive glances.

As Andy hit the call button the whole group strained their ears against the relentless clamour that enveloped the room, but their efforts were in vain.

"I definitely put it back in my bag after I used it," protested Julia hotly.

She could already envisage the lecture that Jim would mete out when she told him she had mislaid her phone on a drunken night out at the pub, with the workmates he neither particularly liked nor trusted around his wife.

She snapped out of her reverie and carried out a frenzied search of her bag, the table they had put their drinks on, and the faces of her friends, just in case they were playing some kind of cruel trick on her. None of these actions bore fruit. Julia looked visibly shaken.

"You need a drink," said Alison with only the bare vestiges of sincerity, adding after a short pause, " and it's your round."

Helena cast a scornful look at Alison but Julia was too deflated to take issue. Andy cut in with an offer of opportunistic chivalry and offered to go to the bar with Julia on the pretext of helping her to carry the drinks back. Though this chivalrous intent was arguably a misogynist trait predating gender equality, he did not seek to insult Julia's feminine agenda further by offering to pay.

For a few moments, as they waited by the bar, Julia became briefly distracted from the loss of her phone by the first proper contact with Andy since he had arrived in the pub. She felt glad to see him but nervous about her reasons for doing so. Having taken this extra step in their clandestine text-based liaison she suddenly felt much less clear about how much further she wanted, or needed it, to go. She was teetering perilously close to 'the line'. If this was a border crossing point she wasn't at all confident that she now wanted her passport stamped.

Andy was far less worried about this element of their growing attachment. The horizon, for Andy, was much closer at hand; ideally it was back at his apartment in a couple of hours. If this was indeed a border checkpoint in their flirtation then Andy anticipated no obstruction to his right to unimpeded travel.

"You OK?" asked Andy, nonchalantly, but struggling for anything more original or engaging to say.

"I'd be a lot better if I knew what I'd done with my phone," replied Julia softly.

"It'll turn up," he reassured her, as he gently snaked his arm around her slim waist.

Trembling nervously she offered no challenge.

A few yards away and in spite of the mass of bodies between them Alison and Helena were quick to spot the movement, and used their feminine telepathy to flash a meaningful look at their flushed and nervous friend.

The young man sporting the reindeer antlers appeared and Julia yelled her order over the incessant din.

"What do you want Andy?" she asked, as the barman dealt with the rest of her order.

"I'm looking at her," he smiled, exuding a slightly irksome, oily charm.

"To drink," Julia's tone was semi-admonishing, but sufficiently tempered so as not to discourage further flirtatious banter.

"A bottled beer, I think they're doing a two for one on one of them."

The antler-clad youth reappeared and looked slightly put out to have a further drink added to the order he had just tapped into the cash register, and he swivelled huffily on his heel back to the chiller cabinet. Julia was far too preoccupied in craning her neck behind her to see what her friends were doing, or more importantly seeing and sensing about her brief 'alone time' with randy Andy. Predictably Alison and Helena were projecting sickly sweet smiles at her, their eyes focused on Andy's arm, their eyebrows bouncing playfully up and down in knowing acknowledgment of the blossoming situation. Seeing this, Julia gently but decisively pushed Andy's arm from around her waist, quickly deflecting his injured protests.

"You take the girls' drinks and I'll bring yours and mine," she said firmly.

Downcast by the rebuff Andy shuffled back to the table with a rattling tray of drinks.

"Twenty-five pounds, seventy-five, please," said the young barman curtly, spitting the word 'please' at her.

Following him to the till with her eyes Julia saw a white 'phone perched next to the bottles of fruit juice. She narrowed her eyes and saw the faintest line of the pink shell that covered the back of the device, the same candy pink that she had on her own 'phone. So absorbed with the randomly abandoned 'phone was she that she ignored the bar tender's outstretched hand with her change cupped in his soft, fleshy palm.

"Your change," he said loudly, after a few seconds of proffering the coins without a response.

"Is that your phone?" Julia blurted.

The barman stared at her, his fluffy antlers standing proudly erect, like a handsome stag surveying the glen below.

"No, some woman handed it in a few minutes ago," he replied questioningly, his hand still fully extended, the coins now dampening with sweat.

"I've lost one in here tonight exactly like that," stated Julia, still oblivious to the money or indeed his very erect horns.

The barman finally tipped the money into Julia's hand whilst he considered how to respond. The three years he had spent drinking in student bars and getting a 2:2 in history and politics had not prepared him for this scenario. He resisted the urge to scratch his antlers in contemplation, but he thought the problem through anyway.

" Well, if you get your boyfriend to ring it, and it goes off, we'll know it's yours and you can have it, " he mused finally, displaying publicly the formidable analytical powers which had justified the years of academic discipline.

It felt slightly surreal, and a little naughty, to hear the barman refer to Andy as her boyfriend, but this was no time to set the record straight.

Andy despite still feeling tender from the rejection of his display of affection towards Julia was still filled with sufficient chivalrous and libidinous intent to acquiesce to the plan. He located her number, stiffly shown as Jules Carter in his phones address book, Jules being a sufficiently asexual name to both arouse his private excitement and subdue any suspicion on the part of his current and beautiful girlfriend,

Sophie. Smiling at Julia he pressed the keypad and after what seemed a painfully long delay the phone behind the bar began to play its reedy melody. It sang brightly and briefly, vibrating on its perch behind the bar, like a trembling, lost child waiting for its mother. The barman could only bow his horns at the weight of evidence proclaiming Julia's title to the slim white 'phone, and he reached across and handed it solemnly to her. The light in her lovely blue eyes was relit.

"Thank you. Where is the lady who handed it in?" she asked, her voice cracking with sheer relief.

The barman scanned the bar in a slow and deliberate 180-degree sweep:

"No sign I'm afraid. Can't help you."

Julia's gaze remained on him, those antlers registering in her consciousness for the first time. She stared at him wordlessly for several seconds, which was sufficient time for the young man to seize his opportunity:

"Your friend's nice looking," he said simply, gazing in the direction of Helena.

"I'll tell her," Julia promised with a smile, "You may want to lose the horns though."

TUESDAY -Taxi Ride

The evening continued with an unabated sense of raucous excitement. In Julia's small group Alison bitched more loudly and more frequently and with considerably less reserve as time and alcohol passed. Her scorn and derision was largely aimed at targets who were not present at the function, but her bile occasionally strayed to some that were. Neither demographic cared especially. Dawn, always more of a listener than contributor, signalled her presence simply by the volume of her nasal laughter, that increased exponentially with the quantity of drink consumed. Helena tried to listen to and even to feign interest in everyone who took the trouble to include her in their part of the conversation, but at the same time expended considerable effort in transmitting 'cow-eyes' at the horny barman/boy.

For their part Julia and Andy tried hard, sometimes too hard, to blend invisibly into the pervading merriment and chatter, making every effort to circulate naturally. However, if the ebb and flow of the group drew one of them too far 'downstream' from the other, they thrashed wildly against the tide until they were safely, and noticeably, back in their intimate bubble. In that bubble they briefly occupied a separate reality to the others, bound by different rules across time and space. Everyone noticed their ritualistic mating dance, but, with the possible exception of the leering Alison, pretended they hadn't.

As the bar clock silently lurched towards the midnight hour Julia interrupted a whispered conversation with Andy:

"Andy, it's nearly mid-night," observed Julia, with a mixture of surprise and disappointment.

"So?" challenged Andy, with an air of injured defiance and not a little concern that Julia was about to make a run for it, "It's Christmas. It only comes once a year, relax, enjoy yourself."

His words rattled out as more of a plea than an invitation.

"I am, but it's late. I should really go home," protested Julia who was caught in a Cinderella moment.

"Want to share a taxi?" ventured Andy, more in hope than expectation.

"I don't live anywhere near you," said Julia, naively failing to spot the thinly veiled implication of the offer from her red-faced and increasingly desperate suitor.

"You might not live there but you could visit,"said Andy, slowly and suggestively, raising his eyebrows and rolling his eyes to reinforce the carnal undertone of his invitation.

She stared at him, taking in what he had said. There was no question that Andy fanned the flame of passion which had dimmed to no more than a flicker in her marriage, and his impudent proposition was the affirmation she craved that she retained her feminine allure. Flirtation and risk faced each other down like gladiators in the ring of battle. The sword of temptation was raised and only the shield of fidelity stood between Julia and capitulation. The crowd roared as the two mighty opponents struggled, but it was Julia's day. It was for Andy to yield this day! Propriety stood victorious, though as a word it was one that Julia could not even attempt to utter, after seven glasses of the debilitating horse urine that had been the house wine.

"I've got to go," she slurred decisively.

Andy shook his head, but offered no further resistance:

"Call me?"

Julia nodded and smiled, her ego satiated for now. Even in her inebriated state she knew that she was being sensible and doing the right thing. A sober mistake is careless at best, a drunken mistake simply reckless.

Julia glanced over at the bar. Helena was leaning forward towards the young barman. There were fresh drinks on the bar that Helena had quite clearly ordered, but she showed no inclination to interrupt her conversation in order to deliver them to her waiting friends. More overt flirtation played out in front of Julia's glassy eyes, as did Helena's chest which had been liberated noticeably by the undoing of a couple of buttons on her blouse. Helena was fighting an offensive campaign and had not shied from bringing in the heavy artillery; the antler-wearing barman was about to have his position overwhelmed. Through the half-light in the pub and between the swaying bodies between herself and the bar, Julia saw Helena scribble something onto a beer mat and hand it to the young man in the antlers. The campaign was over and Helena had handed the barman the terms of surrender, and from the smile on his face as he took the note, they seemed to be reasonable and favourable.

As Helena strode back with the tray of drinks she bore the smile of the cat that had got the cream.

"He's too young for you. Wait till he sees you in daylight," sniped Alison.

"He said I was by far the best looking woman in here," retorted Helena smugly.

"He's obviously drunk then!"

"But not drunk enough to fancy you!"

If Julia had any doubt that it was time to make her exit, the cattish duelling between Alison and Helena eradicated it. She mumbled her goodnights hastily and was about to make a sharp exit, before her designer dress and shoes turned back into affordable high street brands as the clock chimed its twelfth ring, when Andy made one last concerted attempt to stall her:

"You look really nice tonight..." he blurted, "we could go on somewhere ..."

Julia smiled, turned and walked wordlessly towards the exit door, which appeared to be blurring in and out of focus and even spinning a little. She tottered across the floor, pushing her way through the human barrier, apologising unilaterally, frequently and at no one in particular. Her retreat was hurried and ungraceful, leaving Andy watching her disappear with a look of wistful disappointment etched on his youthful countenance.

Her mind whirled in the cold night air. The sudden chill flushed through her sinuses drawing the alcohol lazily drifting through her arteries into her brain with alarming efficiency. In addition to the effect of the booze she suffered an emotional intoxication that was completely independent of the liquor she had consumed. She knew she needed to find a taxi home before baser instincts kicked in and drew her inexorably back to a place she might regret visiting. She looked back towards the pub with a kind of longing as she trotted through the cold, unfriendly town centre street. She had left no glass slipper on the steps of the pub. No call for them these days, certainly not in her size. In any case she didn't believe in fairytales, and in particular fairy tale endings.

Her shoulders were rounded and drawn forward to ward off the freezing night air as she walked briskly into the main part of town. Her purposeful stride, head set firmly down arms clasped tightly across her chest, was only interrupted momentarily as she swerved slightly to allow other pedestrians to go past. They too bowed their heads against the inhospitable weather as they made their way between pub and nightclub, curry house or kebab stall, bus stop or taxi rank. Jim's 'motherly' suggestion that she took a coat, as she had bolted through the front door earlier, now seemed both reasonable and sensible. The withering look she had given him at the time was dismissive and scornful. In years to come there was little doubt that the scenario would be revisited when little Katie reached her middle-teens. But Julia was no teenager ... she had just acted like one.

Julia felt cool now, to the point of being frozen stiff. She felt much less sexy than she had as she sashayed into the pub a few hours earlier. Her perfectly groomed brown hair wilted in the cold night air, her white face was etched with cold, giving her red lipstick the appearance of fresh blood. As she stumbled knock-kneed and hunch-backed to the taxi rank there were no cabs to be seen: 'Typical,' she thought irritably. She shrunk a good couple of inches as she pulled her shoulders up to the bottom of her ears, shielding herself against the relentless chill. She stood with her back very gently resting against the unwelcoming brick wall of the listening bank, which routinely 'cocked a deaf un' to the drunks who frequently used it as a makeshift lavatory. The moon looked disdainfully down upon the *intelligent* nightlife beneath it. Every few hundred yards sodium streetlights glowed pale orange, but like the light on an old electric fire offered no warmth at all.

A message tone cut into the frozen night air. Julia rummaged in her bag and pulled out her mobile 'phone. 'Andy' was the name highlighted in the message bar. Julia opened the message and, summoning what appeared to be the fragments of a smile, she read:

'Missing u already x.'

The smile was brief because it pulled at her chapped lips. She looked around at the desolate streets, inhabited by the odd passer-by shuffling past, hands in pockets, lit eerily by the glow of the street lamps. They looked so dowdy as they trudged on their unknown journeys across the frosty pavement.

There was no one to see her have a last cigarette for the evening she thought, so reached shiftily for her pack of ten mild cigarettes. She struck a match from a book of matches she had taken from a hotel and lit up. As she blew out the match and drew elegantly on the cigarette she extinguished another few minutes from her life expectancy as voguishly as the habit would allow.

At thirty-three Julia was still young and healthy enough to scorn the warnings about smoking. She reasoned that we all have to go sometime and that she might be run over by a bus tomorrow. In her favour this was a diminishing risk thanks to the public service cuts being rigorously applied by her local council. What was the point in living into her seventies wracked with the frailty and illnesses of old age, she had reasoned? A poll of sixty-nine year olds may have thrown a different perspective on her logic.

'In any case,' she mused, swirling the cigarette smoke through her mouth and nostrils, 'do I want to live long enough to become some old and slightly potty hypochondriac constantly visiting the doctor for pointless prescriptions and someone to talk to?' Suddenly and inexplicably her mother's face popped into her head, and stamping the cigarette butt into the pavement she quickly abandoned that particular train of thought.

The town clock struck the half hour, the 'bong' reverberating loudly in the still night air.

'That's it,' she thought, 'I'm going to die of cold right here next to the cash machine. Exposure, that's what'll do it. I'll be found by some young policeman checking shop fronts at about 5am, stiff as a board and my hair all a mess.'

There were two issues here. Firstly proximity to large quantities of cash would ordinarily brighten the blackest of days for Julia. Only one thing excited her more than money and that was spending it, copiously, frivolously and recklessly (not necessarily in that order.) Secondly, the prospect of being found tragically deceased from exposure by a young, good-looking policeman with her hair wild and her makeup dissolved into her lifeless, pale skin. It had not occurred to her that she might be found by a plain or even ugly officer of the law, or worse still by a tubby female officer in a shapeless yellow blouson of indeterminate size and cheap uniform trousers that accentuated the trimmest of rear ends. In the case of the young, good-looking officer it was a fate not in itself unromantic, in a Charlotte Bronte sort of way. However, these were not windswept moors and she was no consumptive heroine of literature. Julia stabbed lipgloss onto her lips, bursting the hallucination in the process.

It was as she dabbed the soothing balm across her chafing lips that her mobile once more sounded an alert. No name appeared, but an unfamiliar number popped onto the screen. Julia was slightly disappointed, but not sufficiently downhearted that she didn't want to slavishly read the message.

'Julia. Have sent a taxi for you. Will be here in a couple of minutes. You look really cold.'

The number in tiny figures at the top of the screen meant nothing to her no matter how long she stood there staring at it. 'You look really cold' she mused, re-reading the end of the short message. Was someone watching her standing at the deserted taxi rank?

In a quantum leap of logic Julia decided that Andy must have come to look for her and seen her shivering at the rank. Rather than face a further snub he had simply done the gentlemanly thing and arranged a taxi for her. It didn't explain the unrecognised number on her 'phone, but she recalled that Andy had complained in the pub that his battery was low. Maybe he simply had a backup 'phone. She'd ask tomorrow, for now all she wanted was a super-heated cab to whisk her home to a warm bed and an unconscious husband.

'Ah, he does care after all.' Her kind thoughts of Andy were not supported by solid evidence, she had simply applied the alchemy of the mind in her search for gold. Many a *man* of science had lost everything in such futile endeavours.

In the distance Julia heard the drone of a car engine. She looked up from her handset and saw a medium sized saloon car snaking its way through the town's one-way system. On its roof a partially lit sign wobbled precariously on its magnetic base, a curly black lead disappeared into the driver's door window. The car pulled up alongside Julia, its diesel engine chugging reassuringly. The passenger window opened stiffly and, it seemed, a little reluctantly. The driver leaned forward to face Julia through the resultant gap.

"Carter?"

"Yes," she said miserably. She approached the rear door of the private hire car nearest the pavement and tugged at the handle. The driver, wrapped up for arctic conditions, made no attempt to get out of the cab to assist, but sat patiently while the slender fare struggled.

"Where to?" he asked amiably, as she finally tumbled onto the hard leather of the back seat.

Julia was a little surprised by the question. If Andy had indeed booked the cab she expected the driver to have his directions already, probably to deliver her to Andy's modern apartment across town. It was a little dejectedly that Julia gave the driver her address, but it was probably best that her little adventure was over, at least for tonight. The car clattered reassuringly back into life as the cabbie pulled away, merging into the gyratory system once more.

"Who booked this for me?" Julia asked tersely as the journey began.

"No idea, love. I get the bookings from the office. Sometimes by radio, sometimes by text if it's busy. I got this one by text. It just said *lone female, name of Carter by the taxi rank*, so I got here as quickly as I could."

The driver's reply was friendly and almost apologetic for not having the information Julia required. His apparent concern to make sure a lone female wasn't left stranded on her own was reassuring and belied his gruff, heavily insulated exterior. The driver was no white knight on a charger, more like a Friday night in a Cortina, but Julia was nevertheless glad he had been sent.

"I can contact control and see who made the booking," he offered, without turning his head, sensing Julia's slight irritation on the point.

"No it's fine, I think it was a friend of mine. It's not important. I really just want to get home now," she replied, her attitude, if not her fingers and toes, thawing.

In the ensuing silence Julia thought about her evening and about what might have been, had she been a little less of a tease and a little more wanton in her flirtations. In a snap poll on infidelity Julia was a positive 'don't know'. No good would come of playing around of course, but conversely she was sure that someone had once said 'a little of what you fancy does you good'. Why was life so full of contradictions? How come the 'right thing to do' was invariably dull and the 'naughty' so invigorating? To Julia ethics were a little like food nutrition; if greens and salad were so good for you why hadn't they been made to taste like chocolate? Contradictions!

The driver, a large, bearded but amiable looking man in his forties, sensed that his fare's evening might have gone a little flat. In a tone designed to gee up the atmosphere for the remainder of the journey, he asked, in a broad Welsh accent:

"Good night then?"

Julia looked at the back of the cabby's large head. She noticed that underneath his woolly hat and above the scarf draping his thick neck, his hair was close cut in contrast to the very full beard he wore. Julia didn't like beards, 'dirty looking', she thought, shuddering at the remnants of dinner that probably lurked, festering in their hairy nest. Nevertheless the bushy facial adornment somehow seemed to suit the large man. He seemed homely and kind, and Julia instinctively warmed to him, his thick Welsh baritone simply completing his kindly façade.

"Not bad," she replied after a brief pause, which was a fair summation.

"Girl's night out?" the driver continued airily. He craned his neck momentarily so he could see his fare through the rear view mirror. Eye contact, however awkward, is the seal of good conversational manners after all.

"Sort of. Bit of an office party really. Mind you," she continued, "it could have ended in tears. I thought I'd lost my 'phone at one point. I can't remember putting it down, but we couldn't find it no matter how hard we looked. Luckily when I went to the bar it was on the shelf near the till. A woman had handed it in."

"That's nice. Good to see there are some honest folk still out there. There's a few would have had it away," said the cab driver sincerely. Julia nodded earnestly.

The 'phone was the latest model; it could speak, if you wanted it to. It could listen too, which was more than the men in Julia's life seemed inclined to do. It had apps and programmes to undertake a range of tasks that Julia had absolutely no need for and probably never would. It had a capacity that would have taken a room full of base stations to produce just a couple of decades ago. More importantly it was a newer model than the one the young girl in Julia's office had, the girl whose boyfriend drove a Porsche and who had just come back from the Maldives with a Sri Lankan gold eternity ring. Julia had been quick to request an upgrade on her contract ... if only it was that simple with men!

"Your lucky day then," he said, Julia catching his warm smile in the rear view mirror.

She could picture Jim's face, had she been forced to admit losing the new handset. He would have become immediately judgemental and sanctimonious and Julia would have had to bite her lip whilst he gave one of his lectures. Jim was actually quite amusing when he became self-righteous, somewhere between evangelical preacher and total knob-head. After almost a decade together Julia diffused such tantrums with ease, invariably infuriating him further by making him laugh. Julia was 'Mission Control' carefully taking her husband from the stratosphere of ill temper to a safe splashdown in a sea of calm. She smiled at the thought of his pouting lip as his annoyance faded and he gave in to a grin that curved from one ear to the other. She felt a warm tingle somewhere deep inside, the place where their love nestled, a snug and safe place, a place where excitement and passion were infrequent visitors these days.

"Lucky I didn't have to explain it to my husband," she laughed.

The exchange lightened the mood in the taxi, and

made up for the fact the car's heater was woefully inadequate and that the driver's window had to be cracked open to admit the lead from the taxi sign on the roof.

Julia was sure they couldn't be far from home now. The cold night air had only increased her level of intoxication, during the time she had waited for the taxi to arrive. She had lost track of the streets as the driver took her homewards at a sedate pace. Suddenly a loud burst of music cut through the sanguine atmosphere of the cab. The chorus of 'Delilah', belted out by Tom Jones, rang out. Even from the confines of the speaker on a mobile 'phone the power of the Welshman's voice filled the entire space they occupied. Julia jumped in her seat.

Defying the rules of the road the cabbie grabbed his 'phone from the passenger seat and clamped it roughly to his ear.

"Yeah, hello. How are you? I know I shouldn't be working but I couldn't let Larry down, could I? What? How many? Well I don't know. Have you rung the hospital? Your mother? What bloody good is that going to do? For heaven's sake … yes, yes, sorry love…" as he spoke the urgency in his voice was unmistakable.

Julia leaned forward, as far as her seat belt would allow, listening and trying to make sense of the conversation which clearly contained an element of desperation to it. He looked over his shoulder, his face etched with worry, and his large grey eyes wide and round like saucers. In spite of his beard, and the rough-hewn features above it, he had an air of real vulnerability about him at that moment. The conversation ceased abruptly and he jabbed the end call button so hard with a stubby finger, which poked through fraying fingerless gloves, that Julia thought it would end up embedded in the circuitry. The 'phone was then planted forcefully back onto the passenger seat. Silence reigned briefly, before he pulled over to the side of the road, looked over his shoulder at the empty road behind him, and turned the car in a wide semi-circle before heading off in the opposite direction.

"Look I'm sorry about this love, " he said, almost breathlessly "but my wife's gone into labour. I wasn't supposed to be working tonight but Nobby went sick, and Larry was desperate and offered me double time. I was supposed to finish at one o'clock but the text came in to pick you up. Well I didn't want to leave a woman on her own and I thought one more fare won't hurt... Oh bloody hell," the burly driver babbled with machine gun rapidity.

His words were enough to bring a temporary sobriety to Julia's aching head:

"Well, let's not hang about then. Where do you live?"

"About a mile away, we'll be there in a few minutes. Look I'll get you sorted with a ride as soon as I get home. I'll get another cab out," he jabbered, his tone increasing in pitch and urgency with each passing second.

"Don't worry, I can sort all that out. Is this your first?" Julia said, briskly and reassuringly.

"Fifth," came the less than anticipated reply, effectively curtailing further conversation.

The car turned into a long, straight road, where cars were parked on either side of the carriageway as far as the eye could see. The cabby saw a vacant spot, which to Julia seemed too small to accommodate a child's pedal car, let alone a bulky old saloon. The time-served cabbie with skill, experience and judicious use of the pavement wedged the taxi between a dumpy looking mini and a small, rusty van.

With little more than a frayed smile the driver leapt from the car, instinctively grabbing his bag of takings, and headed towards the nearest house where an upstairs light glowed behind unlined curtains. Julia, for no good reason she could think of, followed him, tottering on high heels across the uneven pavement, slamming the door of the cab, causing a noise like a gunshot in the quiet and dimly lit street. This was a modern town, no curtains twitched in response to the momentary outburst of 'gun-fire'.

The panicking cabby poked a huge bundle of keys at the peeling wooden front door of the three storey Victorian terraced house and disappeared inside. Julia followed in his wake, gingerly stepping into the unlit hallway of the old house as if she was entering a Pharaoh's tomb. Tentatively she stepped into the house, relying on her other senses while her eyes adjusted to the darkness inside the house. As she stood at the base of a steep stairway with worn wooden treads, she heard the driver's voice chattering excitedly with a female, though the words were indiscernible.

Unsure what to do she stood nervously collecting her thoughts. The smell of hard liquor wafted into her nose and for a moment she frowned in disapproval. 'What sort of den of iniquity is this?' she thought, 'and this woman heavily pregnant too!' At least that's what she thought until she realised that she was the source of the boozy aroma. She blushed slightly, though in the darkness no one could see her colour, but she felt her cheeks burn nonetheless. This was no time for self-recrimination though; this was a time for decisive action. A time to help your fellow man … and woman; a time to offer the robust hand of support in a time of crisis. With a rush of altruism and a jolt of unprocessed Tequila Julia started to ascend the stairs.

TUESDAY - Special Delivery

Julia followed the sound of the voices to the top of the stairs. The landing was long, narrow and barely lit. A single vase shaped lamp glowed vainly from beneath a dull, dust covered shade, giving the landing an eerie gloom.

Edging along the hallway, like a cat burglar, Julia stopped at the entrance to the bedroom where a shaft of brighter light leaked through the crack in an unclosed door. Adult voices whispered loudly and urgently from within. Julia coughed loudly in order to introduce her presence, then hesitantly leaned into the room.

A red-faced woman sat on top of the bedclothes, damp sweat clinging to her forehead. She wore a cheap, loose fitting nightdress which also clung to her ample contours. The woman stopped mid-sentence and her head snapped round suddenly at the intrusion. The woman and the taxi driver stared at Julia and Julia stared at them both, desperately trying to fix them both in her sights, though the alcohol in her system had abandoned control of her eyes.
"I was wondering if there was anything I could do to help?" said Julia plaintively.

Not once during those silent moments of first encounter did it occur to her that it might be courteous, if not a little essential, to explain her presence there to the lady on the bed.

"You must be Barry's fare, I'm so bloody sorry love, but I'm in labour, see. A bloody good way along too," said the red-faced woman kindly, in a broad Welsh accent.

With a strained smile the woman brushed aside the need for any further introduction. There was a warmth in her expression that negated explanation. She looked at her husband, towering above her, shaking her head as though he were a naughty schoolboy. Dragging a stranger along into an intimately private family situation was clearly expected behaviour on his part; he left thinking and planning to his wife. After all that was her strength, not his.

"Sorry love," said Barry sheepishly, " I kind of forgot about you down there."

The large pregnant woman exuded an air of control, which in the circumstances someone needed to do. Barry simply held his wife's hand, stood at the side of the bed, looking awkward and uncomfortable. Sadly the control did not extend to the wild ramblings of her flimsy nightdress, which twisted and rode up with every movement she made. Julia kept her head mobile so as to avoid witnessing anything she might later regret.

"Ooh bugger," exclaimed the woman, her face suddenly contorting with pain and effort.

"Impatient little sod, this one," she breathed, between clenched teeth. She followed this with a mammoth exhaling of breath and still more facial contortion.

Julia noticed that the woman was clutching her husband's hand ever tighter through his hand-knitted, fingerless gloves. Those big stubby fingers were white where the blood was being forcibly starved from them by a vice-like grip. Manfully he said nothing, but the widening of his big brown eyes told their own story. Barry looked at Julia for inspiration:

"What should I do?" he hissed at her, as though his wife wouldn't hear his helplessness.

Firstly it should be understood that Julia was the mother to one seven-year old girl. There was a reason there had been no additions to her family, principally the sworn (in both senses of the word) oath that she would not be going through the *joy* of childbirth again. This despite the fact that Katie's birth, in a hospital, was in all the usual senses uncomplicated, and that Julia had not only had any and every drug offered but had sucked enough gas and air to undertake a mission in space. In any case if this was baby number five then surely this brute of a man should be able to tell a mid-wife what to do.

"Never mind him," chided the woman, "he's useless. He was useless all the other times, no reason he should be any different today. Panics under pressure, see? Probably faint later on."

Julia shook her head as she realised that the bulldog of a man, bursting the stitches across the shoulders of his hooded jacket with his bulk, was the one in the room in need of reassurance, not the woman panting on the bed a couple of pushes short of a textbook home delivery.

"Shouldn't we phone the hospital or something?" asked Julia, sensing it was rather too late for all that.

"Done it already, sweetheart," the woman reassured her, "big crash on the by-pass, no ambulances free, said to make my own way in, otherwise they'd send the midwife."

Of course had Barry not taken that last fare he would have been home in time to do just that. Julia looked at the panting woman; her back wedged against the slowly yielding headboard of the bed, and felt a surge of indescribable guilt.

"Well if Barry helps you down to the car I could pack a few things for you, if you tell me what you want and where it is," offered Julia feebly.

"No tiiiiiimme, luvvy," came the *laboured* reply.

Even with pain etched on her face the woman still had the capacity to show concern for both her helpless, hopeless husband and the total stranger in her bedroom.

The woman reclined further on the disarranged double bed and her wayward nightdress flapped around her hips like a flag of surrender. The time for any remnant of decorum was over, and with a shout like a roar from the terraces on a Saturday afternoon, a baby was launched towards the footboard of the creaking bed. There really was no turning back now.

Barry froze to the spot, staring at the tiny, blood-smeared bundle of arms and legs. He seemed to have stopped breathing.

"Let him go," groaned the woman, her voice collapsing, along with her over-stretched muscles.

Julia looked perplexed, but only momentarily, as Barry toppled forward like a huge tree that had been chopped from its base. Gently he clattered against the wardrobe and slid harmlessly to the floor.

"Useless, I told you," said the woman weakly, her eyes closed. She had gathered the baby in a towel and held it close to her, still connected to the cord, as its first raucous cries filled the room.

"Mu-um, mum are you OK?"

The voice came from behind Julia, from the semi-darkness of the landing. She turned to see a young, frightened looking, tired sounding boy stood behind her.

"I'm fine darlin'," said mum reassuringly, her best smile radiating from beneath clenched teeth, her voice quiet and exhausted.

The boy pushed past Julia's legs and attached himself to the side of his mother's bed.

"Say hello to your sister and then you get back to bed," she commanded, gently, kissing the boy on the top of his bowed head.

"Stand aside please," came a brisk voice, again behind Julia.

It was like Spaghetti Junction on that landing just now. This was a woman's voice, business-like and once more Julia was gently pushed to one side. In a blue blouson and black nylon trousers the midwife busily went about tending to the baby and mum, stepping over the hapless Barry, who was coming to slowly.

"If you want to hold your daughter, you can take off those filthy gloves and wash your hands," snapped the midwife at the helpless hunk hauling himself to his feet. "Take the young man to bed on the way. Mum and baby need rest."

Then the midwife's eyes rested on Julia. Everything about her was out of place, and the midwife scrutinized her with hard pebble like eyes:

"Best thing you can do is put the kettle on," she barked, her tone saying 'I've got my eye on you young woman'. Julia simply jumped to it.

Julia returned with a tray a few minutes later. Given that she had had to locate and navigate an unfamiliar kitchen she had been quite efficient in her tea-making activity. As she walked into the bedroom there was order where chaos had reigned just a short while before. The woman sat in the bed propped up by an assortment of pillows and cushions. Barry sat meekly on the edge of the bed holding his wife's hand, gloves gone hands clean and fresh smelling. The baby was now in a fitful slumber in a cosy and much used crib at the other side of the bed. The midwife quietly and unobtrusively went about doing whatever it was she was doing, which seemed a lot like picking things up, folding them and putting them down, to Julia.

"My name's Julia, by the way," she said quietly, "I'm really sorry to have intruded like this. It just sort of happened."

"Megan," said the woman with a wistful smile, through half-closed eyes. "Thank you," she added, somewhat inexplicably.

Julia handed out the cups of tea, including one for the surly and still faintly suspicious midwife.

"May I?" asked Julia, looking towards the cot.

"Of course sweetheart," replied Megan, sipping gratefully at her hard-earned cup of tea.

There was something very warm and reassuring about these people, a simple love and kindness that seeped into Julia's soul almost without her noticing. She very gently touched the baby's tiny digits, and even as it slept, they curled automatically around her long, slender finger.

"I should go, I'm intruding," said Julia softly, pulling her finger from the infant's feather-like touch.

"Sit down, love," Megan insisted, " have your tea. Celebrate with us, you've been part of it all after all."

Julia perched on the opposite side of the bed to Barry, feeling a little tearful, and almost entirely sober by now. There was a wonderful, contented calm about the room. The baby slept fitfully after its ordeal, Megan sipped at her tea, half asleep, half awake. Barry held his wife's hand and this time it was he who squeezed her fingers, but with a loving clasp. The midwife pottered around like a benevolent ghost watching over mum and baby, and no doubt keeping a weather eye on the mountain with the soft centre – Barry. Somehow this was how Julia felt a family should be.

Suddenly the little boy reappeared:

"I can't sleep mum. Are you ok?"

"Yes darling," Megan nodded, with almost the last strength she had that night.

"Go back to bed, there's a good boy, mummy's very tired and needs her sleep," the midwife urged sweetly.

"I can't sleep though," the boy persisted.

"Do you want to sleep by your mum?" Megan asked her son. He nodded.

In spite of the austere glance from the midwife Barry lifted the boy over Megan and the lad scurried beneath the bedclothes snuggling tight in to his mum.

"The other kids are at my sister's, but young Ryan wouldn't leave his mum," explained Barry, regaining the power of speech. "He's a good boy," he added warmly.

That was Julia's cue to leave. There was simply nothing more this stranger could add to their night or indeed her own. She glanced at her watch, it was almost five a.m. She glared at the dial in horror, but said nothing.

"She's beautiful," Julia said to Megan, casting one last glance at the crib.

"I'll run you home," said Barry, releasing his wife's hand.

Although Megan had begun to snore, and Ryan's blonde head had virtually disappeared beneath the sheets, Barry's place was with his family, not in a ropey old cab on the cold streets of the soon-wakening town.

"No you won't," said Julia firmly but kindly, " I'll sort myself out. I'll be fine."

"I'm done here, I'll give you a lift home. You live in town, don't you?" the midwife interjected.

"Yes, … thank you," replied Julia gratefully.

"I'll be down in a minute then," continued the midwife, dismissing Julia from the cluttered but quiet bedroom.

It was still dark, as Julia stood on the pavement wiping her eyes and feeling a little silly and emotional. It was now even more bitingly cold. Julia shrugged her shoulders and wrapped her arms tightly around her chest, chin firmly down to ward off the bitter wind that was blowing silently down the deserted street. The orange glow of the street lamps did nothing for Julia's early morning pallor. Last night it seemed 'cool' to shun Jim's suggestion of taking a jacket with her. Now she was cool alright, virtually sub-zero. From above her head a baby's wail rang out, but it didn't last long. Someone had quickly tended to its needs. She smiled, but she felt her lips crack as they turned upwards. There was a thick frosting of ice on the windscreen of Barry's abandoned taxi.

"Come on then young lady, I expect there's a warm bed waiting for you at home," chirped the midwife briskly, as she appeared from the direction of the front door of the house. She was warmly wrapped in a thick woollen jacket, which covered the uniform trousers that so unflatteringly exaggerated her already ample bottom.

Julia eagerly took the passenger seat in the midwife's tiny Fiat. She was relieved that the heater in the tiny car was working and efficient, a lot like its owner! In the empty streets the journey home didn't take long. Neither woman wasted breath on much conversation; this was not the start of a lasting friendship. Outside her house Julia thanked the midwife for the lift and the little car churned its way out of view. The house was in darkness, and nothing stirred. The security light at the front door bathed Julia in its spotlight as she fumbled with her keys. Eventually the latches on the double glazed front door clunked sturdily open and she stepped wearily into the hall.

In the house all was quiet, apart from the ticking of the old wooden wall-clock. Steady and constant it marked the seconds of each hour that passed unceasingly by. She kicked off her shoes freeing her feet from the confines of her fashionable, if snugly fitting, shoes. They were in reality at least half a size too small for her and as her feet were liberated from the confines of the unyielding leather the blood rushed warmly and playfully through her toes, making them tingle. The size of Julia's shoe had always had a greater aesthetic significance to her than the inevitable discomfort, and probably damage, they caused to her feet. Kicking them asunder was therefore like plunging both feet into a gentle foot spa.

She tiptoed to her daughter's bedroom and gently eased open the door. The little girl was sprawled outside her duvet and lay crossways on the top of the bed. Her ringlet hair spread was across a pillow that she had dragged with her as she wriggled in her sleep. A teddy bear balanced precariously on the edge of the bed where a tired hand had long since released its grip on the much-loved toy. Julia placed an 'angels kiss' almost imperceptibly on the little girls warm forehead and crept back out of the room, easing the bedroom door to.

Outside the girls bedroom she examined the call register of the 'phone. Still the mystery number meant nothing. The hall clock struck the half hour. It was five-thirty in the morning. Julia felt a huge wave of tiredness wash over her whole body. She yawned so hard it made her jaw click.

Like a ghost she glided into her own bedroom, shed her clothes as quietly as a spider shedding its skin, and wriggled silently into bed. The pulsing green light of the alarm clock cut into the darkness of the room. She glanced at it briefly, cursing it because its piercing call in a couple of hours time was going to cause her great pain. She set her 'phone to silent and stuffed it deep underneath her pillow, away from any prying eyes.

Jim lay with his back to her, breathing slowly and rhythmically. The events of a long and eventful evening flitted across her mind in the few seconds before sleep escorted her to a warm and wonderful place. As she fell fitfully into the shadow world of dreams, her right arm snaked underneath the warm duvet and wrapped itself gently over Jim's stomach, pulling him very gently towards her.

TUESDAY - A Quick Drink After Work

"You darted off very suddenly last night," said Helena bluntly, accusingly even.

Julia blinked and looked up from her desk. Her eyes were watery and vague, her skin unusually pale and vapid. Helena looked unblinkingly at Julia for a few seconds, scrutinising her appearance:

"You've got really black bags under your eyes, and you look blotchy. Did you have a row with Jim when you got back?" she persisted, digging for dirt.

Julia could hear but the words floated in her skull, lazily avoiding the cognitive areas. Only her unwilling body had emerged from her warm and cosy duvet, her soul and spirit were still enmeshed in blanket and pillow. The alarm clock had expertly waited until she had drifted to the deepest recesses of the dream world before screeching mercilessly in her ear. Helena was likewise unrelenting:

"Had words with lover boy?" Julia scrunched her eyes as if she was unable to process the inquiry. "Have you got a hangover? Dawn's got a really bad head; she's been sick twice, she texted me both times," she added informatively. "No-one's even heard from Alison, she started really knocking it back after you went. Some bloke came over and started buying her drinks, so she went onto spritzers. Anyway after he'd bought her about three, he jangled the keys to his BMW at her, just before closing, so she told him she was a lesbian and snogged Dawn. Dawn was so pissed by then she didn't care, she groped Alison's boobs and the bloke disappeared so fast you wouldn't believe it. The doormen asked us to leave then."

Julia found that her vocal function was no more effective than her comprehension skills, and abandoned any attempt to reply just behind her bottom lip. It felt much the way it did after an injection at the dentist.

Helena used her friend's silence only to take a breath and shuffle closer to her, perching elegantly on the edge of Julia's desk. She looked furtively around, then dropped her head so that it was nearer to Julia's and lowered her voice to a secretive whisper:

"Andy didn't stay long after you left. He had one more drink but he was really quiet after you'd gone." Helena looked Julia in the eye, as far as that was possible, in view of the involuntary focusing and refocusing Julia was undertaking in that department. There was again no discernable response, so Helena took it upon herself to fill the void in conversation:

"I think he really *likes* you." Nothing. "You *like* him, don't you? I can tell. Everyone can tell." Still nothing, though Julia's fingers flapped aimlessly at the keyboard on her desk. She didn't know why, it wasn't yet switched on. The void in discussion, like the Universe, continued silently to expand. "Well, you're always sending each other little messages on your 'phones. We all know it's him when you scuttle off to take a message," Helena baited her friend.

It was undoubtedly the word 'phone which magically reactivated Julia. It was as if Helena had input an over-ride code that had instantly re-energised the vast network of microprocessors in the dormant circuitry of her mind.

"I had a text message while I was waiting for a taxi in town, after I left the pub," she blurted, as full functionality was peremptorily returned. So many words had been bottlenecked in her throat they literally burst into conversation, spilling from her tongue with the urgency and intensity of a grid of racing cars sprinting from a green light.

As Julia began to recount the events of the previous night Helena eagerly pinned back her ears waiting for every grimy, sordid detail to spew forth. Her expression changed quickly as the true version of events emerged. True, there was no embarrassing, or better still sleazy aspect to the unlikely tale, but it was unusual, a bizarre turn of events really, all considered.

When the story concluded it was Helena's turn to stay silent. Julia handled the silence much better than Helena had done previously, principally because there was nothing to add. No further embellishment of the tale was likely to make it any more compelling or curious. In fact it was too convoluted to be a clever cover story, to hide a murky pre-arranged liaison with randy Andy. Surely?

"So what did Jim say when you rolled in at 530 a.m., reeking of booze and newborn babies?" sneered Helena, when the power of speech had returned to her lips.

"Jim? He was fast asleep. I doubt if he even noticed when I got into bed," said Julia quietly, not really believing herself.

Julia had tried to be as normal as her sleep deprived, booze wracked mind and body would allow, as she got ready for work. Jim had seemed himself, and other than asking 'how it went' had gone about his morning routine unfazed by his wife's early morning tiptoe into their bedroom.

"So you've no idea who rang for the taxi then?" asked Helena, after momentary deliberation.

"No idea," confirmed Julia, and to prove it she flicked the number up on the screen of her handset and thrust it under Helena's inquisitive nose.

Helena shook her head:

"No, it means nothing to me either. Mind you if it was *me,* and I found out who put me through all that, I'd want to poke them in the eye. What a night!"

"I know, but they wouldn't have known what was going to happen, and in any case it was kind of nice in the end. Being there, with the taxi driver and his wife when the baby was born … well, it made me think …" Julia paused mid-sentence, as she replayed the events in the old Victorian town house. More words simply wouldn't come, they were superfluous to the feelings that consumed her, making her feel warm and tender, like a loving caress.

"Made you think of Andy?" teased Helena, feeling an uncomfortable need to trivialise her friend's fairly momentous experience.

Julia chose not to grace the comment with a reply. In fact the unnecessary and crass comment did prompt thoughts of Andy to lurch awkwardly into her mind. She felt her cheeks warm and her brow knit.

"I'm going to ring the bloody number," she announced angrily at no one in particular.

She jabbed ferociously at the screen on her 'phone and stabbed at the 'call number' command. She jammed the handset so close to her ear that it hurt, but no ring tone sounded from the tiny speaker. There was just silence and the accompanying frustration of a failed connection. She held the device in front of her and stared accusingly at the screen. She dialled again, once more to no avail. Mobiles were temperamental, they did have minds of their own, and they could be contrary, she reasoned. She thought it might be some kind of *small computer syndrome*. There was a time she had dated a small man, and he turned out to be contrary and temperamental as well. 'There you are then' she thought, slamming the inanimate piece of plastic irritably into her desk drawer.

"A mystery then?" remarked Helena, bored now with the whole issue, and slid gracefully from the edge of Julia's desk to return to her own. Julia sat there scowling at her desk computer, willing it to play up - if it dared!

Julia found it difficult to concentrate for the rest of the morning. Her senses had to contend with the sensation that someone had poured wet cement into her cranium as well as the emotional aftermath of her birthing experience. She also felt a rising sense of irritation that she couldn't identify her mystery caller.

Of all the days for Julia's boss to pop his head affably into the office this would not be her choice. Of course it wasn't Julia's choice, it was his and inevitably he had a window somewhere between a post-breakfast tee-off at the golf club and a liquid lunch at 'The Striding Horse'.

"Hello trusty underling," he crowed as he sauntered into the office, swaggering nonchalantly as only the boss can do. He tossed his overcoat neatly onto the chair on the opposite side of her desk, an overcoat that showed little signs of wear on the basis he rarely wore it. It was more of an accessory that he slung over his arm. The coat spent most of its life draped on the leather seat in the back of his luxury saloon, like a pampered dog in front of a crackling coal fire.

"Coffee on?"

Julia flicked a cursory nod to the coffee filter in the corner of the office, which seemed to be blending a form of tar in a heavily stained glass jug. David Barnes sauntered over to the machine and stared dubiously at it:

"Has this been on all morning?" he asked, a look of distaste forming on his lips.

"Don't know. I didn't put it on David," Julia replied abruptly, keeping her head down in an effort to stop him seeing the 'morning after' reddening to her eyes.

Barnes looked at the coffee pot suspiciously once more before reaching out a tentative hand in the direction of the handle. Ignoring the obvious and immediate threat to his digestive system he shrugged his shoulders and poured a measure of the liquid into a clean but time-stained mug nearby.

"You've never got sweeteners have you?" he complained light-heartedly.

"You should decide whether you want sugar or not. Sweeteners are a cop out, they're the nicotine patch of the teeth," said Julia a little caustically.

"Oh dear, got out of the wrong side of the bed today?" Then Barnes experienced a brief light bulb moment, "Of course, yesterday was the big night out, Feeling a bit fragile?"

Julia snapped her head round and glared at him. One look into her tiny reddened eyes, and the greyish pallor of her face answered his question.

"It wasn't like that …" grumbled Julia impatiently.

"Never is, never is. Went on a boy's night out a week or so back, had a meeting the next day. Couldn't think straight. Came out of the meeting, didn't have a clue what had gone on, or come to that what I'd agreed to, but we went to the pub afterwards anyway. That soon sorted me out. Hair of the dog, infallible cure for a hangover."

Barnes left Julia to reflect on his words of wisdom while he took a substantial swig from his mug. His benevolent smile instantly transformed to a bitter wince. He gamely swallowed the potion down succeeding only in infusing the acrid after-taste deep into his palate, lips and throat where it lodged for the foreseeable future.

"Good God, that's foul," he said shuddering, thrusting the mug back on the counter. " You need a proper drink. Hair of the dog; unlike this muck, which is more like Hound of the Baskervilles. Look I'm going out with a couple of lads from the other office for a late lunch, something in a basket, do they still do things in baskets? A couple of beers, job done. Right I'll go and check my emails, send Barbara for an early lunch, I know she'll go shopping for three hours, and I'll pop back for you in an hour or so. Up for it? Good girl!"

The opportunity to decline evaporated with his perfunctory disappearance; in any case Julia knew that refusal was pointless. Not that Barnes was in any way a bully - to anyone. In fact he really liked, and most importantly trusted, Julia. She was his 'right-hand man'. If anything he was an outgoing, genuinely good-natured bloke with the infectious enthusiasm of a faithful dog. He had an astute head for business, but adopted the philosophy of catching his flies with honey rather than vinegar. Therefore he amassed a circle of good friends and a flock of loyal customers, and once you entered his court you were there for life.

He had 'adopted' Julia some years back when she was a young stick insect in the dispatch team. A happily married man, his interest in Julia had been paternal and platonic from the start and she had flourished under his fond mentoring. If he had a character flaw it was that he was polygamous; he was married to Jeanette, his wife (spoken of affectionately but rarely seen in public), the business, the golf club, his sports car and his rugby team, though not necessarily in that order.

So, in the words of many a bad wartime movie 'resistance was futile', and Julia steeled herself to a boisterous afternoon with David and his rowdy acolytes.

Sure enough an hour later David reappeared, coat slung over the arm of his dapper Italian design suit. Wordlessly Julia simply grabbed her coat and bag and followed in the tailwind of her boss all the way to the car park.

David and Julia were first there. Whoever David had planned to meet hadn't yet arrived. Julia stood quietly behind her boss looking around at the busy and festive little pub. David took care of drinks dismissing Julia's initial request for a diet cola and substituting it, for her benefit, with a large glass of wine. Julia stood facing David's broad back as he took a clutch of menus from the harassed looking bar staff and set up a (tax deductible) tab. He was in fine form, and he joked with the staff at the bar and they shared his humour, politely and dutifully. It was going to be a loud and laddish afternoon and Julia was not looking forward to it one little bit. Her head still ached and her tummy grumbled spitefully. 'Take me out on the lash and abuse me will you?' it grumbled poisonously, underneath her blouse. What she really wanted to do was to go home and lie on the settee for an hour.

She stood behind David looking miserable and working on the energy to summon up a fake smile, which would carry her through the hideous afternoon to come. It was then that she felt a light tap on her shoulder. Instinctively she moved to one side, assuming she was obstructing someone's path to the bar.

"Hello Cinders," came the cheeky retort. It was Andy. Julia felt her cheeks burn and she was unable to stop the surge of blood to her face as she reddened visibly. In that instant her sense of discomfort immediately doubled.

"What are you doing here?" she hissed at him irritably.

It wasn't that she was totally disappointed to see his handsome features; it was just that his appearance failed the 'time and place' test.

"Nice to see you too. Get home ok?"

"Eventually," she said mysteriously, eyeing him suspiciously.

"Oh! Struck lucky after you left me despondent and heartbroken?"

"No, just a bit of a game getting a cab. Long story. I'll tell you another time," she said in a low, almost conspiratorial voice.

"So there's going to be another time. I'm looking forward to it already," oozed Andy confidently.

"Maybe," Julia rasped dismissively, " now go away I'm in here with my boss and a couple of preferred clients."

"Am I one of your preferred clients?" he persisted, a broad grin across the light field of designer chin stubble he sported above the year round tan he seemed to retain.

"Look, another time. Get your drink and go back to your friends. I'll text you tomorrow," she said to him through clenched teeth.

"Andy!" crowed Barnes, turning round with his brace of menus.

"David," replied Andy coolly.

"Do you know each other?" asked Barnes, looking at Julia. She flushed again, but not so dramatically this time:

"We've met," she replied, turning on the sweetest of her smiles.

"Oh, that's good," enthused Barnes, "we're just waiting for Phillip and we're quorate. Over there I think." Barnes pointed to a booth in the corner and Julia and Andy trotted behind him to take their place as his guests for the afternoon.

Julia felt as if she had been placed under a microscope. There was no immediate sign that David had inferred anything untoward about herself and Andy, but he was the last person she wanted to place her complicated affections under his lens. If Andy was destined to be a pleasure, then he had to remain a *secret* pleasure, a gut-wrenchingly guilty pleasure.

"Well, now we're here, I'm really looking forward to this," said Andy, looking at David but addressing Julia.

After about fifteen minutes they were joined by a flustered looking man who David introduced as Phillip Daniels, a buyer from a local firm, whose contracts David Barnes sought greedily when they came up. He apologised for running late and shuffled awkwardly into the bench seat beside Julia, brushing accidentally into her as he did so:

"Sorry, sorry. Clumsy. Sorry."

Julia dismissed the matter with a winning smile and shuffled an inch or two across the seat to allow the young man a bit more room. That squirm was the first of many during the good-natured ribaldry of the next three or more hours. Squirming and avoiding eye contact with a very lairy and mischievous Andy turned out to be the order of the afternoon.

After a three long hours of smiling sweetly at the laddish quips, good-naturedly raising her eyebrows at their hilarious double-entendres and nodding agreeably at their disjointed banter, Julia began to cast longer and more obvious glances at her watch.

"You're a bit quiet this afternoon," said David to Julia, spotting her repeated clock-watching.

"I had a late night yesterday, I shouldn't be too late home tonight," she replied weakly.

"Happens to the best of us," agreed Phillip, smiling directly at Julia through small, piggy eyes.

"It wasn't like that," she protested, but she knew further explanation would be wasted on them, particularly the younger men, who had egged each other along all afternoon.

David shot her a paternal glance then turning his attention to Andy and Phil he tapped his nose and winked:

"Poor Julia, tank's running on empty. We should get the poor girl home," then, redirecting his words to Julia, "shall I get you a taxi?"

Julia must have looked momentarily aghast. At any rate her expression surprised her boss, who protested that he was just trying to be considerate.

"I know, David, I'm sorry. Long story, but I'm right off taxis just now. I can get the bus, there's a stop not far from the pub," she said, equally concerned that she had caused David any offence.

Ordinarily the chance to spend an afternoon with

Andy would have been a clandestine treat, but the preceding hours had not at all been how she had imagined, or hoped, it might be. When they exchanged texts it was intimate and private, away from the prying eyes of the world around them. The stolen moments, the brief messages, the secret chats were theirs and theirs alone. She had Andy's sole focus on these occasions, and sharing him that afternoon had not been easy, especially as Andy had become the boorish epitome of a salesman on the road, loud, hard drinking and brutish. She preferred the softer, gentler Andy. The person that said nice things, encouraging things, the person who made her feel special. Special in a way she had long consigned to her emotional archive. This afternoon, however, had been raucous and impersonal. She knew full well how the wheels of business were oiled, but she didn't have to like it. Now, it was time to go home.

Suddenly in spite of the din in the pub she heard the message tone tinkling from within her handbag. She rummaged amongst the keys, chewing gum packets, tissues and lipstick until she unearthed her 'phone. As discreetly as she could she read the message emblazoned on the screen: *"Julia, time 2 go, sum1 will give u a lift."*

Julia frowned at the curt message. 'Bloody cheek' she thought, immediately deciding that Jim was the author of the message. Jim wasn't being unreasonable, even if he was urging his wife to leave the pub. The last twenty hours or so hadn't gone as Julia had anticipated, and her hapless husband was a fair target for her irritation at the fact. It was only a cursory second glance at the screen, which revealed a number, which was unknown to her displayed there. She stared at the screen for longer than was usual, catching the attention of Andy.

"Everything ok sweetheart? Is the 'old man' on your case?" he asked, with a sneer.

"Nothing to do with you, nosy," she retorted sharply.

Andy made a handbag gesture at her, and carried on talking to David Barnes.

"Look, I'm all done here, I have to get home myself," began Phillip, a little more earnest in his tone now, "if you live in town I can give you a lift."

In spite of the ribaldry Phillip had not been drinking, at least not beyond a couple of bottles of lager with lunch, and only soft drinks for the best part of the last hour or so. Julia glanced once more at the clock. It was five thirty, just twelve hours since she had collapsed into bed albeit for just two hours sleep. Julia hadn't taken to Phillip particularly, he seemed a little full of himself, but then again all three men seemed that way that afternoon. Maybe it was the male-bonding thing. Julia was out of sorts, and probably out of place in this macho pissing session. In any case, whether summoned or not, she did need to get home, and she felt she could stand Phillip's company for as long as it took to get her safely back to Jim and Katie. If it turned out to be Jim who had sent the message she would sort him out when she got home. *When* she got home.

"Ok Phillip, that's very kind of you. Can we go now please? I really need to get home, I'm dead on my feet."

"Fine," smiled Phillip, "I'll just make a quick call and I'll be with you."

With that he wriggled awkwardly out from the bench seat he'd been sharing with Julia during the long afternoon. Once again he brushed against her as he manouevred out of his place. Julia felt a sudden sense of relief, in addition to her growing exasperation with the noisy, apish antics of the three men, she'd resented Phillip's close proximity to her. Maybe tiredness had made her edgy and intolerant, maybe it enhanced a sense of claustrophobia, but she knew when she didn't feel comfortable. It felt great to regain a little space around her.

Phillip, oblivious to any irritation he had caused Julia, trotted to a less raucous area of the pub, clamping his neat, slim mobile to his ear as he walked. Julia followed him with her eyes for a moment before turning back to Andy and David.

"Sorry to be a killjoy David, but I'm flaking out and I should be at home, with Katie," she said, deliberately omitting any reference to Jim, in deference to Andy.

"No problem. Glad you came this afternoon, you know what

a soft spot I've got for my trusted deputy, my personal apprentice" said David affectionately. "Have you enjoyed yourself? That's all I care about."

"Yes, it's been fun," she lied, matching the fib with a false smile.

"Good. Good," said David, in a state of mellow semi-intoxication, only hearing what he wanted to hear.

Phillip reappeared, sliding his 'phone into the inside pocket of his jacket.

"I'm ready if you are," he announced airily. Julia nodded, and gracefully extricated herself from her seat.

"Goodnight David," she said, giving her amiable, and half-cut, boss a daughterly peck on the cheek. David grinned and winked at Julia his eyes twinkling.

"See you Andy," she mumbled at a very disappointed Lothario as she flung on her coat.

"Huh! Where's my kiss?" he grumbled loudly, mainly for David's benefit. His eyes though fixed on Julia's, which in turn darted floor-ward for cover.

David and Andy laughed in unison.

"You're backing the wrong horse there Andy, I've known our Julia for ten years and I only get a kiss on the cheek on my birthday and at Christmas," David chortled.

"So I have to wait ten years?" teased Andy, homing in on Julia's obvious discomfort.

"At least," was all she could think of, by way of countering his remark.

"All done with your so called banter?" Phillip interjected, "Because if you have exhausted your witty repartee for the afternoon, I can take this young lady home."

"I'm saving the best till you've gone," Andy fired back.

"Obviously!"

That was Julia's cue to fling one last smile at each of her still seated companions and lead the short march to the pub's exit. Phillip issued a casual wave in David and Andy's direction, mouthing the salute 'so long, losers' as he did so. It was all very juvenile but it made the three men happy, facile insults seemed to be the universal language of bonhomie.

"After you," said Phillip, holding the door open for Julia.

She smiled at him by way of thanks and stepped outside, the cold air hitting her like a moving train. Julia didn't like the cold, so why did it follow her around like a faithful puppy dog lapping at her heels?

TUESDAY – Diversions in Place

Phillip strode confidently ahead of Julia towards a large four-wheel drive car that seemed to have spread itself across at least two parking spaces. Julia pulled her trendy sapphire blue lightweight raincoat tightly across her chest and shivered.

"Freezing isn't it?" commented Phillip cheerily, a remark borne of some kind of sixth sense as he had not looked around to see her hunch and tremble against the cold. It was almost as if he had sensed her physical discomfort, or simply had eyes in the back of his neatly coiffured head.

There was a baritone double clunk followed a high pitched squeak as the car announced audibly that it's security systems had been disabled. He opened the driver's door with a deliberate flourish and hopped lightly up and into the impressive SUV, as the Americans prefer to call them. Julia tottered to the passenger door her arms still wrapped tightly across her chest against the chill evening air. As Phillip had not chivalrously opened the door for her, she was forced to unclasp one arm to heave open the passenger door and took her seat with a kind of bunny hop motion.

"Make yourself comfortable Julia," said Phillip, an arrogant smirk playing on the corner of his mouth, "soon thaw those icicles in here."

Phillip was right. Whatever make of wagon this was, the heating system was remarkably quick and efficient. The cold night air was swiftly banished and Julia bathed in the sudden warmth that radiated invisibly and noiselessly from the slatted vents in front of her. Phillip flicked on the radio and a woman with honeyed tones oozed the news, from the vehicle's multi speaker system, with crystal clarity. The woman's unhurried dulcet delivery filled the interior of the car, her reassuring voice as soft and supple as the beige leather seats that supported them. Phillip smiled at Julia, revealing a row of gleaming white teeth, a smile that lingered for just a second or two too long, which Julia found unflattering and mildly unnerving. It put Julia in mind of the wolf in 'Little Red Riding Hood'. She shuddered under her designer raincoat, but not this time, with the cold.

"Where would you like to go then?" he asked ambiguously.

"Home," said Julia plaintively.

"I see, that's fine, but you might want to tell me where you live," replied Phillip, remaining marginally on the right side of condescension.

Julia felt a little embarrassed. Perhaps she had unreasonably misinterpreted Phillip's attempt at a friendly smile as being vaguely predatory. She was tired and eager to get home, she had experienced an eventful and unusual night, and maybe her judgment was temporarily letting her down, or her guard drawn up too high. Either way she felt an apology was necessary:

"Sorry," she said meekly, and provided the necessary directions.

Imperceptibly she breathed out, and the tense knot in the pit of her stomach which had begun to constrict her in the pub, relaxed. Phillip nodded earnestly but couldn't resist saying:

"Well, we shan't need the on screen Sat-Nav in this baby to get there," and raised one eyebrow, Roger Moore style.

The large car gave a low pitched snarl as it rolled forward, slowly and precisely manouevering out of the car park onto the open road.

"She's a magnificent machine, isn't she?" commented Phillip entirely rhetorically.

Julia nodded, oblivious to the pedigree or type of the 'magnificent beast' as long as it got her home. Phillip in any case wasn't looking at her, his eyes were fixed on the road ahead and his mind was wandering far beyond that. Julia again snatched an agitated looked at her watch.

"Will the tea be in the dog by now?" teased Phillip, once more deploying his, apparently, all-seeing eye.

"No, not at all," she replied hastily, "it's just that my husband will have to take my daughter to Brownies, I hope he's remembered, that's all."

Julia had no idea why she felt the need to explain herself so emphatically and Phillip nodded empathetically, though it was patently clear that his attention span for Julia's domestic arrangements had long been exceeded. After a pause of a few seconds, whilst they sat in a queue of commuter traffic he commented:

"You do that a lot, look at your watch. Are you a natural clock-watcher? Or has your husband got you on a tight rein?"

It was an unnecessary and facile remark, and instantly caused Julia to snap back in irritation:

"Neither, I lead a busy life and I do my best to be in the right place at the right time. I'm sure you're the same."

Phillip didn't reply, he simply sneered to himself. He seemed to enjoy baiting the attractive young woman for some reason. There was a latent streak of misogyny lurking not far beneath the ostensibly smooth surface of the young man. Phillip had a healthy respect for the time and the place; it was just that as a rule he liked to be in control of both. He glanced discreetly at his passenger. 'Not bad' he thought, 'got some spirit.'

The rush hour traffic seemed especially relentless tonight. It took an age for the prestige vehicle to snake the short distance from the pub through the traffic lights. The radio provided little respite as the queue moved tortuously forward, a cars length at a time, the rapid sequencing of the lights frustrating any attempt to make ground.

The journey, though relatively short in distance, was

taking an age. Julia felt frustrated. Frustrated at the unrelenting traffic and the dispassionate traffic light system that loosely controlled it. Frustrated at the selfish drivers who cut lanes to gain a cars length on other road users and obstructing progress through the queue. Frustrated with her flirtation with Andy, and frustrated that she had shied away from brazening it out a little longer in the pub the previous night. Frustrated with Jim … she wasn't sure why, but she felt that he was somehow to blame for all her frustration. Frustrated that she couldn't simply seek sanctuary from the mad pre-Christmas world. Frustrated with her 'phone … then the message tone sounded:

'Looking gud, J. Y cudnt u stay? Wish u were here. A x'.

Julia couldn't resist a girlish smile at Andy's schoolboy message. It was so juvenile, so Andy. She couldn't explain why the merest contact sent a tingle into her stomach, but it did. She wanted to respond but her sense of discretion took hold and yet another feeling of irritation zipped across her chest and shoulders. She was right to resist the urge to reply as Phillip's inbuilt sensor sweep had taken in the momentary interruption to their silence:

"Alright?" he asked with nonchalant concern.

"Fine," was Julia's initially curt reply, but then her manners pushed themselves forcibly to the surface, " ... thank you." Her manners retreated quickly, reproaching themselves soundly as they disappeared back into her 'better self'.

Thereafter silence between the two was resumed, apart from the incessant babble of the radio presenter, albeit in perfect diction. It was a soulless mechanical tune which interrupted the stiff silence. Phillip looked from one side of the car to the other then began to pat himself down.

"Sorry Julia," he explained distractedly, as he continued his strange contortions, "'phone."

Julia watched him, unimpressed, as he fumbled beneath his coat. The traffic began to move in their lane but Phillip's car remained stationary while he wrestled with an inside pocket made largely inaccessible by the seatbelt. She watched helplessly as the cars in front moved off ahead, one by one. They stayed stubbornly where they were, Phillip annoyingly oblivious to the sudden movement of traffic. The car behind sounded its horn loudly and impatiently. Phillip looked briefly in the mirror:

"Big horn for a small tin can!" he sneered. However, the look of disdain transformed into a triumphant grin as he whipped the 'phone, which had desisted its call by now, into the open. He turned to share the moment with Julia, but she did not share his sense of joy at the retrieval of the handset. Her expressionless stare was directed wholly at a bare expanse of tarmac and in the distance those emotionless, weary, unyielding traffic lights turning stoically back to red. She felt her stomach churn.

One handed he steered his car slowly forward, the

'phone now perched precariously on a hunched shoulder: "Voice mail message," he explained.

Phillip was sublimely oblivious to Julia's look of distaste; he was listening intently to his message. 'Surely this awesome driving machine had a hands-free amongst its various gadgets?' she thought irritably. The car behind beeped angrily again, but it's hooting was in vain because the lights once again changed to red before Phillip had gathered sufficient speed, or indeed concentration, to cross them. The driver in the trailing car threw his arms up in the air in anger and irritation, emotions that echoed along the entire line of cars stuck behind the dawdling SUV. The mass frustration he caused to the snaking line of homeward bound travellers made no impact on Phillip. Instead he listened intently to his message, a deep frown creasing his brow as he did so. Re-pocketing the phone he remained strangely silent. In spite of every instinct to the contrary Julia could not help filling the void:

"Everything alright?" she ventured, with laboured concern.

"Not exactly," he began. Julia's heart sank, "girlfriend's gone out to evening class and she's sure that she's forgotten to turn the gas out under some vegetables she was getting ready for tea. She gets the tea on the go, I finish off, then we can eat when she gets back from college it's a kind of a routine."

Julia nodded dismissively, though she didn't really

care about Phillip's domestic arrangements with his unlucky girlfriend.

"I'll have to go and turn it off, otherwise I'll have a burnt pan, a kitchen full of smoke, and earache till Christmas Day."

'Oh, great! All I wanted was a straightforward lift home!' thought Julia angrily. She felt her lips tighten across her clenched teeth in sheer vexation. With that the lights changed, and what should have been a short journey home became another unscheduled detour as Phillip's car growled into life and rolled smoothly forwards. But instead of following the other traffic onto the busy ring road Phillip deftly switched lanes and drove onto the one lane system through town, to the collective annoyance of the tailback of drivers who had been stuck behind him.

They were there in a matter of minutes, parked outside Phillip's smart townhouse. The street was empty, bathed in a sterile white light from a single lamp, it looked icy and inhospitable, matching Julia's fast deteriorating mood.

"Coming in then?" Phillip called cheerily, as he jumped out of the driver's seat onto the pavement outside the house. "Too cold to sit out here."

"I'll be fine," said Julia icily, "you won't be long will you?"

"Depends what state the saucepan's in," he replied simply. "Come on in, I'll be as quick as I can. The heating will be on, at least you'll be warm."

It sounded an innocent and reasonable enough offer,

and after all she had endured enough time in a cold, deserted street the previous night for one winter. Julia reluctantly descended from the large car and followed Phillip unenthusiastically along the short block-paved pathway leading to his house. There was the familiar double clunk and squeak as Phillip locked the vehicle, now behind her. As the hazards flashed in confirmation of the cars high-security status the front of the house was briefly illuminated with an eerie orange light.

Phillip opened the highly glossed, red, wooden front door and walked briskly inside, flicking on the hall light in one flowing movement. He casually tossed his keys onto an oak console table in the hallway. The house had a new smell, and the walls were unmarked, the plaster fresh, powdery and overwhelmingly magnolia. Julia crossed the threshold and stood quietly on the mat behind the door, which she pushed to gently. Phillip ambled unhurriedly along the hall and disappeared behind a gleaming white, wooden panelled interior door. For a man responding to a domestic emergency Phillip's nonchalant manner belay any sense of great urgency.

"Go into the lounge, it's nice and warm in there. Heating's been on," called Phillip's disembodied breezily.

'Shouldn't you be checking your pan?' thought Julia as she shuffled grudgingly into the lounge.

It was a cosy room inevitably dominated by a large

Adam's style marble fireplace. The gas fire in the form of a fire basket was unlit, but the shelf was adorned with a couple of candlesticks with red coloured candles in them, and an array of Christmas cards. There was a deep, floppy sofa opposite the fire, the sort that reached out and snuggled up to you as you sat down. A couple of table lamps in brass and dark metal glowed softly, the whole effect being soothing and inviting. The low-lit room, festooned in sumptuous fabrics and natural woods, was a place to kick off your shoes, tuck your feet under your bottom and sink, lazily, into the cosy settee, wine glass clutched tightly in both hands. The ambient warmth of the preset heating combined with the subtle charm of the surroundings drew you in beguilingly. Unconsciously, Julia began to thaw, physically and emotionally, under its spell.

Phillip reappeared carrying two large glasses of red wine:
"Thanks for being so patient. Disaster averted. I though a quick one for the road by way of an apology"

Phillip stood there in his shirtsleeves, already divested of his suit jacket and tie, smiling benignly. Julia knew she should still be feeling annoyed, she should have been home more than a quarter of an hour ago. But she had already consigned her efforts to be in time to take Katie to Brownies to the waste-bin. The cosiness and warmth of the room had washed over her, dispossessing her of her growing anxiety.

She did just want to sit down, kick off her shoes and relax, even if it was for just ten minutes. She looked at her watch, Jim would be in the car with Katie now, it would be a while before he got back. She looked at Phillip standing there coyly, against the backdrop of his lovely home and he seemed somehow less of a jackass. Maybe she had misjudged him, transposed the irritations of the last twenty or so hours onto his undeserving shoulders. It was Phillip, after all, who had stayed sober during the afternoon's frivolities, and it was he who had broken away from his friends to offer her a lift home when she so desperately needed one. OK, so there had been a slight detour, who hadn't left a pan on the boil at some time? In a way it just went to show that it wasn't just her week that wasn't going to plan. 'What the heck,' she thought recklessly.

"OK, one for the road," she said, exhaling deeply.

She took the glass from Phillip's hand and sat in front of the unlit fire, perching on the very edge of the sofa cushion.

"Just twenty minutes, then I must get back, I really must."

"That's fine, I'll just take a couple of sips then, I can finish my wine later," said Phillip amiably, reaching in down to ignite the flames on the fire basket.

Phillip took a seat on the sofa, next to Julia, but leaving a respectable gap between them.

"Take your coat off, kick your shoes off, make yourself

comfortable," he said genially.

"Known Andy long?" he continued, leading the conversation.

"Not long, he works in the same office complex, but for a supplier," replied Julia civilly, discreetly easing her feet out of her shoes, just for a moment. It felt blissful, like an impromptu foot sauna.

"Do you like the wine? It's a claret. Always nice at Christmas, don't you think? I get it from my wine merchant. There's no point buying cheap plonk is there?"

"I don't normally like claret but this is quite nice," replied Julia honestly.

For a moment the conversation froze awkwardly. The two didn't really know each other after all, their connection was through their mutual associations, and they were most likely still guffawing at each other's bad jokes in the pub. Julia took it upon herself to break the silence:

"I like your fireplace," she enthused, the wine warming her inside and out.

"Thanks, came with the house. It was a bit of a selling point, gives the room a focal point."

Julia nodded in agreement, once again scanning the room, noticing how precise and tidy everything was about it. The reflection of the flames from the gas fire danced on the surface of the wine, the yellow and deep red melding in a warm kaleidoscope of colours. The flames were as hypnotic as they were warm. Julia shuffled back just a little, retreating from the wave of heat which lapped at her lower legs. As she did, Phillip moved imperceptibly a little closer to the middle of the sofa.

Julia stared, mesmerised by the flicker of the yellow and blue flames, sipping daintily from the large bowl of the wine glass Phillip had given her. Phillip meanwhile stared at Julia, equally mesmerized by the attractive profile of his guest. She sensed him examining her and turned towards him, catching him out.

"Sorry, I was miles away," he started.

There was an awkward pause.

"Why don't you take off your coat while you finish your wine? You won't feel the benefit when you go outside," he suggested quietly.

"Hardly worth it, I'll have to go in a minute," she said a little frostily, but curiously and inexplicably she met him half way and unbuttoned it so that it hung open across her shapely knees. It was almost as if she didn't want to be rude to her host.

Again it went quiet, Julia took a longer sip of wine and glanced at the clock in the corner of the room. Phillip seemed consumed with an air of anticipation.

"Almost seven already," she declared matter-of-factly, "I really should go."

Time was not Julia's friend this week it seemed. With that she tipped back her glass and drained it to the bottom.

Without further comment she stood up and began to re-button her coat.

"Thanks for the drink, Phillip," she said coolly, holding out the empty glass for him to take from her.

"Have another glass, there's no rush. In for a penny, eh? It's nearly Christmas, go wild!" he suggested, giving her a friendly wink.

"No, I really must get home." Julia replied quite emphatically.

"Half a glass then," persisted the host hopefully.

Julia smiled, but this time her smile was a little strained and tinged with suspicion. She fastened the belt of her raincoat across her stomach and turned towards the living room door.

"Oh well. At least I offered," said Phillip in a good-natured tone.

Phillip strode quickly to the door, overtaking her and holding it open like a doorman at The Savoy. He stood clutching the door handle, a little nervous perspiration apparent on his top lip. However, Phillip had effectively restricted the exit route with his body half turned to Julia in the doorway. Julia put her head down to avoid making eye contact with Phillip, whose cheeks were visibly flushed. She did up the higher buttons on her mac all the way to her neck as she manoeuvred awkwardly past him. As she did she caught Phillip lightly with her elbow:

"Sorry Phillip," she began.

However, Phillip had already taken hold of her trailing elbow, edging across the open doorway so they were face to face. Julia was taken by surprise, for a few split seconds she failed to see what was happening. She hesitated just long enough for Phillip to pull her firmly towards him. Julia felt a sense of growing alarm as they stared at each other, eye to eye.

His arms were by now snaking round her back. His right arm stayed in the small of her back while the left descended towards her bottom. As he pulled her towards him Julia found herself locked in a powerful but uninvited embrace. A frightened squeak of protest leapt from her throat before his mouth pressed firmly against hers and his hips thrust into her midriff. Her mac was being pulled in all directions and the lower flaps of the coat separated to reveal her skirt underneath. Fortunately the buttons she had fastened all the way up to her throat held strong.

She froze under his assault for what seemed like an eternity. He pushed his lips harder and harder against her mouth, urging her to respond. She felt his hot breath on her face. His arms snaked about her body, exploring the contours of her back, shoulders and buttocks. It was like being enveloped by an octopus. It was unexpected, unwelcome and overwhelming. She couldn't find the strength to pull away and escape his roving grip. It was almost as if everything had stopped and she was no longer part of what was going on. She was disoriented, in a strange, half-lit house, her body rigid against a stranger's roaming arms, mouth and tongue. It was like an horrific out of body experience, or one of those vile, sweat-inducing nightmares that terrify your unconscious mind in the dead of night.

Her mouth stayed closed against the repeated foray of his lips and the attempted incursion of his tongue into her unwilling mouth. She closed her eyes tightly, feeling somehow that if she didn't look it might all go away. Phillip interpreted that simple act quite differently, and his meandering lustful actions intensified, physically pushing Julia back into the living room and towards the sofa. They were intertwined in a ghoulish shuffling dance with Phillip leading. He forced Julia into taking tiny backward steps, fighting against the urge to fall and at the same time prevented from doing so by his strong arms which were wrapped roughly around her back. Was he stronger than he looked, or was her strength deserting her in her hour of need? Was this some form of defensive capitulation?

She felt the shock of the dramatic encounter passing and turning into raw fear. She felt robbed of oxygen, her breathing shallow and shaky, her lungs refusing to draw in sufficient air. Her body became a desert, she was numb all over, she felt nothing physically, just fear.

Within a few seconds she felt the arm of the settee against the back of her leg. Phillip's mouth by now had strayed to her neck where he pecked and nibbled. Her coat was tangled around her chest constricting her further. As it pulled in one direction and the other it restricted the movement of her arms stopping her from pushing him away. Valiantly she tried to maintain her balance but momentum and gravity were with Phillip. Her knee length skirt rose and fell with the gyration of his body against hers, his hands dropped to squeeze her buttocks through her panties as though he was kneading dough. She felt like a helpless spectator, a gaping bystander, unable to act and unable to scream, just watching in terror, watching in slow motion. As Phillip pawed and nibbled he made little groaning noises that cruelly added to the whole craziness of the situation.

He bore down on Julia's unresponsive body; his body weight caused her back to arc painfully, as he explored her with his hands and mouth, desperately seeking a response. Suddenly the pressure became too great to resist and Julia toppled helplessly backwards onto the sofa, taking Phillip with her. He bit his lip as he tumbled, and he yelped like a frightened puppy.

Suddenly the groping stopped as they lay one on top of the other regaining their breath. Phillip dabbed his finger at his bleeding lip and felt aggrieved to have suffered injury.

"I've split my bloody lip," he moaned, "I hope it hasn't gone on the settee."

It was the sheer matter-of-factness of his impassive

statement that roused Julia's hibernating faculties. The muscles and tendons, sinew and joints that had been impotent spectators for the last couple of minutes were suddenly reanimated. In her veins and arteries, lungs and heart adrenalin fuelled rage surged like an acid bath.

Her arms, momentarily freed from his tentacle like grip, swung ferociously into life. One pulled furiously at his wiry blonde hair, the other disentangled his roaming hand from her backside. This sudden act of resistance caused a jolt to Phillip's senses. Suddenly the tide had turned. Julia glared at her assailant, her blue eyes flashing with pure anger. Her vice-like grip on his hair was resolute. Phillip felt the sting of pain in the roots of his scalp, and sudden, naked fear registered in his wide, watery eyes. Phillip tried to look away, but found it easier to just close his eyes, to shut out the hate pouring into them.

"You total dick-head," she screamed, with the full power of her re-functioning lungs. "What the hell was that about? What did I do or say to deserve that, you utter moron?"

There was no response. What could he possibly say? She felt his body go limp as latent energy leaked from every pore of his deflated body. Now it was his turn to feel helpless. His primitive male ego retreated in abject defeat and he was rendered a whimpering shell.He raised himself off Julia's disheveled form, his arms locked out straight on the arm of the settee.

"I thought you liked me. That's why you came in. I thought it's what you wanted," he twittered feebly.

Feeling no compassion for her tormentor Julia drew back her knee sharply and positively, and even in the confined bundle in which they now found themselves, she aimed it upwards with uncanny power and accuracy.

Phillip howled like a coyote. The hands which had just minutes before been straying unrepentantly over Julia now darted with some immediacy downwards towards his own, now redundant, reproductive zone. For a second time that evening he collapsed downwards, his spectacular demolition once more pinning Julia to the cushions on the sofa. This time however, Phillip's body lay limply in place and Julia simply rolled from under him, landing on the soft, shaggy rug beside the settee.

Julia lay on the mat, panting and trying to regain composure, smoothing the clothes that had ridden around her body back into some semblance of order and decency. Phillip lay face down on the sofa groaning, one hand cradling his genitals the other dangling loosely to the floor. As sanity threatened to return to the soft lit, tastefully adorned living room, there sounded the distinctive click of a key in a lock.

"Phillip … Phillip. I'm home. The lecturer gave us an early finish at college, I think it was the staff Christmas do tonight."

There was a pause and the owner of the voice could be heard shuffling around in the hall. Chances are she was hanging up her coat, glancing at the mail, her usual routine when she arrived home. Home sweet home: sanctuary from a busy and wicked world outside.

"Did you get my voicemail? Did you put the tea on like I asked you to? I bet you haven't," she called brightly.

It was like watching a disaster happen in slow motion from a vantage point too far away to warn the hapless victims. Julia shuffled onto her bottom so that she was in a sitting position on the rug, but her clothes were creased and disarranged, her hair in disarray and her senses still desperately trying to reconnect with reality. She watched the shadows cast by the fire cavorting over the brilliant white plaster ceiling like a macabre puppet show, a sense of doom flooding her mind.

Phillip remained partly oblivious to the new drama that was about to unfold in his living room. He was too busy worrying about how far inside him Julia had transported his testicles.

TUESDAY - Wake Up Call

Terri Fisher is a nice girl. She works as an assistant buyer for a high street fashion store chain. One evening a week she studies conversational French at college, in the hope she might get to visit the fashion houses of Paris one day. Once a week she meets old school friends for a drink and a meal. They chat about old times and new loves. She is an innocent, even at the age of twenty-six, it's one of her many endearing attributes.

Terri is pretty; she has large, trusting brown eyes. She has a willowy figure and her tasteful, designer clothes hang from her as though she were a beautiful mannequin. Nevertheless, taking nothing for granted, Terri is a regular participant at the Zumba and Body Pump classes at her local gym. Never will Terri Fisher be a slave to an occasionally naughty or exotic diet. In habit and politics she is conservative with a small *c*, discrete, law-abiding and still loves her parents, very much in fact. Terri is the epitome of a nice, well-balanced, hard-working young woman. Too good to be true? Not at all, Terri is what she is, but she has one grave vice…

… and *he* is currently writhing on the sofa, that they had chosen together just a month or two before, clutching his violently aching crotch. Phillip is her blindside. Those envious of her might argue that he is what a divine spirit sent down to balance out her over-abundance of positive traits. However, the blunt truth is that he is simply a shallow, egocentric, woman chasing, misogynist, amoral knob-head. Phillip is Terri's Achilles heel. Most of her friends can see it, but lovely, trusting, sweet-natured Terri cannot. She suffers from emotional colour blindness of the most chronic variety.

Their love blew in on a wind; in Terri's case it was the steamy, sandy caress of a desert sirocco; in Phillip's case, the destructive gust of a hurricane. Terri simply existed in the eye of the storm; blind to the carnage he left in his wake. How often it is that the Phillips of this world rely upon the stormy dust-swirl created by their ego to mask the grainy fragility of their limited potential. It cannot be denied that Phillip is good at his job, makes decent money, is decent looking and knows how to live and have a laugh. It's just that overall, all things considered, by and large, and as Julia succinctly and accurately put it, he is a total dick-head.

Terri hovered innocuously in the hallway, still safe and untouched, in the eye of the gathering storm, waiting for Phillip to respond. Then her hand reached gently for the door handle, it was the first teetering, unconscious step toward the black swirl of the tornado.

On the other side of the door, and despite her dishevellment and shock, Julia had entered a state of almost transcendental calm. She, unlike her recent nemesis, had heard the front door open. She had heard the cheerful trill of

Terri's voice calling to her man, her rock, her lover, her protector. Terri's imminent entry into this perverse pantomime raced through Julia's mind with the speed of a tilting train in open countryside. Julia knew the next few moments would be testing mentally and emotionally but as she sat upright and watched the doorknob twist her mind remained calm and focused with an ethereal strength drawn from the aftermath of her ordeal.

In the hallway Terri hesitated, surprised that Phillip had not called back to her, from his usual position in front the HD, surround sound, Smart TV. After all his car was outside taking up an obscene amount of the roadside and the lights were on in the kitchen. Perhaps he had abandoned the telly for his iPod? Perhaps his 'Beats' were drilling something raucous into his eardrums? She loosened her grip on the door handle and considered going upstairs to change out of her smart suit into something more suited to lounging lazily in front of the TV, with a tray and a small glass of Chardonnay. With her body half turned towards the stairs a hoarse cry broke the silence. The voice was that of her boyfriend, the noise he made was the call of destiny.

"For f****...sake!" was the sound that crashed through the neatly painted interior door and slid unapologetically into Terri's very charming ear canal. Not the kind of French she was taught at night school, but she understood it easily enough.

It was an unexpected bawling that alerted Terri immediately to something quite out of the ordinary. It demanded investigation and her grip re-tightened on the door handle. This time she twisted it more forcibly. The only noise made by the door, as it swept open was a very slight *swoosh* as it caught the generous pile of the pale lounge carpet.

Still clutching his throbbing testes Phillip sat bolt upright and swivelled round as the door brushed the surface of the floor covering. His eyes widened to a manic, terrified stare. Terri froze to the spot as their eyes locked across the room. Terri saw Phillip hunch-backed on the sofa his hands thrust into his lap, his head snapping sharply towards her. His eyes were like saucers, filled with fear, which ironically brought a sudden dull numbness to his throbbing nuts. He foraged helplessly in his brain for a credible story to make sense of the disastrous scenario before Terri, as she paused mid-stride into the romantically lit room. Unsurprisingly the internal search engine he lodged between his ears came up *'no matching results for your search'*. Oddly, the same function in Terri's mind instantly flooded her with a variety of corresponding answers. Her eyes swept the room in disbelief. No-one spoke, words were momentarily superfluous.

"What's happening?" ventured Terri nervously, her voice tiny and shaking. "Are you OK?" she continued, her concern a lingering testament to her feelings for the worthless man in front of her.

The sound of her voice was enough to sweep the temporary 'anaesthetic' from his groin. Suddenly the pain returned in a surge, and with an injured, helpless smile, he slumped forward and groaned. He was a man trapped with nowhere to run, a hopeless man.

Terri's took a couple of hesitant steps forward. Phillip straddled the settee awkwardly, his shirt creased and the tails draping over his trouser belt. He wore the look of guilt like a luminous badge of shame. Below him, on the rug in front of the fire, lit by the flickering light of the imitation flames, sat a reasonably attractive woman, whose clothes, hair and lip-stick, bore the marks of recent disarray. On her shoulders the woman had a coat which was either half on or half off, neither scenario boding especially well to the confused young woman who surveyed the scene, through increasingly watery eyes.

Terri's response was not typically incendiary; she did not know how to respond to what she saw. There was so much information to process, so many questions, so few alternatives. Eventually as her thoughts began slowly to converge through the confusion it seemed to Terri that hysteria and tears were probably appropriate. In a microsecond her conscious mind turned the reaction into tears which cascaded uncontrollably down Terri's cheeks and which seeped less attractively from her pretty nose. At first there was no noise, her ribs and lungs were still frozen, but silently both Julia and Phillip watched the emotion well deep inside the young woman counting the seconds before the hurt burst, unrestrained, from her aching lungs.

As the wailing sound rose to a crescendo Julia's Zen-like calm was shattered by the woman's cries. It wasn't so much the noise but the sheer silent power of the deep gulps, which preceded each agonised yell, which shook Julia. It was like watching a distressed baby depriving itself of oxygen in the throes of a tantrum. It was horrific. When her cries filled every corner of the sizeable living room, it actually came as a relief.

Julia quickly became the sole focus of Terri's tear flooded, accusing eyes. Julia had no desire to engage Terri in eye contact and instead nervously patted down and adjusted her disarranged clothing. However, this simple act had the effect of bringing Terri's furious attention upon her even more. Julia wisely chose not to speak, there was no point. She sat there on the rug, like a naughty puppy that had chewed the sofa.

Phillip, unsurprisingly, 'hid' quietly in the background of Terri's wrath, glad that her attention was focused on the victim rather than the perpetrator. Under the cover of the, so far, wordless confrontation he wriggled painfully to the edge of the sofa and sat himself upright so that he was facing his girlfriend's back, and most importantly remained out of her eye line. Julia looked up and watched the young woman as she stood resolutely in front of her, fighting to stem the flow of tears so that the power of speech might be returned to her. Julia braced herself for an onslaught, verbal, physical or possibly both. In her position sat on the rug retreat was not an option, and getting to her feet would have been tantamount to someone shouting 'seconds out'. Though Julia was the victim she understood that Terri could not know this. Ultimately Terri was a victim too, of a different sort, but a victim, and Julia couldn't help empathising.

Phillip let out an involuntary cough. It was only nervous impulse but it was enough to draw Terri's attention back to him, though she kept a steady, if watery eye on Julia. All the time Terri was assessing and reassessing this unknown woman, evaluating her threat to her relationship and as an interloper to her home.

"Bastard," was the only word that Terri managed to squeeze from her mouth. She flicked out the word with the speed of a snake's tongue and with just as much venom.

Phillip looked away guiltily. The source of the bullshit, which ordinarily flowed easily from his mouth, had dried up. Terri's eyes flicked briefly to the empty wine glasses:

"So this is what you do when I'm at college?" she began quietly, but with each word her tone rose in pitch minutely, "and on the one occasion I get to finish early I come home to find you shagging some old slapper you've picked up goodness knows where," she continued, ignoring the hurt on Julia's face, her voice rising by degrees to a crescendo.

Phillip groaned, though whether in physical or mental pain was unclear.

"What's the matter? Why are you making that stupid noise?" Terri demanded tersely of Phillip, the well of tears drying by the second.

Julia seized her chance and took it coldly:

"Because I kneed him in the balls," she announced, glaring at the crestfallen man cringing on the sofa.

Terri rounded on Julia straight away, glaring maniacally at her, her nostrils flaring her eyes and brain formulating an attack plan.

"Tell her. Tell her you dipstick," Julia shouted at Phillip angrily. "Be a man for once in your life. Tell her what you did. Tell your girlfriend what you did ... *to me!*"

"Tell me what?" screamed Terri at her wretched boyfriend, ignoring Julia in a grand and obvious way.

She was met by a cowardly silence, but Julia was not in the mood to let the lecherous sex pest off the hook. She turned to the Terri, who was inflamed with rage and uncertainty, and, using her conviction as a blunt weapon, said:

"Your boyfriend kindly offered to give me a lift home from the pub, where we'd been with some other work colleagues. I was stuck there without a car and I was in a rush to get home. On the way he said that you had left a voicemail to say you'd left some vegetables on the oven and the saucepan might boil dry, or something like that. So, 'Sir Galahad' said he would have to go home to sort that out first."

It was more of a rambling account than Julia had intended and Terri was beginning to look impatient. She stood hands on hips, eyes dark and narrowed, her body language screaming *'get on with it, you whore, and it had better be good'*.

Julia picked up the pace and almost garbled:

"I offered to wait outside in the car, but the *white knight* wouldn't hear of it, *'come in, it's too cold to wait outside'*.

Terri's expression remained fixed, and the rigid set of her otherwise attractive jawline suggested strongly that she was not being convinced by any of the words uttered by the tart that had taken advantage of her good-natured boyfriend. Julia could see she wasn't reaching the young woman who glowered at her.

"You tell her the rest. *You* tell her what happened next … and don't try and turn the blame," she demanded of Phillip, who still cowered from both of them on the sofa.

"Yes, why don't you take the story from there," said Terri in a low growl, turning her fiery glare on Phillip, and dismissing Julia with a single sneer.

Phillip made some noises from deep within his throat but he seemed incapable of forming these into actual words. The colour had drained from his face, the dim light making him look grey with dark shadows under his eyes and beneath his bottom lip. He looked every inch the monster who had been beaten back into its dingy lair.

"He can't speak. *You* tell me," snarled Terri, turning back to Julia, who had used the brief interlude in interrogation to stand up.

"I waited in the lounge while he sorted out whatever kitchen crisis there was ..."

"There was no kitchen crisis, as you call it," said Terri icily.

"I didn't know that," replied Julia defensively, "anyway, when he came back out of the kitchen he brought two glasses of wine with him. I was too late to take my daughter to Brownies and I didn't want to be rude to someone who was doing me a favour ..."

"So you thought you'd shag him to say 'thank you'?"

"No!" Julia's response was firm and emphatic. She suddenly tired of being the villain of the piece. It was unjust and unfair, and now that the young woman had had time to adjust to the circumstances Julia was no longer content to be the 'whipping boy' for the situation.

"*He* grabbed *me* when I asked him to take me home. He forced himself on me, groping me all over, trying to force his tongue down my throat; it was horrible. I struggled but he pushed me backwards onto the sofa. His arms were everywhere, I fell backwards and that's when I got the chance to put my knee where it would do the most damage."

Julia looked Philip directly in the eye, but he looked away as if he was flinching from bright sunlight. Terri also stared at him, her expression demanding that he gainsay the stranger in her midst. Phillip almost seemed to be melting away in front of both women. Julia sensed the minutely changing dynamics and looked at Terri, directly and unwaveringly.

"So are you saying he tried to rape you? Is that what you're telling me?" asked the young woman desperately, not knowing now how to channel her anger.

"I'm saying that he's a chancer who fancies himself and thinks he's God's gift to women. How could a mere woman resist his chat and his charm? Well I bloody did."

After the shortest of silences Phillip briefly reanimated. He threw his arms indignantly into the air, shaking his head vigorously:

"Don't listen," he sneered, "stupid tart came on to me. She'd been giving me the eye all afternoon. Couldn't wait to get me on her own. I said it was time to get going and she was all over me like a rash ..."

Terri responded in a quiet, slow, deliberate voice:

"So why bring a woman who's been coming on to you all afternoon here? To our house?" she said quietly, mulling over the words of the unknown woman and the loud, brash protest of her significant other. "Why pour a woman, who you think is a predatory 'man-hunter', a glass of wine in *our* living room? Most of all what was all the bullshit about me leaving a saucepan on the hob? I left you a voicemail to tell you which pizza I fancied. You know very well that we always have pizza from the freezer after I've been to college. We pig out in front of the telly. Well now we know which one of us is the pig!"

As much as she wanted Julia branded as a harlot, a liar, a tart, too many things rang true, factually and instinctively. After a very brief contemplative silence Terri spat out the words she had tried to deny to herself on many occasions and not least of all this evening:

"Phillip you really *are* a tosser! A *class A*- knob, a dick-head and a loser..."

Whether poor Terri ran out of defamatory references or simply decided less was more in terms of verbal abuse, she stopped there. The deflation of anger in her breast was apparent. Instead she was consumed by a wave of crushing disappointment. She knew there would be other consequences, far reaching ones, but they would have to be faced later. Julia watched the emotional spectrum play out on the pretty features of the young woman. Was it a consolation that Julia's horrible ordeal might have saved Terri from a life of continual deception and hurt? Any feeling of sisterhood was savagely cut short by Terri's next words: "Ok, you've had your say, now get lost! I want you out of my house and out of my life ... NOW!"

Julia was momentarily taken aback. 'I'm a victim here too you know' she thought indignantly, but wisely chose not to put her protest into words. Instead she decided to leave quietly, avoiding the indignity of further assault, as unjust as her peremptory dismissal might have been.

Terri neither moved nor flinched as Julia sidled past her. Julia satisfied herself by throwing a glance of contempt at Phillip who hung his head like a guilty schoolboy. Terri maintained a steady resolute glare at her soon-to-be former partner, determined not to give Julia the satisfaction of seeing the anguish in her young eyes.

Phillip shrugged his shoulders weakly at Terri in a fairly pathetic attempt to deny any wrongdoing. Terri's eyes burnt through him, she had finally witnessed *the end* and there was no coming back. He would beg and whimper over the coming weeks, he would 'phone and email, text and send flowers but none of it would matter.

Terri would suffer pain and heartache, she would search her soul and relive the good times in disbelief but in spite of moments of crushing uncertainty and vulnerability she would reach the conclusion that 'this bird had flown'. These were wounds that wouldn't mend, blood would flow until the heart of this relationship stopped beating once and for all.

Outside Julia took a deep breath of the cold, crisp air. She dug her hands deep into her coat pockets. As she walked along the harshly lit street, cars littered on the kerb-side of both sides of the road, she began to tremble. Not this time with cold, but with the latent shock of her disturbing encounter. Her entire body quivered, her nerves flowing in waves like a ripples in a pond. She stopped and sat on a wall her eyes watering and dry, noiseless sobs beating against her chest.

A young lad ambled by gorging on a steaming bag of chips. He looked at Julia from beneath his hoodie and stopped hoovering hot chips into his mouth for a moment:
"You ok missus?" he asked gruffly, but with a genuine concern.

Julia nodded feebly, though it was clear she was far from alright.
"Can I do anything?" he asked, not really knowing what help he could be.

Julia smiled through her tears and said, simply:
"No, thanks."

The lad walked away, stopping a few yards further on and looking back down the street to where Julia sat. He hesitated; he didn't feel right about leaving her there, distressed and alone. As he walked reluctantly on he tossed the bag and the rest of his chips over the wall of a house, he suddenly felt too sad to finish his meal, without knowing why.

It was dark and bitingly cold. Julia wanted to go home now more than ever, but to walk would take ages and she really wasn't in the mood for a long trek through the wintry streets. Her fingers, toes and ears tingled uncomfortably with the cold. The message tone sounded on her 'phone and she pulled it from her bag with icy fingers. The screen lit and the message read:

'Go home, quiet night in. You'll be fine.'

The number attached to the message was the same unknown number as before. Whoever was sending these messages was really starting to annoy her now. If someone thought they were being funny, they weren't. It was uncanny and a little scary, Julia felt as though someone was watching her.

"If you've got something to say, say it," she said out loud, to no one and everyone.

An old man on his way to the pub looked at her as though she was a mad woman. He carried on watching her warily as he continued along the street and almost walked into a lamppost in the process; that at least brought a smile to Julia's pale, drawn face.

She decided not to ring Jim and drag both him and Katie out into the cold. She caught a bus, which rattled and bounced its winding course to where she lived. It had been an age since Julia had used public transport, but the journey on the virtually empty single decker was strangely enjoyable. In the stark, harsh tube lighting of the bus she dabbed at her face in the reflection of the mirror of her compact to remove any tear stains or runs of mascara. Deftly she brushed a layer of lip-gloss onto her lips and tousled her hair to bring some body and shape back to it before pinging the bell to bring the rattling, plodding bus to a halt at the stop near her house.

Needless to say Jim and Katie were back from Brownies, Katie waiting excitedly for mum to appear before she would submit to bedtime. Julia apologised to them both and made some lame excuse for her tardiness, but as it turned out neither Jim nor Katie was listening.

At bedtime as Julia got undressed Jim sensed that his wife was subdued. He thought about asking her what was the matter but she seemed unusually tired so he didn't bother. 'Probably a heavy day,' he reasoned. He didn't know the half of it.

Julia snuggled under the covers and turned onto her side, her back facing Jim. He reached over to switch off the bedside lamp and already his wife's was breathing steadily, her eyes clamped shut.

Julia wasn't asleep; she was fretting about what had happened. She worried about poor Terri. She wondered what she should do. Julia had been a victim; she had every right to go to the police, maybe even a duty to do so. Men like Phillip needed to be brought to book, taught a lesson. Maybe he had. Did men like Phillip ever learn? The questions and dilemmas whirled round and round in her mind. Julia had been a victim today, but like thousands of victims she would choose to take matters no further. Not this time. That was her right, the same as it was her right not to be manhandled and molested by a man. 'What a world we live in' she thought as she turned herself towards Jim, wrapping her arms over his sleeping form and pulling him gently towards her. Finally, the tiredness of the last 48 hours washed over her, warming her body from top to toe and dragging her deep into the shadow-world of sleep.

WEDNESDAY - What's Love Got To Do With It?

Julia got up unenthusiastically, showered mechanically and threw on the nearest work suit she could find. She poked the tail of her blouse clumsily into her waistband, happily oblivious to the escaped material that waved in the breeze behind her. She dragged a brush through her wet hair, grimaced in the mirror and gave it up as a bad job. She gathered a little momentum as she bounded down the stairs, briefly skating through her expensively fitted kitchen with its range of hi-tech, lightly used cooking equipment to grab a hastily buttered slice of toast and gulp down a mouthful of orange juice, almost whilst still in motion. She grabbed her car keys and handbag, taking care to make sure that her 'phone was inside, and, still on autopilot, glided to her car. Jim had already taken Katie to her mum's for the day and as she pulled the front door to she left behind the quiet echo of an empty household.

Struggling against her instincts and a distinct lack of zest she headed off to work. The events of the previous evening replayed in her tired mind and she shuddered. She was determined that Phillip's unforgiveable groping was not going to ruin her Christmas, and neither was a police investigation, her decision not to inform the Constabulary being a final one.

'*The creep deserves a visit from the police*'. she thought angrily, but satisfied herself with the thought that he would get what was coming to him in many other ways over the next few weeks. The pain Julia had bestowed upon him with her accurate and powerful knee-strike would be replicated several times on his ego by his (ex?) girlfriend; that would have to suffice.

Absently, her mind far away in thought, Julia drove to work and though she had her hands firmly on the steering wheel and her feet were squeezing the pedals at the right times, it was a testament to her subconscious that the car was heading safely in the right direction.

In this semi dreamlike state she pulled the car into first available parking space in the grounds of her office complex. As the seatbelt reeled smoothly across her shoulder she heard her phone tinkle its delicate message tone. There was the usual brief rummage around for the device before she pulled it clear of the other contents of her handbag. The message began a mobile treasure hunt as the text led to a voicemail, which had to be retrieved, then a verbal message which had to be listened to, which often included a further number, which required a repeat listening so that it could be scribbled down on a receipt in eyebrow pencil. This, as it happened, was no exception.

"*Hi, it's David. Really sorry to catch you on the way in. I have a customer complaint to deal with but for some reason I can't fathom my alarm clock didn't go off. When I finally got out to the car the front tyre was flat to the floor. Not a great start to the day, would you go for me please? I'll text you the house number and postcode. Thanks Julia I owe you one."*

The message ended there and a perky automated female voice resumed with an impressive new array of further options. Julia ignored the voice's kind menu choices and jabbed the 'end call' icon irritably.

'Just what I don't need,' she mouthed to herself, flinging her head back against the headrest. 'Flat tyre my rear end! Too much beer at the pub, and the only reason he missed his alarm is because Mrs. Barnes consigned him to the spare room. I don't blame her.''

Before she could get out of the car the 'phone tinkled sweetly once more. There it was; a postcode and house number, no names, no detail of the problem and not even a thank you to round off the text. 'No problem, David, my pleasure, I'll catch up with my work when I get back then shall I? Rearrange this famous phrase or saying: backside, broom, sweep!' she thought irritably.

Julia virtually threw the 'phone back into her handbag and heard it clunk against the other ephemera with which it shared the space. She clenched her teeth in frustration and snatched the Sat-Nav from the glove box of her car. *'Not in the mood,'* she intoned, as she poked the letters and numbers onto the screen of the device.

'Searching for satellites' it announced on the screen.

"Well search a bit harder then you moronic overblown compass," growled Julia. The machine, though ordinarily ambivalent to threats and insults, dutifully brought forth the tiny segment of map that filled its display. Immediately an uncompassionate, tritely polite and vaguely robotic voice announced:

'In 50 meters at the main road, turn right.'

Julia glanced ungratefully at the map segment as she plopped the holder onto the windscreen: 'Great, 28 miles to destination,' she read with disdain. 'Once again fortune rains on the barbeque of life!'

Today was not a day she felt like placating a couple of 'moaning Minnie's' whinging on about their out of date warranty and why the repair should still be done for free; or why her firm should mend a bodged DIY repair. Today Julia Carter was not made of apologies and courteous smiles, today Julia Carter was made of pulsing green bile and rumbling irritation. Today would no doubt test her sense of duty and loyalty to the firm and to David personally. Today was going to be a right royal pain!

As she steeled herself for the journey and for the customer experience at journey's end, her phone bleeped once more. She patiently extricated the handset from the bunch of keys against which it was now lodged deep in the recesses of her handbag and dabbed resignedly at the screen. This time the message was from Andy:

'Meet me @ lunchtime? xx' it read.

Julia's tummy tingled for a second or two, it was a girlish, silly sensation and she felt guilty for entertaining it, but today she felt that she deserved a little attention. A few stolen moments of 'innocent' flattery and fawning might help to put the horror of the previous night into some sort of manageable perspective. It was a foolish and self-indulgent impulse, but 'what the heck', at least someone was noticing her for the right reasons, a feeling that had lain dormant for too long. A smile creased her face as she texted back:

'Seeing customer out of town, will text when back. xx'.

Barely had the message left her screen than a reply came back:

'Looking forward to it already xx'.

Turning the ignition key she glowered in the direction of the Sat-Nav, which sat imperiously and unemotionally on the windscreen:

"Don't you dare get me lost, you little rat-bag," she growled menacingly.

As she drove away from work and out towards the countryside she was determined that no griping half-wit was going to take up all of her morning, or spoil her day in any way. This was going to be customer service delivered Clint Eastwood style; eyes narrowed, lean on words and a clean 'kill'. This cowboy would be riding out of town, on the last strike of mid-day, gun still smoking.

The journey was not without adventure. The cold weather had the sun racing for cover beneath thick grey cloudy skies. A Nordic pall cast a gloom across the countryside. In front of her and behind her and littering every side road were those drivers who would ordinarily be sitting in front of a gas fire, blazing like a furnace, engrossed in the mind-wash that masquerades as day-time TV. It fascinated Julia that the very weather one would imagine would deter the nervous or reluctant driver contrived to produce the very conditions that seemed to bring them out in force. In short every highway and byway had become a wintry vehicular obstacle course. Drivers in hats, a danger sign in itself, clogged the tarmac, plodding slowly along obstructing every opportunity to put your foot down. Every manoeuvre was exaggerated because it was cold outside. Brakes were dabbed liberally at every turn and bend of any 'B' road. Of course Julia's route was comprised principally of such thoroughfares, contradiction in terms though that expression turned out to be. The blood pumping through Julia's heart fizzed and bubbled with a rage that had nowhere to go. The Sat-Nav inevitably contributed to her growing annoyance by directing her on a puzzlingly circuitous route which introduced her to many unfamiliar country tracks and dead-ends, sometimes more than once. If it really wanted to push her button, which by now was operating on a hair trigger, it would simply say: *'please make a U turn as soon as possible.'*

By the end of her tortuous journey Julia felt frazzled and spiky. She pulled up outside a row of cottages that lay in a tiny village, which was little more than a row of houses dotted either side of a winding lane. It was not a place that Julia had been to before. It was quiet and quaint and had an almost instant calming effect on those taking in the view.

The house number, which corresponded to the second text, was a pretty white stone cottage, which sat at the end of a row of similar properties. They were small and low with a tiny front garden, which in summer would be a palette of colour from the meticulously tended border plants, hanging baskets and dwarf shrubs. Thin wisps of grey smoke swirled from one or two of the stone chimneys that pierced the thatched roofs. The narrow pavement, in front of the houses, glistened with overnight frost that showed no sign of dissipating in the brisk morning air.

As Julia stepped onto the pavement she paused a while to drink in the rural tranquility. The air and the ambient noise were different here to that of the town; it seemed gentle and soothing. She still had no idea who it was that she was going to see, or the nature of their grievance. David simply hadn't bothered to add substance to his garbled voicemail. His faith in his protégé was satisfying but sometimes it teetered close to the point of taking her for granted.

Her plan was to give them no more than thirty minutes to vent their spleen after which she would conduct a no-nonsense negotiation concluding in a mutually acceptable compromise. Her strategy was to talk big and offer little, leaving the beaming clients feeling as if they had negotiated a cease-fire in the Middle East. She would bid her farewells, flashing her most ingratiating smile, before the local peasants realised they'd been fobbed off with a bag of coloured beads. That was the plan at any rate.

Reaching the heavy wooden door, with its iron rivets and small inset bubble glass window, she knocked at it confidently and rapidly, producing a sound like the sharp rap of machine gun fire.

After a short while the door was heaved open by a very young looking woman in jeans, Australian suede boots and a designer hoodie. The girl had dark hair and unlined, pale, blemish free skin. She was disarmingly attractive and youthful and not at all the kind of person Julia had expected to encounter. This put Julia slightly on the back foot. The girl looked engagingly blank upon seeing a smartly dressed businesswoman on the doorstep, company briefcase in hand.

"Hello, my name is Julia Carter. I'm from Heat Solutions, I understand you have contacted my company and that you have a complaint."

Still the girl looked none the wiser.

"You may have been expecting Mr. Barnes, the M.D., but he's very busy with the run up to Christmas, so he's asked me to deal with the problem. I'm sure I'll be able to help."

The smile, which accompanied the introduction, was broad but forced but the girl hardly blinked, maintaining unerring eye contact with Julia. Julia wavered, wondering briefly if the girl was deaf, or morbidly stupid. Glancing over the girl's shoulder Julia saw a man of late middle age pottering about in the back of the small cottage.

"Perhaps your dad called us?" Julia said, a little condescendingly, lifting herself slightly and looking deliberately over the girl's shoulder into the house.

"I don't think so," the girl replied simply, but sweetly, "he doesn't know where I live. I haven't spoken to him for nearly two years."

"Oh!" was the best Julia could muster by way of response.

There was now a complete impasse at the door and Julia was starting to shiver. Her suit was smart but hardly insulated against the bitter cold of a winter morning. When she got out of the car it never occurred to her that even the act of crossing the threshold of the house in question was likely to be a drawn out negotiation in itself. In her experience the ardent complainer was inevitably only too willing to invite access in order that their tirade of dissatisfaction can commence. The girl, however, stood her ground but seemed visibly unsure what to do next.

The man who was pottering in the background had tentatively started to edge towards the door, a quizzical expression forming across his craggy features. After a seemingly endless interlude whilst the two women were locked in uninspired silence he appeared over the girl's shoulder and stared at Julia's pale and very cold face.

"Let the lady in Lauren," said the man in a warm, kind voice.

At that the girl stood gracefully aside and Julia stepped gratefully into the cosy, if sparsely furnished living room. If nothing else an open fire flickered in the small inglenook fireplace. Julia automatically navigated her way to the ash-splattered hearthrug and let the warmth of the crackling log fire 'do its worst' on the backs of her freezing cold legs. She tucked her briefcase under her arm so that she could rub her icy fingers together in an effort to restart the circulation in them.

Before Julia could reintroduce herself, this time to both parties, the girl started to laugh. It was a lovely tinkling laugh, which perfectly complemented her girlish prettiness.

"You thought Steve was my dad," she giggled, throwing a disarming look at the man.

Julia just turned her lips upward in a smile which acknowledged what the girl had said but clearly conveyed the message ' I don't know what the heck you're on about.'

"Oh, don't worry, it happens all the time," said the man, joining in the amusement, which still bypassed Julia.

He stepped forward and offered his hand to Julia, who took it and found hers immediately gripped in a firm, welcoming handshake.

"Put the kettle on Lauren. If we're going to be talking business we need a cuppa. Tea ok?"

Julia nodded appreciatively, any additional infusion of warmth into her dithering body seemed like a good thing at that moment.

"Take a seat, anywhere you like," invited Steve cordially, and with a broad smile.

Julia looked around her and saw that she wasn't spoiled for choice. Behind her was a well-worn but comfy looking two-seater settee, to her left was a patterned fabric bucket chair, which had seen much better times, and on the other side of the fireplace were two mismatched wooden dining chairs with cushion pads tied to their seats. Julia plumped for the bucket chair and perched uncomfortably on the edge of the shiny, worn cushion, balancing her briefcase awkwardly on her lap. She opened her mouth to recommence her introduction but was quickly cut short by the sound of the younger woman's voice:

"How do you like it? Milk? Sugar?"

"Erm, just milk, thanks."

Steve sat on one of the dining chairs and stared long and hard at Julia.

"I don't know you do I?" he asked, as if he should know her.

"No, I don't think so," Julia replied cautiously, wondering if this was a special client whom she should recognise or at least know of.

A contemplative silence between them broke out as they searched deep for reasons they might know each other. There were none, as it happened.

Steve was by nature an affable sort. Never one to slam the door in the face of a canvasser or door-to-door salesman, never the type to send a roving evangelist on their way, irrespective of their chosen faith. In fact the occasional visitor broke the isolation in which Steve and Lauren lived. The only visitor Steve feared and avoided was his estranged and fearsome wife, or any emissary sent by her. He studied Julia carefully and quickly decided that, whoever she was, she wasn't on a mission for 'the Witch'.

Lauren tottered into the room partially underneath a large tray bearing a teapot, cups, milk jug and so forth. The rattle of the tea things was at that moment the only sound in the small room. Lauren carefully balanced the tray on a small and slightly wobbly coffee table. Maintaining the silence Lauren noiselessly poured a cup of tea from the pot and handed it to Julia. The cup was made of fine china and Julia thought that it was dainty, slight and pretty, like Lauren. Steve took his tea in a more manly pottery mug, more rounded in shape and plain in design. However, there was no analogy with Steve there, he was slightly built, medium height and had an intelligent, thoughtful demeanour emanating from his grey eyes.

Lauren settled herself next to Steve on the other dining chair and sipped delicately from a bottle of spring water.

Now both of them stared quizzically at Julia across the room, as she sipped her tea, cup in one hand, saucer in the other, briefcase balanced uncomfortably on her lap. Someone desperately needed to break the silence, and it was Steve who took the initiative:

"Right," he said, in a brisk but friendly tone, "how can we help you, er ..."

"Julia. Julia Carter. I'm from Heat Solutions, I understand you have a complaint...?"

Neither Steve nor Lauren reacted to her statement in any noticeable way.

"You have a problem with one of our installations?" she asked, in a more inviting manner.

Still nothing, just blank looks from two such contrasting faces.

"Have you got the right address?" asked Steve, his craggy brow furrowed as he tried to place Julia or her company's name.

"Well my boss, the M.D. of Heat Solutions, sent me your house number and post-code, and it's such a small village I can't imagine this is the wrong address."

Steve nodded in acknowledgement, it was a fair point and well made.

"Well we must have something your firm supplied then. We've not long moved in here, could it be the previous owners who made the complaint?" he suggested, trying hard to be helpful and cooperative.

Julia glanced at her watch. The tiresome guessing game was trying her patience, not so much with the blank faced residents of the cottage but with David, who had doubtless forwarded some duff information. If she was going to get out of here and meet Andy she needed to make progress with these 'Hillbillies'. She instantly regretted her harshness towards the mismatched couple, if that's what they were; after all there was something instinctively nice about both of them. The ornate mantel clock above the fire ticked away languorously reminding townie Julia that you didn't rush things in the country, there was always time, to take time. She hated the damned clock already.

"We are suppliers of heating systems, boilers, insulation products, free standing heaters, air-conditioners, we supply to commercial and domestic customers ...have you bought something from us, something that's gone wrong? A missing part? Damage to a casing?"

Julia had rattled out the list of options with increasing desperation. Surely such an extensive list had to trigger a response? She might as well have been speaking in Latin, because no flicker of illumination registered on either of the bewildered faces that stared vacantly back at her. They glanced at each other for inspiration but to no avail.

"To be honest we haven't got a great deal of stuff between us, and most of it is stuff we already had or is second hand. Any fixtures in the cottage were in full working order when we signed the lease," said Steve apologetically, after another agonising pause.

"I'll ring the office," said Julia patiently, masking her growing irritation and wondering if these outwardly nice people were quite 'the full ticket'.

With that she whisked her 'phone out of her handbag. Lauren shook her head, pursing her lips, as though this was a bad idea:

"No signal Julia. Not out here. No 'phone signal, nothing through a TV aerial and the slowest broadband outside the third world I'm afraid," she explained apologetically.

"Oh, right, ok then, would you mind if I used your phone then, please?"

"Of course ... if we had one. The telephone company can't fit us in until after the holidays," said Steve, somewhat inevitably.

Julia sat cradling her cup and saucer, looking despondently into the fire, which spat and crackled as if taunting her. After what seemed an eternity of conversational silence, during which Julia finished her tea and considered her options, she stood up and faced Steve and Lauren resolutely:

"Well I'm sure I have the right address, although it would have been nice if my boss had rung and confirmed the details of the complaint. I don't think there's anything I can do at the moment without more information, I can only apologise for interrupting your morning."

Julia stopped there, because as she faced them she saw that they were holding hands, tightly and tenderly. She looked into their faces which were staring earnestly back at her waiting on her next sentence. What Julia saw was a staggeringly pretty young girl in her early twenties and a timeworn, greying man, advancing at a gallop through his fifties. It wasn't that Steve was an unattractive man, for his age, he had a certain character that nature bestows on some men of late middle-age; it suited him, and gave him a worldliness that complemented his evidently gentle nature. However, the age gap between the two was stark.

"I told you she thought you were my dad," said Lauren softly to Steve, smiling a sweet smile, which bore no malice or injury.

"I - er, well that's none of my - er...," Julia stumbled around for the right thing to say, without actually finding it.

"Understandable," said Steve warmly, "a beautiful young woman with a middle-aged fossil like me."

"Oh, I wouldn't have said that," said Julia reddening, knowing that though she hadn't said it she had thought it, sufficiently obviously for the pair to pick up on.

"Age is just a number Julia. Love doesn't see lines and wrinkles; it sees laughter and kindness," cooed Lauren, a little poetically for Julia's taste.

"Well I'd better go," mumbled Julia awkwardly, gathering herself together, and avoiding further, potentially embarrassing, eye contact with love's young and old dream combined.

"I'll ring you ...oh no I can't, can I? Well perhaps you could contact us in the New Year when you remember what it is you needed us for. I'll leave you my business card."

Julia placed her cup on the hearth and left a card beside it. Smiling at the couple she walked towards the old oak front door with its black, hammered iron hinges. She had to admit that despite the sparseness of the furniture and the tiredness of the decor the house exuded a relaxed, homely charm. It suited the generation spanning lovers who lived beneath its ancient timber beams, in their hideaway love-nest.

She dipped her head so that she could see out of the low set quarter panes, in their bowed wooden frame, that formed the only window in the room. All she could see was the colour white. Steve, meanwhile, had got up from his chair to open the door for Julia, on the basis that it sometimes stuck in the cold weather. As he tugged the door ajar he had been sprayed liberally with tiny white flakes that swirled and flurried into the room from the grey sky outside. Snowflakes settled, like celestial icing sugar, on the plants and shrubs in the tiny front garden.

"Put the kettle on again Lauren," he smiled, shaking his head, "I don't think Julia will be going anywhere for a while."

With that he pulled the heavy door to. The living room had darkened as the snowfall blotted out the daylight. Steve flicked on a couple of lamps shrouded with over-sized shades made of thick patterned fabric. Only a fraction of the light from the low energy bulbs escaped into the room, giving the surroundings no more than an intimate glow.

Julia sank back into the bucket chair. Steve was right. The snow had settled on the wood dividing each pane of glass like a scene from a Christmas card. Outside the snow whipped wildly through the sky coating everything in its wake, with the wild, flamboyant strokes of an otherworldly artist, to create a study in white. In the street Julia's car became no more than an outline in a winter pencil sketch. The sudden fall of snow had consumed the countryside and Julia's tryst in one capricious mood-swing of nature.

"Home-made soup and bread on the menu, French onion, a favourite of ours," said Steve cheerfully, stepping back into the living room from where he had been supervising Lauren in the kitchen. "Lauren makes the bread, it's great, you'll love it. Cheer up Julia we won't let you starve."

Julia sighed inwardly but managed to feign a pitiful smile for the benefit of the effervescent Steve. Lauren meanwhile busied herself in the kitchen like a true country housewife, a role that seemed to be many years ahead of the young woman's chronological age and youthful appearance.

Sitting watching the flames on the open fire, Julia stoically accepted that, in cricket terms, play, with Andy, had stopped at lunch due to bad light. As the covers were drawn on the pitch of love, or was it lust, she was already consigned to the pavilion. A 'pavilion' with no satellite signal and therefore no means of warning Andy that their midday tryst had been postponed. How many times do we long for the days before we became enslaved by the mobile 'phone and its instantaneous demands? It is ironic, therefore, that when our wish is granted we feel such intense frustration at suddenly being signal free.

Andy was destined to survive the crushing disappointment of Julia's no-show by making a spontaneous visit to his girlfriend's office, and to her delight whisking her off into town and to the shops, perchance to spend a little extra on making Christmas magical. Well, no point moping!

While Lauren donned an apron that wrapped round her slender frame more than once, and had to be knotted from behind to hitch it comfortably to her neck, Steve entertained Julia in the living room, telling her *their* story: "We've been together almost two years," he explained "but we've known each other for much longer."

Julia found this difficult to fully comprehend on the basis that she felt that Lauren had not been on the planet a great deal longer. 'Maybe,' she thought, 'my prejudices are getting the better of me?' She simply couldn't imagine being with anyone so much older. In Julia's case that would make Jim almost seventy. That was inconceivable to Julia, unimaginable that his physical age would match his current outlook. That was a cruel observation and she scolded herself internally, but half-heartedly.

It was as if Steve had hijacked her silent train of thought, perhaps there was something in her eyes that gave it away.

"Oh yes Julia, a long time before. Many years ago I was Lauren's teacher, when she was about eleven. Coincidence really, I moved schools, went on to be the Head of the local

Grammar School. I would see her in the village where I lived, with my ex-wife," he added quickly, the pitch of his voice dipping to a mumble at the mention of 'the ex', " fares, fetes that sort of thing. Then she got a Saturday job in the local grocery shop when she was about fifteen, I suppose. She was, is, such a pretty girl. Hard for a chap not to notice, but that was all … at the time."

Julia nodded, but it was a qualified acknowledgement, she was still unsure where the story was going, and whether she would morally approve of its direction.

"Then I took early retirement from teaching. There's a lot of stress in the profession and I'd just got to the point where enough was enough. The kids are ok, and most of the teachers the same, but the politics and bureaucracy and the constant interference were a nightmare. I'd been careful and prudent and I was lucky enough to be in a position, with a nest egg from my parents, God rest them, to get the hell out. That provided me with a lot of free time. Well, I might have been out of a job but I'm a pretty active sort of chap and a born organiser. I got myself on a rake of committees, including the Parish Council and the thing they have in common is the pub. We either met there, in a back room or debunked there after meetings. Either way it was dry sherries all round by eight o'clock."

It all sounded very 'country set' to Julia, but it fascinated her to find out how the two cottage dwellers had got together, so she nodded, encouraging him to go on.

"By now I reckon Lauren must have been about eighteen, maybe just nineteen. She had begun to work evenings in the pub while she took her 'A' levels, and carried on when she went to College. Of course I recognised her, from school all those years before, and from being about the village, and working in the grocers. By now she had really blossomed into a gorgeous young woman. I could hardly be blamed for noticing, except by my wife, who thought I was no more than an old letch."

'What a coincidence,' mused Julia, whose thought processes had taken the same journey as Steve's former wife by now.

"I suppose she was right … in a way," he admitted, once more seeming to anticipate Julia's line of thinking. "But apart from the obvious outward sexual appeal there was always more to it than that. When Sheila, that's my ex-wife, wasn't with me Lauren would always chat to me. Sometimes it seemed that she singled me out to talk to, you know, when the meetings in the pub had fizzled out. She really seemed interested in me, but I tried to blot it out. 'Impossible,' I'd think, 'Young girl like that, you'll be making a fool of yourself, an *old* fool.' As time went on though I really started to fall for her, and worse still, I believed she actually fancied me. Can you imagine?"

Julia shook her head without thinking, agreeing with him then realising that her honesty might offend her host.

"No, nor could I," he replied warmly, untroubled by Julia's response, and quickly putting her at ease, "but she did, she couldn't help it any more than I could. I can't explain it, and I'm damned sure she can't – otherwise she might still be on speaking terms with her parents. They took it badly … but not as badly as my ex, of course. At first Lauren and I sneaked off on a couple of dates, well, harmless walks in the countryside, cream teas in other villages, that sort of thing, but the more we talked the more we fell … *for each other*. I didn't want to be without her and I knew she felt the same. I know it's a real May to December relationship, but if it feels right surely you have to go with your instincts?"

Julia sensed the passion building in Steve's voice. She supposed that the chance for him to talk about, and maybe justify, his unconventional romance was rare. For her part she smiled politely without commenting, her eyes looking back at him were non-committal.

"Eventually we had to face up to everyone, and it wasn't pretty. I was ousted from about every committee I was on, lost my seat on the Parish council and embarked on the divorce from Hell itself. Lauren fared no better, mind you. Her parents were appalled, understandably I suppose, and her family turned their back on her. The Landlord of the pub had to let her go because some of the customers were getting very sniffy about our … *relationship* … and in a nutshell we ended up out here, in the sticks, ostracised from our community, pretty much in hiding really, but very much in love."

Something about the power with which Steve had ended his sentence touched Julia deeply. His words resonated with the purity of real, unrelenting love and Julia almost instantaneously saw him in a different light. 'Love is love,' she thought, 'it doesn't really matter where you find it.' Whether that would help or hinder her own needs and insecurities was another matter, but perhaps she suddenly had a better idea of what to look for.

"It's ready," called Lauren brightly, from the kitchen.

"Oh lunch, good, I'm ready for this," said Steve cheerily. "I'm sorry for going on, it's so rare to see a friendly face … or even a neutral one," he continued as an aside, as they rose to go and get their lunch.

The kitchen was truly rustic. There were quarry tiles on the floor scored with years of ingrained dirt, a coal black Aga pumping out a ferocious heat, and an old oak table covered with a homely checked tablecloth where they sat.

Lauren dished the thick, steaming soup into bowls and placed a plate of chunky home-made bread in the centre of the table.

"Tuck in," she said happily, "I've made loads."

Lauren took her seat, sidling past Steve to get to it. Julia noticed that she gently stroked his forearm as she went past. It was a fleeting but telling gesture. The sparkle in her dark eyes as she smiled at her partner was unmistakable; it was the twinkle of real love.

"I suppose Steve's been telling you *our* story," she said with a smile.

"Yes. If ever the course of true love didn't run smooth, it didn't for you," commented Julia between spoonfuls of the wholesome, tasty soup.

"Perhaps that's what made it special," offered the young girl, looking wistfully at her man.

"I think we'll be putting Julia off her soup at this rate," laughed Steve, " a captive audience is one thing, but I really think she's heard enough about us."

Julia paused mid slurp and smiled at the pair. She liked them, they were genuine and nice; she believed in their love, or whatever it was.

"I understand it can't have been easy," said Julia thoughtfully, "especially for your parents Lauren. Do you think they'll come round eventually?"

"I can't see it," replied the girl sadly, "but who knows?"

"And did you have children Steve? It must be difficult for them."

"No, no children involved," he said simply, with the tiniest element of regret in his voice.

"Not yet anyway," teased Lauren, with a hint of mischief in her response.

Julia bowed her head so she was looking intently at the bowl of soup and at her spoon. As open-minded as she had become about this generation spanning arrangement the hint of procreation in the turn of conversation proved to be a step too far, at least for the soup course. Once again sensing Julia's discomfort Steve neatly 'changed lanes' on the conversational highway.

"I can see how awkward it is for people to come to terms with us, Julia. Especially those who are close to us, and, come to that, those people that don't know us at all. It's all too easy to write me off as a dirty old man and Lauren as a young, rebellious girl who doesn't know her own mind. Neither of us are those things, we love each other and it has nothing to do with age. They say the soul is ageless, it's a pity most people can't apply that logic to physical appearance. It's not 'the norm', I can see that, we both can, but these days what is? There are plenty of couples of the same age fighting like cat and dog, airing their hatred for each other, their sex lives, their bad language and their crass tattoos on the daytime schedules. Or should we take our lead from the air-headed, perma-tanned, celebrity obsessed nonentities of 'Reality TV'? Either way, if that's becoming the norm I'm not embarrassed to step outside of it."

"You've thought that through quite carefully, haven't you Steve," said Julia, a little shocked by his passionate indictment of contemporary society.

"I just don't see what harm we're doing," he replied, in a more even tone, "we just happen to love each other, deeply. We don't want to hurt anyone, not intentionally."

"Well maybe your ex-wife's reaction is understandable?" suggested Julia tactfully.

"I suppose, but if you can't see your relationship is stale and stagnant after almost thirty years then maybe you're a little blind to the truth … whoever comes into your life."

Julia felt that the transfer of any sort of blame to Steve's wife was a little lame, but nevertheless the point he was trying to make resonated with her. Her mind flicked to Jim, boring, predictable Jim; then to Andy, buoyant, confident Andy. For a moment she questioned herself. What was she trying to achieve? Where was she trying to go on life's short journey? She must have gone noticeably quiet because in a very timid voice, as though she was trying to wake Julia from a light nap, Lauren said:

"More soup Julia? I've made plenty."

Julia looked up and she glanced at Lauren, smiling a faraway smile. She shook her head and placed her spoon gently into the bowl to show she had finished eating.

"It's still snowing," said Steve, peering out of the kitchen window, "I'll go and get some wood from the wood-store,

Lauren would you make some coffee please. We can take it in the living room. It's more comfortable in there."

Lauren nodded sweetly and began to gather up the bowls and side-plates with the remnants of crusty bread abandoned on them.

"Thank you, it was lovely," said Julia, "can I help clear up?"

"No that's fine. I'll pop the bowls in the sink; Steve can wash them up later. Come on through to the living room."

Julia took a long, hard look at the kitchen clock. What daylight there was left in the afternoon was fading quickly and the old kitchen was slowly being consumed by dark shadows. The back door thumped shut as Steve braved the elements to collect a few more logs for the fire.

"I should really be getting back. I don't want anyone to worry about me," said Julia fretfully.

"You should wait for the snow to stop falling at least," Lauren responded, standing patiently by the door to the living room, waiting for Julia to get up from the table and join her, "otherwise Steve and I would be worried about you too!"

Julia believed her. Even though she had known the pair just a couple of hours she sensed that their friendly concern for their uninvited guest ran deeper than simple hospitality. She felt instinctively that Lauren and Steve were just caring people After her brief deliberation she stood up and followed Lauren into the tiny living room.

"I know Steve goes on a bit," Lauren began as they took their seats by the orange glow of the dying embers, " but he's right you know. My parents were outraged when I told them about Steve and me. They'd spent my teen years warning me about *boys* who would use me for sex, draw me into a life dependent on drugs, or risk my life on the back of a motorbike, so I really don't know what they expected. I could have settled for a smart, sincere young boy of my own age, fresh from university, but there's no guarantee that I'd have been happy. I am happy with Steve though, happy here in our lovely cottage. We've got nothing, you know, things, I mean. Just enough money from Steve's pension to pay the bills and to eat, but in other ways, the important ways, we've got everything we need."

Steve, on cue, reappeared in the living room laden with roughly chopped logs.

"Did you put the coffee pot on?"

"No, I thought I'd wait till you were back inside. I'll do it now."

Now Julia was alone with Steve. She watched as he knelt by the fire off loading the blocks onto the flagstone beside the fire grate. He prodded at the ash pile in the hearth with an iron poker. A weak flame flickered reluctantly. Steve placed a couple of new logs onto the smouldering pile of soot and patiently manipulated them until a meatier blue flame began to spit angrily, at which point he withdrew and turned to Julia.

"Are you married Julia?" he asked.

"Yes, I've been married almost ten years. I've got a daughter, Katie, she's almost eight."

"Lovely. Your daughter must be looking forward to Christmas then?"

"Yes. She's getting very excited, it's lucky I've got mum to entertain her while she's off school."

"Yes, it must be tricky managing a full time job and a family."

"Thousands of families do it, we're no different. It's just a juggling act, but we manage."

"You're lucky. Like I said I don't have any children. It would have been nice, but we were both so darned busy with our careers. We couldn't seem to find the time …" he trailed off, staring at the flames as they flared up towards the fire canopy, turning into thick, dark smoke which was sucked into the brick chimney above them.

Lucky? It was not a word Julia often deployed in relation to her domestic situation. Getting up at 'silly o'clock', prepping lunches, school runs, work, after school clubs, Brownies, swimming, taking mum shopping, getting something ready for tea, the endless, spiraling bills … no, *lucky* was a word consigned to a dark corner of her vocabulary. *Lucky*? Surely that was when you won the Lottery or got 'something for nothing', not for simply being part of a happy, healthy family. That was just life … surely? She wasn't taking anything for granted, was she? Everyone wanted to win millions, it would change everything. Only money, and lots of it, can make you truly, blissfully happy … everyone knows that, *don't they*? You only had to look at all those happy, well-balanced, contented, altruistic millionaires out there to see that … didn't you?

Suddenly the room was filled with the aroma of freshly brewed coffee. The smell wafted through the increasingly darkening room before Lauren pushed open the door from the kitchen with the toe of her suede boot. She bustled into the room, the tray of cups rattling, the cafetiere, almost full to the top, balanced precariously in the centre.

"Ooh, lovely, you've got the fire going," she cooed, as she placed the tray down on a small table.

Steve circled the small room lighting candles on saucers and slate bases in various nooks and crannies. Outside the window Julia could see that the snow still swirled in the ever-greying sky, but the flakes seemed wispy and less dense.

"Saving electricity?" she asked.

"There's light, and there's candle light. Which makes you feel nicer Julia? "

It was a rhetorical question. Julia watched the candle flames as they danced in the semi-light, casting hazy patterns on the dark austere beams that had witnessed centuries pass by. She had to admit that the common light bulb couldn't *hold a candle* to candles.

"It's very nice, particularly for the time of year, but I notice you don't have a Christmas tree. Don't you celebrate … ?"

"There's only one proper place for a tree Julia," laughed Steve, " let me show you."

Julia followed Steve into a well-tended garden at the back of the house, and Lauren followed Julia, a broad beam illuminating her pretty, young face. The garden was modest in size but well stocked and mature. A small circle of grass played host to a rusting table and chair set and a stone birdbath that needed a thorough clean. Beyond the tiny lawn there stretched a hedge of intertwined holly and hawthorn. They formed a natural, tangled border with the fields behind that had been worked by man, animal and machine for centuries. The patchwork quilt of arable fields undulated peacefully into the horizon, under the rapidly darkening sky.

Amongst the other snow strewn bushes and shrubs a fir tree stood tall and sturdy to the side of the lawn. It was tall and largely green, though it bore a few brown sections of leaf, which spoke of the ravages of time, and maybe a little neglect. Through the dark, and even though it was a few yards distant, there was something else which seemed to be embedded in its spiky foliage.

"Ho ho ho!" Steve guffawed with the deep voice of a man but with the excited tremor of a child.

With a deft flick of a garden switch the tree burst into a kaleidoscope of colour. Chunky light bulbs of all hues adorned the outside of the tree, their festive light shining merrily through the crisp white snowflakes that covered each branch.

"Tad-da," Steve sang out, the little boy peeking out excitedly from within the grown man.

"Can't do that with candles!"

Julia glanced at Lauren who was clutching Steve's right arm, drawing her body close to his. She watched as the tiny snowflakes that were now flurrying above them settled on their hair and clothes. Lauren's eyes sparkled with joy as she clung excitedly to her man; Steve's much older eyes twinkled just as brightly as he drank in the instant magic of it all.

The three of them stood hunched against the cold air, the colours of the bulbs reflected in their eyes, the snow tickling their noses and ears. Suddenly Julia felt like a millionaire.

After a few minutes of drinking in the charm of the surroundings, the cold began to bite rather than tickle. The flakes dissipated to a kind of clinging wetness in the air as finally darkness descended like a veil on the countryside around them.

"I really should be going," said Julia with a genuine reluctance, "but thank you for lunch and shelter from the snow storm, especially as we never got to the bottom of why you called my company."

"It was no trouble. It's nice to have visitors, even unexpected ones. I really have no recollection of calling your company, I would have remembered, but if it was a mistake it had a very pleasant consequence," Steve said sincerely.

Julia smiled coyly; the pleasure had been unexpectedly satisfying and mutual.

"I'll help you clear your car," he offered, and extinguished the pretty light show with a simple flick of a switch.

Between them Julia and Steve made short work of clearing the screens and digging a trench for the tyres to take a grip of the road surface. The snow hadn't settled as deeply as Julia had first feared.

As she climbed into her car she paused to wave at Steve and Lauren as they stood, arms linked, in the doorway to the lovely little cottage. Behind them and through the window she saw the orange and yellow flicker of the firelight and the assorted candles. They waved back, their smiles of happiness and contentment quite genuine.

She wondered, as she settled into the driver's seat and started the engine, what the future held for the couple. How would they navigate Steve's journey into old age with Lauren still a young woman? There was an unhealthy obsession with longevity that transcended happiness in the present, it seemed. They were happy, now, in this moment. Maybe there would be many, many more moments for them to share; to share with the passion they possessed now -

she hoped so at any rate. In any case how do you compare a single day of intense joy against a lifetime of tortuous misery? However long fate had allocated for their personal happiness, at least they had found it, some people expended a wasted lifetime searching for love and contentment in places where it didn't exist.

As the engine turned and the headlights lit, piercing the inky darkness of the unlit lane, Steve and Lauren turned and stepped back into the cottage. The heavy wooden door thudded shut and she pushed the gear stick into first with a strangely heavy feeling in her breast. They seemed so happy with nothing, and Julia seemed to be permanently frustrated and discontent with everything she had.

She had barely begun to lift her foot off the clutch when her 'phone began to beep wildly. She looked at it in astonishment. She was still just a few short feet from the cottage where there was no signal to be had, and yet here, in her car, the dots indicating signal strength lit up like Steve's Christmas tree.

She poked the screen to retrieve the first text. It was a message from David:
'Forget complaint, bit of a mix up, will sort it after the holiday, DB.'

Furiously she scrolled through her inbox for earlier in the day, but she couldn't find the text containing the postcode and house number.

'Bloody smart-phones' she cursed under her breath, 'bloody thick, annoying phones.'

With that she scrunched the tyres through the icy snow and drove into the wintry darkness towards the distant orange glow of roadside lamps and civilisaton.

THURSDAY - Thursday's Child

As Julia pottered about in the kitchen she peered through the window, daylight was starting to break through the sooty coloured dawn sky. It was a watery, nondescript light making the world look grey and uninteresting. The snow still lay across the lawn like a badly iced cake with patches of stubborn, stubbly grass poking through. Just looking at the uninspiring, shabby landscape made Julia feel cold to the bone.

'Another winter wonderland' mused Julia cynically, pushing last night's washing up around the bowl without any cleansing zeal.

She thought of Steve and Lauren's cosy cottage, the firelight, the candles, the effortless love, and wondered who'd poured water over the smoking embers of her own love life.

"Mom," came a croaky little voice from just inside the kitchen doorway, "are we still going to see Santa later?"

Katie stood in the doorway, buried beneath an over-sized dressing gown. Crazy hair tumbled all over her face and her eyes were still struggling to open fully. Her words tumbled out from between a pair of sleepy lips. She clutched her toy rabbit with a limp grip and it swung upside down, its ears brushing the wooden floor.

Julia smiled at her daughter and nodded:

"If you're good and eat all your breakfast," she said kindly, but she was thinking, 'bugger, I'd forgotten that was today.'

Julia had carefully negotiated the day off, and she had masses to do to get ready for Christmas Day. The roads into town would be choked, and this would not be just an hour's deviation from her plans. The semi-conscious Katie was oblivious to her mother's machinations, instead she stood rooted to the spot staring, as far as her half open eyes would permit, into the middle distance.

"Go and put the Christmas tree lights on," Julia suggested brightly, still urgently reorganising the day in her mind. It was typical that Jim was working on her Christmas prep day, and wasn't going to be there to distract and entertain Katie. In fact, it wasn't typical at all, and her reliable spouse did more than his share of parenting Katie, and he did it happily, most of the time.

Katie shuffled forward, still in a zombie like trance, and pressed the rocker switch that brought the twinkling white lights to life. She stared vacantly as the lights began their sequenced dance, but deep inside those glassy brown eyes her little heart skipped.

"What's for breakfast, mum?" she asked idly, transfixed by the lights which flickered and chased around the tree. She reached out with a little finger to touch the trinkets, which hung from its spiky branches, with childish tactile curiosity.

"Porridge," said Julia firmly, not offering anything else by way of choice.

"Ok," said the little girl meekly, "can I have some juice please?"

"Morning, beautiful. Excited?" said Jim as he bounded in, scooping Katie into his arms.

"Da-ad," she protested, giggling as he nuzzled her cheek with his nose.

"Off to see Santa today? Hope you've got your list?" he said, as he spun his daughter round, making her giggle, before placing her gently onto the sofa. Katie grinned and produced a crumpled piece of paper from her dressing gown pocket.

"Good girl. Well, have fun, I've got to go to work today, but I'll be back later and we can get Christmas started properly. Yeah?"

"Ye-ah!" she squealed.

Julia looked over at her husband and scowled as discreetly as she could. Her message was simple and required no words: 'Don't get her all excited first thing in the morning!' He just shot her a half-baked smile and grabbed his jacket from the back of one of the dining chairs. He strode the couple of paces to where Julia was busy microwaving Katie's porridge and planted a kiss on her head. The kiss would have been on her cheek if Julia hadn't ducked, for all intents and purposes to reach a bowl from beneath the kitchen counter. Instead Jim got a mouthful of yesterday's hair spray. Along with the residue of the spray he caught a waft of her perfume, it was a smell he adored, especially when it had faded almost to nothing. Somehow it mixed with her natural odour and to Jim it was as unique as a fingerprint.

"See you later then," said Julia absently, avoiding direct eye contact, as she straightened up with the bowl in her hand. She couldn't explain why she found it easier not to look him in the eye, but that was just the way it was lately.

"Yes, see you later," he replied, his manner a little deflated. "Be good for Santa," he called to Katie with forced buoyancy in his voice.

"Porridge and juice, I want to see you finish it all, ok? Or no Santa," warned Julia, adding the obligatory seasonal sanction to her instruction. Christmas, after all, isn't just for wide-eyed children; it's also a time for heavy-eyed adults to exploit the season for its opportunities to blackmail their offspring into compliant behaviour. Thanks Santa, nice one! Of course the threatened sanction was like a politician's promise, rarely, if ever, followed through.

It took the best part of an hour to get through the unending line of traffic snaking into town. Every side road of any note fed the line still further and the traffic lights became even more Bolshie at these busy times. The cars mimicked the Wagon Trains of the Old West as they made their painful progress to the crowded car parks and multi-storeys. There really wasn't much 'good will to all men' evident in the shoppers edging slowly forward on their tortuous journey.

Parking was a nightmare, having circled like a vulture Julia finally thrust her car into the first vacant spot she saw, much to the beady-eyed contempt of other cars hungry to feast on the fresh carcass of an empty bay. The car parked, or more accurately abandoned, next to hers occupied a jaunty angle between the markings of the bay. It meant that Julia, as slim as she was, required some gymnastic ability to exit her vehicle. As she twisted out of the car she was forced to lift her left arm, complete with handbag, above her head, giving the impression of executing a graceful pirouette. As she tottered backwards out of the bay, emerging on tiptoes she cursed the examiner who had granted the imbecile in the adjacent car a driving licence. In the spirit of Christmas she also mentally lambasted the half-witted architect who had designed the parking bays for vehicles no larger than a child's go-kart. Julia was rarely filled with hate, but somehow 'this most wonderful time of the year' brought out the worst in her.

She strode towards the entrance to the shopping centre clutching Katie firmly by the hand, almost dragging the little girl in her wake. On the plus side the wear and tear on the child's new shoes was minimal in that her feet hardly seemed to touch the ground.

Inside the shopping mall it looked like a hive. There were people packed into every walkway and thoroughfare. They created an ambient buzz as they traipsed and crisscrossed the halls and malls. Everywhere there were seasonal adornments, in the display windows of the shops, in the wide-open department store entrances to entice the Christmas shopper inside, on billboards, signs and freestanding stalls. Festive muzak provided an endless, muffled soundtrack to this frenetic example of human activity. Everywhere there were representations of an idealised Christmas, posters depicting red cheeked children playing in crisp, white snow, hoardings showing good looking consumer families swapping perfectly wrapped gifts, and scrolling electronic displays of men in paper hats wielding carving knives above golden, succulent turkeys a twinkling smile etched on their acceptably time-worn faces. The real Christmas turkeys were the stressed and harassed shopping public staggering from shop to shop with a myriad of carrier bags cutting welts into their fingers. All these people were engaged in creating a lost myth, searching for a white Christmas where chestnuts roasted on an open fire and sleigh bills jingled gently in the distance. Anyone over ten knew in their heart that the day was more likely to be an indigestion-fuelled disappointment. Perhaps if they focused on the spirit of the most wonderful day of the year instead of the consumerist hype, it might just live up to its promise!

Julia was in no mood for this nonsense. She was no longer hoodwinked by its uglier traditions, the excess, the expense, and the anti-climax, she was free of those grubbier attractions of the season, but she had a responsibility to Katie, and she wasn't about to let her down. She made a bee-line for the garish and crudely put together grotto provided by the centre management which was staffed at the entrance by bored looking young women dressed as elves. The line was as seemingly relentless as the line of traffic they had endured to get here. Inwardly she winced, but feeling Katie pull at her hand as they shuffled into place, she warmed a little. This was Katie's special time, and in a few short years the unquestioning magic she felt inside her little stomach would evaporate forever. She smiled down at the little girl whose eyes glowed in anticipation. That was all the reason she needed to suffer the torment.

As they shuffled forward a few short inches at a time Julia glanced around, her eyes fixing on the clothes shops and jewellers where she would have felt far more at home. Instead she was trapped in a winding queue listening to the excited babble of clinging children and the muted and exasperated admonishments of their parents, as patience on both sides diminished. Some youngsters recited the list of things they were going to ask Santa for. Many would be struck dumb by the 'great man' when they gravitated to his side, others would bawl in terror. All would emerge with a tacky toy wrapped in cheap paper that only cost their beleaguered parent a fiver!

The man in the red suit was, in fact, a late middle-aged amateur thespian and stamp collector who hadn't worked in months who had been recruited by the job centre in May, so that the police checks could be done in time. Such were the times we lived in. Beneath the white woolly beard was a man who had long since tired of listening to a procession of snotty, spoilt, eager, gobby children tell him how many hundreds of pounds they expected their parents to spend on toys and gadgets. The crappy nylon suit brought him out in spots and the woolly beard gave him a rash for the entire six hours a day he had to wear it. All he wanted to do was get back to his flat, and watch mindless television and start on another bottle of brandy. It was therefore little wonder that some of the kids complained to their mother's that Santa's breath smelt funny. This Santa really didn't give a shit what these brats wanted for Christmas, it was seven years ago this Christmas his wife had cleared off taking all his good will and both of his savings accounts with her. Still, it was regular work, as long as he remembered not to backhand the little sods who tried to kick him or pull at his beard to see if he was 'real'.

Katie was getting more excited and nervous in equal measures as the queue inched forward.

"Don't forget to tell Santa exactly what you want," said Julia, replicating repeated briefings by bored mums throughout the line. "Have you remembered your list?"

Katie fumbled in her coat pocket and brandished the crumpled sheet of paper. She nodded solemnly:
"Will he give me a toy after I've talked to him?" she asked anxiously.
"I think so," said Julia shuffling forward.

After a while they reached the 'money elf' who smiled disdainfully as she took five pounds from Julia for the fleetingly brief pleasure of Santa's company,
"Two pounds goes to local charities," she grunted mechanically.

Katie clutched the ticket bestowed by the 'elf' in trembling hands. She could see Santa now as she was at the very entrance to the tented grotto, with its plastic reindeer and sleigh parked just inside.

Job Centre Santa had an efficient production line of children moving past him. Each child got about a minute of his time, including a very quick snap taken by a very weary helper, who looked more like one of the Seven Dwarves than Santa's helper. It was soon Katie's big moment.
"Ho Ho Ho little girl," he boomed in a stereotypically deep voice. The script was hardly tasking for a man who had once, in his theatrical prime, graced the stage of the Town Hall in an amateur production of 'Waiting for Godot'.

That was it, at the man's booming theatrical introduction, Katie's eyes opened wide, her lip began to quiver and in the blink of a terrified eye she began to wail like an outraged bagpipe. So, Katie was a crier! It was a shock to Julia; she usually left this element of Katie's Christmas to Jim.

"Don't cry Katie, just tell Santa what you want for Christmas," urged Julia soothingly, with a hint of desperation in her voice.

But the floodgates were open and the shut-off mechanism appeared to be jammed. "Waaaaaaaaaah!" came the echo from Santa's tent.

Santa tried to be jolly and sat 'ho-ho-ho-ing' and inviting Katie to show him her list, but there was no consoling her. A supervisor 'elf' tried her hand at calming the little girl but quickly abandoned the effort with one eye on a line of increasingly nervous children behind her.

"Would you like a special toy?" she said to Katie, gently guiding her to the large straw-filled barrel where the gifts were kept. It was a masterstroke. The further she pushed her from Santa the less she hollered.

This wasn't the 'elf' supervisor's dream job. She was a law graduate with a first from a blue brick university. The high of launching her mortar board into the air on a summer's day in July with her fellow graduates had been tempered by the low of a string of failed applications to law firms during a long, desolate autumn. She needed money to see her into the New Year when she could start the application process again. With her head in her books she had dreamed of taking complex briefs for a law firm with at least three surnames in its grand title. It was something of a burst bubble sensation when she came to work in green tights and a doublet that barely covered her bottom for minimum wage.

She stood by Katie at the barrel talking quietly and reassuringly into her ear while she chose not one but two presents. The little girl's shrieks had subsided to long drawn out sobs that rose dramatically from the pit of her stomach, however, the decibel level was infinitely better.

"Thank you. I'm really sorry about this," Julia half whispered to the 'elf', her face flushed with embarrassment and annoyance.

"Don't worry, the kids react that way sometimes. I suppose a big man with a hairy white beard can be an intimidating sight when you're only young."

"I don't understand though, she's really been looking forward to seeing Santa."

"You ok now Katie?" asked the 'elf' soothingly.

Katie nodded forlornly, clasping hold of her presents, wrapped in flimsy paper. The 'elf' smiled warmly at the child and Katie responded with a wobbly, crooked smile, which was as much as her distressed face would allow.

"Here," said the 'elf' pushing the five pound note back in Julia's hand, "hardly seems fair when you didn't get to see Santa properly."

"But she's had the presents," Julia protested.

"Merry Christmas," said the young woman warmly, "you have a lovely Christmas Katie, I hope Santa brings you lots of presents."

"Say thank you," Julia urged her daughter. Katie made a mumbling sound between sniffs, but it was unintelligible.

Santa's chief 'elf' shuffled off as gracefully as her pointy, satin overshoes would allow, waving cheerily. Julia stood there at the exit to the grotto looking at her daughter who returned her mother's stare with wide, innocent eyes. Tucked under the girls arm were her presents, and she wasn't letting them go.

"Shall we put them under the tree with the other presents?"

Katie nodded meekly, and Julia expelled a lengthy sigh upon which the anxiety of the traffic, the queue for the grotto and the crying incident seemed to evaporate. She considered what to do next. The whole experience had left her a little deflated. She needed a coffee and a sit down, she knew that much, so she scanned the immediate area of the mall to identify a suitable café. As her head swept left to right for a second time a familiar face interrupted the busy horizon.

"Oh dear, someone doesn't look very happy," said a man's voice, examining the pale, tear streaked face of the little girl standing beside Julia.

There stood Andy, smiling confidently, his white teeth gleaming. He wore a crisply tailored navy wool suit, with a button down shirt and no tie, his clothes hanging from his slim frame as though he'd stepped straight from the pages of a trendy catalogue.

"What brings you here?" stuttered Julia, feeling quite mumsy and very wrong-footed.

"Finished a little early today and I needed to get a couple of last minute gifts," replied Andy casually.

"Santa give you a fright?" he asked, dropping to his knee and giving Katie his best cool smile.

For her part Katie returned a quizzical look, saying nothing but instead retreating to the safety of her mum's coat tails.

"Time to get a quick coffee?" asked Andy, smiling at Julia, "I'm sure we can find you a coke or something to cheer you up missy," he continued, as he straightened up from his semi-kneeling position.

"I don't like coke," replied Katie curtly, curling her lip disapprovingly. It was not clear whether the look of disdain, which she had copied from her mother's recent facial repertoire, was intended at the sugary drink or the even more sugary Andy.

"Oh Katie, you do. You had coke at Timmy's party last week," Julia said in a mildly rebuking tone.

"Well I don't want any now," Katie insisted and flicked her head away from both her mother and Andy's gaze.

"That's ok," Andy continued undeterred, "I'm sure we can find something you do like, a cake or an ice-cream, what do you think Katie?"

Katie slowly rotated her head back towards her mum and *that silly man*, but there was a grudging interest in her little eyes. Maybe cake would make her feel better? As an accomplished salesman Andy identified the 'buy sign' immediately, and was quick, as always, to close the deal. If only it had been this simple to close the deal on his pursuit of Julia the office 'ice-queen'. He scooped Julia's elbow in his hand and gently guided her towards a café, identified by a colourful coffee bean design emblazoned across its window. Even for a girl of Katie's young age she sensed that the touching between this man and her mum was too familiar for her liking. She shrunk a little further into the folds of Julia's coat from which she narrowed her eyes and threw a glare of suspicion at Andy, who was oblivious to the little girl's intense scrutiny. 'He wouldn't do that if my dad was here' she thought crossly.

The three of them walked past the line of parents and children still queuing relentlessly for an audience with Santa. Some of the children looked rather nervous in the wake of the screaming a few moments before. What awaited them in the dark confines of the tent? Santa or a Cyberman? The source of the terror skulked meekly past them, partly hidden beneath her mother's coat. One or two of the children peered through the rope barrier to see if there were signs of blood, to see if some grisly metal monster had assimilated her. That wasn't the case of course, but she was negotiating a journey between a frustrated, alcoholic actor/Santa and a smarmy salesman determined to breach her mother's pants. Maybe the Cyberman wasn't such a bad option after all.

In the coffee shop they pounced on a table which was in the process of being vacated by a fat couple, who left behind a mountain of sandwich and cake wrappers, straws and giant plastic beakers sucked dry of their sticky contents all but a vague chocolaty residue which clung to the side of the cup in streaky globules. The couple looked perturbed to have this 'family' hovering over them as they shoe-horned themselves from their seats, but Christmas in Lotsa Coffee was a dog eat dog environment.

Andy trotted off to the counter whilst Julia did her best to confine the remnants of the previous occupants mighty feast, or in their case modest snack, to one of the two trays they had left in their wake. She looked towards the counter, which was besieged by customers, and immediately gave up hope that the table would be cleared any time soon. The staff were pinned back to their positions, their arms flailing helplessly across the counter at the unending demand for cake, pastries and sandwiches for toasting. The baristas clicked and pressed and twisted and sloshed, but their harassed faces showed that they were overwhelmed and underpaid for these conditions.

Andy by and by returned with coffees for himself and Julia and a towering ice-cream sundae of some description for Katie. At last Katie's po-faced expression creased into a smile, but as the adults returned her smile with benign grins of their own, she frowned, just to show 'it wasn't over. No sir, it wasn't over!'

Thereafter Katie returned her attention to the serious matter of transferring the glutinous mound into her pint-sized mouth. It was a mechanical process, with equal amounts of ice cream sliding down her throat and plastering her face, but the little girl showed great tenacity and endurance in the face of her almost Herculean task. With Katie thus distracted Andy slid his chair a little closer to Julia and he leaned intimately towards her and they chatted in low, whispered voices, pausing only to smile in Katie's direction and to see if she was listening to them. Julia now and then lifted the bowl-sized cup of frothy, coffee-stained milk to her lips mostly to disguise the girlish giggles induced by Andy's polished and suggestive flattery. She flushed as Andy brushed her leg with a barely perceptible movement of his hand under the cover of the tabletop. Perhaps it wasn't such a stressful day after all? Then again children are legendary for their ability to burst a bubble and that's what Katie ably did by announcing abruptly:

"I'm bored now."

"We won't be long, just sit there nicely for a while," Julia coaxed her daughter, whilst dabbing at the child's chocolate ice cream full beard and 'tache with a paper napkin.

"Ow, that hurts. You're being rough," whined the girl sulkily.

Julia then did what all exasperated mother's do with surly children; she smiled sweetly at her and said:

"Come on Katie, don't be naughty. Please." Then turned and gave the person with her, Andy, the same condescending smile which said 'Kids huh? What can you do with them?'

Andy had some inner thoughts on the subject, but wisely kept his own counsel. Katie, on the other hand, was not bound by any code of adult behaviour and threw them both a look of defiance.

Julia tried the tactic of ignoring her daughter and carrying on the conversation with Andy in a light airy tone, as though Katie wasn't there. It was a flawed tactic from the outset. Katie simply simmered for a few seconds before playing the ace up her sleeve:

"Dad said he was coming home early and he said Christmas could start properly then. I want to go home to see if he's there."

It was a short, well delivered statement and had completely the desired effect.

"Right, say thank you to Andy for your ice-cream," Julia sighed, an air of resignation in her tone. Grudgingly Katie mumbled 'thank you'.

"Did you enjoy it sweetie?" asked Andy, a little condescendingly even for a seven year old.

"I feel sick now," replied the girl moodily.

"Oh dear, it's not your day today, is it?" said Julia, covering her embarrassment at her daughter's ill-mannered response with a false laugh.

"Excited about Christmas?" Andy persevered, "you have to be good for mummy or Santa won't come," he continued, trying hard but failing on all levels.

"Mummy *and* daddy," said Katie dryly, "I have to be good for them both, and nanny."

"Good, that's good," said Andy, "You have a lovely Christmas then."

Katie slid down from her chair and didn't bother with any response. She simply stood stiffly waiting for her mum to make a move, a haughty expression on her ice-cream stained face.

"I'd best make tracks," said Julia a little reluctantly.

"Ok, I've still got a little shopping to do," replied Andy.

"Who for?" asked Julia, fishing a little.

"Oh, no-one special," Andy replied evasively.

With that they got up from their seats, adding their more modest leavings to the pile abandoned by the previous occupants. As Julia slowly and deliberately fastened her coat, much to Katie's growing impatience, Andy, who had been hovering awkwardly said:

"Happy Christmas, it was nice to see you."

He stole the opportunity and kissed her briefly on the cheek, whispering something in her ear as he disengaged from the slightly lingering peck. Julia flushed slightly once more and the corners of her mouth turned upwards almost imperceptibly. Katie pulled angrily at her mother's hand and the three of them left the cafe and went their separate ways.

As they drove back home both Katie and Julia were quiet. Julia didn't let Katie put the radio on, she wasn't in the mood to be brainwashed by the same Christmas background tunes she had heard since she was a kid. She felt peculiar. Here she was going to her lovely home, with a daughter she loved more than life itself, to a husband who, in turn, adored them both. It wasn't enough though. She felt invigorated and enlivened deep inside by the whispered conversation and the furtive brush of Andy's hand. Something tingled in her head and in her tummy that hadn't tingled that way in a long time. Suddenly she felt despondent and deflated, almost as if she'd had a big row which she regretted as soon as it was over. She felt a kind of emptiness that she found hard to explain. It was in this wave of unsourced vexation that she said to Katie:

"You were a bit rude to Andy. That's not nice, especially when he bought you that lovely ice cream."

"He's a tosser mum," replied the little girl, surprising Julia with her unexpected use of the vernacular.

"Where did you learn that word? It's very rude?"

"Dad says it," said Katie unapologetically.

"Well it's a naughty word and I'll tell your dad off for saying it when we get home."

"He said it when *that man* dropped those books off the other week," Katie continued regardless, "He's a right tosser. That's what he said."

Julia coloured slightly, Katie was quite right, Andy had dropped off some technical pamphlets, a couple of weeks before and she'd eagerly invited him in for coffee. Inevitably that was the one day that Jim had finished work early. It was only coffee and the two men had seemed to chat breezily enough at the time. However the brief encounter had been sufficient time for Jim to form an instinctively adverse impression of the young salesman and he'd disclosed as much, in an unguarded moment, within earshot of his impressionable daughter. Nevertheless, in spite of her tender years, it seemed that Katie had formed much the same impression of the man who sat far too close to her mum, and whispered secrets to her.

"Well no more tossers Katie, or Santa won't come," directed Julia decisively.

"Well I hope Santa doesn't go to that tosser," persisted Katie, enjoying the freedom of expression allowed by bad language.

"That's enough," said Julia emphatically, "quite enough."

Katie simply smiled a self-satisfied smile and said no more.

THURSDAY – With My Body I Thee Worship

It was much later that day, after Katie was all 'tossered out', that Julia and Jim decided to call it a night. Jim had been held up at work and as a consequence, notwithstanding her not-so-romantic liaison in town, that Julia had fallen behind the gruelling schedule of pre-Christmas tasks she had set herself. As she knelt on the floor robotically wrapping the last of Katie's mountain of presents (and not a silver shilling, orange or bag of nuts in sight) the will to continue folding and sellotaping finally left her. Jim sat on the settee facing the TV, which chirped and flickered in the background like an unattended budgie. He was snoozing, his head flopped uncomfortably to one side, his body slouched in an untidy heap.

It was glancing at her semi-comatose husband that proved to be the straw that broke the camel's back on a long and trying day. She stood up stiffly and reached over to Jim, shaking him somewhat roughly on the shoulder.

"Come on, Rip Van Winkle, if you're going to snore you'd better do it in bed."

"Uh? What? … What time is it?"

"Bedtime, Sleepy … or is it Dopey? … and definitely Grumpy!"

Sluggishly they went about their pre-stairs routine, switching things off, unplugging things, scooping things up from the floor and the chairs to be dealt with in the morning, collecting a glass of water from the kitchen, all at the pace of a very depressed and unenthusiastic snail.

After the climb up the wooden hill they took turns in the bathroom to perform their night-time ablutions. Tonight it was Julia who was consigned to second turn. That was always a pain because there would be the fall-out from Jim's visit to sort out first; water splashed carelessly on the floor, toothpaste spat into the sink that he hadn't fully swilled away, the abandoned toothbrush he'd not returned to the holder on the wall, the toilet seat left up and the disarrayed towel that he'd thrown carelessly back onto the rail.

After the brief rescue operation Julia stood brushing her teeth staring at herself in the mirror. Even as she drew the toothbrush energetically back and forth across her mouth she managed to let a sigh escape. She examined her reflection; a tired woman stared back at her with dark circles under her eyes. She stopped brushing for a second and scrutinised the unflattering image before her. That woman wasn't just tired, it was true her complexion and features gave the impression of fatigue, but her eyes told another story. They were the dull, listless eyes of a woman who was dragged down by routine, a woman lacking stimulus in her life, a woman who was screamingly bored.

When she returned to their spacious bedroom she found Jim was already in bed. He had rolled over into his sleeping position; his pillows stacked high, just how he liked them. The duvet was pulled over him obscuring his body all the way to his ears.

Julia undressed in silence. It had been a long time since she'd gone to bed naked, relishing the fleeting touch of their bare flesh as they moved in their contented sleep. Tonight was no exception. As she divided her clothes between the washing basket and a chair that stood in front of the dressing table, she glanced once more to the bundle under the bedclothes that was Jim. She pulled on a satin nightdress that fell lightly over her womanly contours. Thin straps held the garment onto her slender shoulders, leaving her neck, arms and the gentle skin of her upper chest and throat exposed. The hem of the nightdress ended just on the knee, and the contour of her thigh was visible through the fine material, as the light from her bedside lamp accentuated the pleasing shape of her leg, by casting shadows onto the hollows that formed naturally in the sheer fabric.

Julia lowered herself into the bed quite gently, so as not to wake Jim, and switched off the light. His breathing was slow and steady; it would be only a short time before he began to snore. At least that's what she thought.

She lay on her back and though she felt bodily tired her mind seemed reluctant to close down. It was as if Jim heard her mind ticking. He stirred slightly causing Julia to go rigid, holding her breath in case her breathing disturbed him, or worse still brought him back to life. It was too late for such precautions; he began to rouse in a form of hazy consciousness, fuelled by an innate sexual drive that transcended the need to be fully wakened.

As she lay there, keeping very still, Julia felt her husband gently turn towards her. He inched across the bottom sheet until there was barely room to insert a sheet of tin foil between them. She recognised the lustful breathing pattern and felt his left arm coil around her waist, like a python preparing to suffocate its victim. He drew his knee softly upwards across her thigh pulling the hem of her nightie with it. His hot breath was now just millimeters from her ear. "Happy Christmas darling," he whispered, his voice sounding dry more than sensual.

Jim had manoeuvred up close and very personal in the space of just a few seconds; he was a sex ninja, working under the cover of darkness and silence. His intentions were pretty clear, in fact his intentions were jabbing the top of her thigh.

"I thought I could give you an early Christmas present," he purred, as seductively as he knew how.

This was one present that Julia instantly wanted to rush back to the returns counter for a full refund. Unfortunately for her she had lost the receipt on her wedding day and had been trying to claim on the warranty ever since!

Now he was rubbing her tummy, deliberately stroking her breasts with the upper edge of his palm as he did so. He nibbled on the side of her neck, but his warm, wet caresses simply weren't having the desired effect on his wife. Luckily Jim was blissfully oblivious to his wife's growing revulsion, or that she diverted herself from his groping advances by wondering how this would feel with Andy. Meanwhile he pressed ever closer to Julia, and she was unwilling that he should be allowed the opportunity to un-holster the concealed weapon that he was driving determinedly into her upper leg.

"Jim," she sighed softly, "it's really late, it's been a long day and we're going shopping in the morning."

If that was Julia's attempt to put Jim off, it was ineffective, to say the least.

"Don't tease, Julia," he breathed, 'you smell great."

It hardly seemed possible that Jim could get any closer to her without their bodies actually merging, but he shuffled his body nearer, immobilising her left arm in the process and pinning her to the bed by drawing his left leg over hers so that his knee was poised just on the line of her stomach.

"Mmmm, your body feels great. You're so sexy," he said in a low growl, which was somehow supposed to be sultry.

"You need to keep that thing you keep digging into my leg under control. Santa won't come if you're naughty you know," she teased, in the misguided hope that Jim would there and then desist his amorous advances.

"It's not Santa's turn it's mine," he leered.

"Santa made Katie cry this afternoon," said Julia, matter-of-factly, but with a hidden sense of increasing desperation. In a few seconds she knew she would have to give in.

Julia, without necessarily realising it, had spoken the magic word; the word that countermanded the launch sequence and instantly aborted 'take off'. The word was 'Katie'. As soon as any thought of his daughter entered his head the beast was effectively caged.

"What are you talking about that for?" he cried, rolling angrily onto his back and reaching out to switch on his bedside light.

"It just popped into my head. I thought I'd tell you," said Julia plaintively.

"Now?"

"Sorry."

The couple lay there, silent, on their backs looking at the dark shadows the single bulb cast on the ceiling from beneath its pale cream shade.

"You didn't want to make love to me, did you?" Jim complained tersely.

'Oh, it's *making love*, is it? Because you didn't get it?' thought Julia bitterly, 'The words you normally use in your seduction technique are much cruder; shag, hump, have sex, screw. It's no wonder it puts me off.'

"Well?" he demanded, intent on knowing the ugly truth.

"I suppose I just wasn't really in the mood," she said without conviction.

"You never are just lately," Jim grumbled.

"There's just a lot to think about," offered Julia, a little more brightly, hoping that Jim was becoming more conciliatory. Fat chance!

"It's *who* you're thinking about, not *what*, that worries me."

"What do you mean?" This time it was Julia's tone that was demanding. She felt a little exposed for a moment, she had lobbed a grenade at him; would he pick it up and throw it back or would he run for cover?

"Nothing!" he replied sulkily, running for cover.

Inwardly Julia breathed a sigh of relief. Now was not the time to argue over her marital fidelity or otherwise, Andy was not yet a cause worth fighting for – not yet.

"Come on, just give me a cuddle and let's get some sleep. There's no point arguing," she said, snuggling up to Jim. Jim bristled for a second or two but it didn't last, and he looped his arm over his wife's shoulder.

"I thought you honoured me with your body, or something, when we got married. It's in the vows, you're contractually bound," he muttered, with the residue of hurt in his voice.

"It's been a hectic week. You know what it's like in the run up to Christmas. So much to do. Anyway, you can *honour* my body when we have more time, when it can be romantic, not just a quick *shag*," Julia said, in what she hoped was a tone of reassurance rather than censure.

There was no more either of them could say now. Jim stretched out his free arm and switched off the light. They lay there in the darkness, Julia cradled in Jim's embrace, both silent. Neither fell asleep for some time. Jim lay still, his eyes closed, fretting about the sexual health of his marriage, worrying that he'd missed something in the preceding months that might explain his wife's apparent indifference to him. Julia lay with her eyes open, wondering what lay in front of her, and where her happiness would lie. If only fate would lend a hand, or give her a sign … if only.

FRIDAY – Freezers and Fairy Tales

Whether it was inspired by his wife's cold rebuff in the night, or that cold thoughts had helped to cool his libido, Jim woke up with the notion that the household was in urgent need of an American style fridge freezer complete with ice dispenser. It was not untypical of Jim to dream up some such hare brained scheme when the spectre of work had been laid to rest for a few days. He had sat bolt upright at about 7.30 am and announced his plan to a weary-eyed Julia. In her case it was doubtless a manifestation of the guilt she felt about spurning her husband's advances that she agreed to go with him on this random and slightly spurious quest. 'Perhaps he can stick his willy in the ice-maker the next time it gets a bit heated,' she thought, perhaps a little cruelly.

Katie was shoehorned reluctantly out of bed an hour later and decanted to Julia's mum's house for breakfast, still in her pyjamas. This was an all too regular feature of little Katie's life, and for that matter Julia's put upon mum, but they all seemed to cope. So whilst Jim drove off his mother-in-law's driveway with an air of anticipation, Julia was less enthused. They already had some last minute groceries to get and she was not relishing the forthcoming battle with the overloaded trolley brigade at the supermarket. This was an urge of her husband's she needed to satisfy quickly so that she could get on with the rest of her day. Satisfying Jim's urges quickly, when it happened at all, was not usually a problem for Julia.

Meanwhile she sat rigidly in the passenger seat of the car staring vacantly out of the window at the dreary sky, the boring pavements and the drab, grey people who inhabited them. The roads were inevitably busy and the journey was laborious. They didn't converse. Not because of any lingering disharmony over the sex incident, but because Jim could be very single-minded when he was pursuing one of his schemes, and when his focus was on the retail park, and the electrical superstore that was housed there, other considerations, such as chatter, were superfluous.

Eventually Jim found a vacant parking slot, just a few miles from the store entrance; at least that's how it appeared to Julia. The whole retail park was abuzz with activity. Even as relative early birds Jim and Julia were behind the pace. Anorak clad customers wheeled all manner of goods on trolleys and carts back to their waiting vehicles. As they padded towards the electrical superstore huge screen televisions rolled past them, Christmas trees, real and artificial, were wheeled to waiting vehicles and men in woolly hats staggered back to their car with large boxes containing stereo systems or computers, a woman trotting in front, car keys in hand.

"We should have got here earlier," observed Julia coolly.

"It'll be fine, it won't take long. I'm pretty sure I know what I'm looking for," Jim reassured her.

"Good," said Julia unenthusiastically.

They walked into the store and it was alive with people. The layout was arranged in a grid according to product type and there were folk milling around every display tailed by sales staff eager to introduce themselves and help them to find what they were looking for. One such salesman, dressed in the brightly coloured shirt provided for its employees by the nationwide company, with his name badge bordered in tinsel, foolishly volunteered to assist Jim. Thereafter he suffered Jim's continuous commentary on his needs, likes and requirements over one shoulder and Julia's grumpy rebuttals over the other. Jim questioned the young man about the cubic capacity and economy ratings, always concluding with the vital query about it having a built in ice and cold-water dispenser. Apparently some even had built in wine coolers, how fabulous; what home could be without one? To Julia they all looked as big as a Tardis but without the advantage of being able to transport her husband to a parallel universe. She tried to smile as the salesman gave his pitch, she really did, but through clenched teeth and cheeks that were rigid with boredom, it came out as a glower.

Having expended significant energy on impressing Jim, ever hopeful of a late surge in his commission figures, the sales person sloped away with an air of deflation when he met with:

"Thanks for your help, we'll give it some thought."

After all that, and with no firm decision from Jim, Julia cast him a glance that belied any immediate need for an ice-maker; there was one staring at him, as other eager shoppers twisted and sidled around her on their continuing quest for superfluous gadgets.

"I'm just not sure. I can't make my mind up," said Jim feebly, shrugging his shoulders, "it seemed like a good idea, but I'd no idea they were so hellish expensive; to get all the features we need."

"Need?" repeated Julia crossly, "Need? What we *need* is cold milk for our cereals in the morning and somewhere to put the fish fingers so they don't defrost before we cook them for Katie's tea! We already have a working fridge and a functioning freezer. I can't believe I let you drag me here on almost the last full shopping day before Christmas to spend money we haven't got!"

"I thought it would be nice. It would look good in the kitchen, and we've got the space for it. I thought you'd like it," he protested, meekly.

There was a pause while a fat woman with a stony face squeezed past Julia:

"Excuse me," she said haughtily, clearly annoyed that Julia was taking up a normal person sized part of the gangway.

Julia shook her head as the woman waddled away, towards the section where they sold microwave ovens, followed by a nervous looking rake of a man who was quite probably married to her, on the basis she provided no obvious alternative reason for a man to actively pursue her. There stepped a woman with little time to wait for a conventional oven to prepare food that she could have in a matter of seconds with the appropriate technology.

"Well, yes, I suppose it would look nice in our kitchen, and we have had the other stuff since we were married," Julia conceded, resuming the conversation with Jim at a more measured level.

"So, should we have another browse here, or we could go to the place near the motorway?"

"No," said Julia firmly but gently, "we can sort it out after Christmas. Let's get the food shopping sorted and maybe we can relax a little this weekend."

Jim nodded and grudgingly made his way towards the exit.

"Have you decided on a model?" called the young salesman sprinting towards them, in response to their hasty retreat.

"We're going to leave it until after Christmas," Jim replied, engaging the very minimum in acceptable eye contact to avoid being rude.

"Ok, merry Christmas," the lad replied smiling outwardly and giving a cheery wave. 'Yeah, season's chuffing greetings, you bloody time-wasters," was what he actually thought, as his commission skulked away through the grey rails of the alarmed exit.

"The salesman seemed a nice lad," Jim commented as he started the car.
"Keen," was all Julia could think to add.

Jim's progress through the car park was decidedly stop-start due to the sheer volume of cars circling for spaces. The hold-ups were usually caused by those cars lucky enough to spot a parking opportunity either waiting for the current occupier to manouevre carefully out the space or so that they could painstakingly squeeze into it. Occasionally a member of the shopper's infantry would march across the roadway their quarry tucked under their arm or swinging within an over-sized, festively emblazoned, carrier bag. Julia just closed her eyes and utilised a controlled breathing technique to get her through the experience.

Eventually they emerged onto the open road network, but even here the platoons of shoppers were being deployed to the seasonal battlefield. No stocked shelf would be immune from attack until the 'all clear' was sounded, as the electronic doors silently shut to, at about 10 o'clock that night. Once they were clear of the main part of the ring road, which served the town and the main retail outlets, their progress became a little less inhibited. At one point Jim was toying with the idea of engaging fifth gear such was his excitement, and it was at that moment his 'phone emitted its message tone.

"That had better not be your work, you are not going in today, not even if the place is burning down!" she warned ominously.

"Take a look would you?" he said frowning, as he finally reached a road where he could drive at the speed limit.

Julia grabbed the 'phone from the well in the centre console and poked at the buttons to bring up the message. She studied the screen for what seemed like an age. She was, in fact, re-reading the message, several times.

"Well what does it say?" cried Jim impatiently.

Julia just kept staring at the screen:

'This has to be a joke," she said, shaking her head in disbelief.

"Joke?" said Jim, "who from?"

His heartbeat hiked for a second or two, some of the jokes circulated by his workmates could occasionally be a little ... *inappropriate*? To his mild relief Julia replied quietly:

"No, not *that* kind of joke,"

Again she paused, transfixed by the tiny screen. For Jim this bordered on mental terrorism.

"What the hell does it say?" he demanded.

"It says," Julia replied slowly, building the tension further, "that you've won a bloody fridge freezer."

Jim was as nonplussed as his wife.

"What?"

"It says to take this text to the Albion at Meredith Hotel."

"Nice," said Jim simply.

"But how?" Julia stuttered, still not believing what her own eyes told her.

"I bought a load of tickets for the raffles they have at work. There are loads of them this time of year, all linked to various good causes, one of them has obviously come up trumps. They text alert everything these days – who's the daddy? Who is the daddy?"

"Never say that again," winced Julia, as Jim swept the car through a U-turn at the next traffic island.

The Albion at Meredith Hotel is a tall modern building constructed largely of steel and tinted glass. The reception is accessed through two large automated doors that swish almost noiselessly open at the slightest footfall of the weary traveller.

For the rich and privileged clientele there is a tarmacked driveway, which sweeps in a crescent in front of the entrance. Here important people can be dropped by limousine, so that the same dirt endured by the ordinary traveller didn't taint the soles of their Italian leather shoes. For everyone else there are the visitor's car parks a short hike away from the main building. This gives the common visitor the opportunity to struggle gamely with their luggage, exposed to whatever weather prevails in the unpredictable English climate. Both the privileged and common traveller, however, share the cheery salute of the liveried doorman, though his unbridled toadying is generally reserved for those that look 'posh and minted'.

The hotel's interior conveyed a look of contemporary chic, whereas the reception desk was staffed by altogether more traditionally attired staff with smiles as automatic as the operation of the entrance doors.

Today there was a queue at reception and the staff behind the large ergonomically curved counter seemed to glide to and fro as if they were on castors. They greeted each guest, guiding them through the check in procedure, with repetitive, grinning efficiency; these were the leisure industry version of the Stepford Wives.

"I'll sort this," said Jim, clutching his 'phone excitedly, "I can't believe I've won something. I never win anything."

He joined the sprawling queue of people checking in and checking out and the uncertain ones who dithered in the reception area because they just weren't sure what it was that they actually wanted. The floor in front of him was an obstacle course of discarded cases many with coats, windcheaters and cardigans draped across them. He turned and beamed at Julia, giving her a discreet thumbs-up. The boyish glee painted on his face reminded her, a little anyway, of why she still liked him – a little.

"I need the loo," she mouthed at him. He nodded and turned to face the counter, waiting eagerly for his turn to engage one of the calmly gliding swans in uniform that nobly patrolled 'Lake Reception'.

Julia headed towards the lifts, looking on the neutrally decorated wall space for a sign that might direct her to a public facility. She saw nothing that stood out to her as a universal symbol for a toilet, but then again, she reasoned, such signs might be considered unseemly in such an establishment. There again the hotel must be obliged to provide publicly accessible toilets in their common areas under whatever licence or legislation governed them, she thought. She looked around to see if there was a room maid loitering in a passageway who she could ask, but the corridors were silent and empty. It seemed that today all the activity was focused on the reception area. As it was a Friday maybe that made sense, this would be when the corporate weekday clients handed over to the weekend revellers.

She walked with a little trepidation further into the corridors, past the metal-framed artworks that were neatly screwed to the walls, all following the commissioned artist's theme in soothing shades of pastel. Here and there she shimmied past an abandoned trolley with its pile of clean towels, plastic tubs filled with tea and coffee sachets and shrink-wrapped packets of tiny shampoo, soap and bath gel. She moved stealthily as if she was a bird watcher stalking a rare avian breed, in this case the lesser spotted room maid – lesser spotted being the operative term in this corridor of the hotel.

As she prowled she caught sight of little packets of biscuits spilling across the middle tier of the trolley. It reminded her suddenly that she had not eaten because Jim had rushed them out of the house, to beat the traffic. That had worked well – not! Now she felt hungry and needed the toilet. It was all Jim's fault when it came down to it, and yet it was Jim who had been rewarded with a top prize in the works raffle, 'Trust him,' she thought irritably.

She briefly toyed with the idea of taking a packet of the tiny cookies, reasoning that her hunger constituted a medical emergency. She erred on the side of caution, and the fear that, if caught, the hotel may interpret her action as simple theft, allowing no room for the mitigation of 'thoughtless dick of a husband'.

'I never get what I want ... ever," she chuntered to herself.

She decided that she had strayed deep enough into uncharted territory and turned round in order to head back towards the main lobby of the hotel. After a few steps she saw that a door was propped open that she had missed on her original trek into the corridor. Daylight originating from the wide window of the large bedroom spilled out into the subdued lighting in the hotel corridor. She peeked inside as subtly as she could, hoping that she would see a maid inside going about her business, who might finally point her towards a toilet.

There was someone in the room, but the person seemed to be perched on the end of the bed with her head in her hands. Because the hallway was so quiet the sound of tiny sobs reached Julia's ear. From the shallow tremor in the persons breathing and the way they snatched back the tiny sob almost as soon as it emerged told Julia that it was a woman. It sounded very much like the residual sobbing that follows a damn good cry; Julia was something of an expert on the subject, having done it many times of late. She wondered if it was a new room maid, lonely and far from home, missing her family, overwhelmed by her lowly place in the bustling high-end hotel. Julia had always been a hopeless romantic at heart. It was her Achilles heel.

She wrestled with her conscience, should she interfere with this poor woman's privacy and try to help her or should she leave her to vent her sadness privately? She watched the woman's shoulders rise and fall with each involuntary spasm. The woman had shining honey blond hair cascading in ringlets from a tastefully discreet tiara. Her hair shone in the pale morning sunlight that burst through the six-foot window panels at the far end of the room. She wore a cream satin dress that exposed bare flesh across her shoulders and neck. Her arms were visible from just above her elbow upwards, as her lower arm seemed to be covered by a long sheer glove. Her skin was pale and youthful and she appeared to be slender and lithe. The dress billowed up around her waist where she sat, as if it was of the bodice and petticoat design favoured in the eighteenth century. If she didn't know better it was if she was looking at Cinderella.

Watching the poor young woman trying to suppress the aggressive convulsions caused by whatever deep emotion had taken her was too much for Julia. She knocked at the door with a feather like touch creating only the tiniest tapping noise.

"Are you alright?" she called to the girl in little more than a whisper.

The girl did not change her position, but from beneath the hands, which were cupping her sorrowful face, she said, in tiny, muffled voice:

"No."

The sheer vulnerability in that single, sad word drew Julia into the room as if she were a single metal tack drawn by the power of a thousand conjoined magnets.

FRIDAY – No Glass Slipper, No Coaches and No Balls

Julia cautiously approached the girl, like a hunter stalking their prey, nervous that the crack of a single twig would send it scampering away. The girl, however, did not flinch she simply shuffled along the end of the bed leaving a space for Julia to sit on, next to her. Julia dropped gently onto the duvet, which had been tightly tucked under the mattress and which hardly moved as she sat down. The mattress itself, however, was pleasingly pliant, though not soft, and made a comfortable seat. The girl hadn't even turned to look at Julia and continued to sob; sobs that started with a deep, deep intake of breath that reached to the very pit of her stomach. A few seconds elapsed while the exhalation rose like an air bubble in a mighty fish tank until it burst onto the surface with the familiar throb of inconsolable despair. Though Julia's instinct to help was strong she felt slightly at a loss now that she was so close to the young woman.

The opulent gown, for that was the only way to describe it, flounced on top of the bedclothes forming a partial barrier between them. On the netting, which covered the skirt, were sewn tiny costume diamonds, and the stiff cream bodice was fitted precisely across the girl's alabaster skin. The whole effect was Disneyesque. Julia placed her hand gently and tentatively on the soft, youthful skin of the girl's bare shoulder:

"What's the matter?" Julia asked in a quiet, caring voice.

"Look at me," the girl snorted through the free-flowing tears.

"Fancy dress?" offered Julia cautiously.

"No, no it's my ... wedding," which was as much as the girl could blurt out before the tears consumed her again.

It would be no understatement to say that this threw Julia somewhat. The dress was certainly extravagant and no doubt expensively made, but was unlike any wedding dress Julia had seen before, even taking account of the examples she had seen worn by members of the travelling fraternity on TV. She looked at the girl once again, this time more critically. She appeared to be in her mid-twenties, and had natural untanned, unblemished skin with no obvious tattoos on display. Her hair was set in cascading ringlets and her make-up, with allowances for the girl's mascara, which had taken a battering, was simple and beautifully understated. Julia's eyes dropped to the floor so that she could see the girl's feet. Her shoes also appeared to be made of white satin, modest heels and no adornments. There was a tiny part of Julia that half expected to see her wearing a single glass slipper – but, sadly, she was not.

"I know what you're thinking. That I'm dressed like a Disney character, *at my age* ..." she paused, partly to see if she could continue without an intervening sob, and partly to raise the pitch of her voice, "wedding? It's a bloody circus."

There was indignation in her statement which sliced through the tears like a knife through butter. Her head flopped back down into her gloved hands and her shoulders started to go up and down again.

"So when is the ceremony?" asked Julia, bereft of any other inspiration as to how she might further engage the forlorn young woman in conversation.

"Three o'clock," whispered the girl between whimpers.

"You're ready very early then," commented Julia.

"I was at the wedding breakfast, but I walked out. I said I was going to the toilet, but I ran here as soon as I got out of the room."

Julia paused, she could see how distressed the young woman was, so the matter was obviously not a trifling one, but how should she continue? She plumped for:

"Nerves? Got to you all at once?"

"It's a bit more than that," she sniffled, after a slight delay. "I'm Penny, by the way."

"Julia."

"It was very kind of you to see if I was ok. I guess most people would have walked past and pretended they hadn't seen me."

Julia just smiled and squeezed the girl's gloved hand. Now that she had a confidante the tears began to abate.

"I don't think I'm doing the right thing," blurted Penny, "in fact, I'm pretty sure I'm not. I'm awful aren't I? I should have said something before, but things had gone so far and I was afraid to let everyone down."

"Weddings can sweep you along," said Julia sagely, "you're not the first bride to get second thoughts on the day itself. In fact I doubt if many brides don't panic, at least for a few seconds."

"That's the problem, I've been having doubts for a few weeks."

Julia now knew that she was on very shaky ground. Not only was she comforting a young woman on the cusp of making a very momentous decision it also brought her own doubts about the estate of marriage to the fore. Surely someone from the wedding party would be out looking for the bride-to-be by now? Likewise she imagined that Jim would be pacing the hotel lobby wondering what she was up to. She squeezed the girl's hand a little tighter, but she wasn't sure whether it was the for the girl's reassurance or, in fact, her own.

Then there were footsteps, heavy, urgent footsteps getting closer and closer. Julia sat a little more upright, expectant and hopeful that salvation was at hand. She was not disappointed, perplexed, but not disappointed.

What every fair maiden needs in a time of great crisis is her own Prince to right the wrongs and steal her to safety on a white charger. There was no horse, and Julia looked twice to make absolutely sure, because now nothing could be certain. A man strode into the room, a man tall and bold, straight-backed and fair of face. Standing before the seated women was ... Prince Charming. Julia looked up and the man looked down. Julia was open-mouthed; the man was tight-lipped. In fact his lips weren't the only thing that was tight, and as Julia dropped her head to its normal position she was faced by a pair of well-tailored but unduly revealing britches.

The man was a good looking specimen, with longish brown hair, dark swarthy looking skin, ice blue eyes and neatly trimmed facial hair that was more than stubble but less than a beard. His apparel was equally attention grabbing, even allowing for the snugly fitting britches. He wore a flamboyant shirt open to the breastbone, velvet tunic, *those* britches and knee length boots. Attached to a wide leather belt there was a scabbard in which a rapier appeared to be sheathed.

Julia blinked, but the evidence of her eyes was undeniable, there stood every girl's idea of Prince Charming. She knew she hadn't suffered a head trauma, she doubted that the hotel corridor was a time portal so this really had to be happening.

"How could you embarrass me like this Penelope?" demanded the man, in a deep baritone voice that filled the room.

"The whole thing is embarrassing, it's a farce," muttered Penny, avoiding the man's eyes.

"It was our dream, the fairy-tale ending to our fairy-tale romance," he countered grandly.

'Prince Charming' had a certain presence about him, delivering his words with measured, theatrical effect.

"My entire family are here, supporting us, witnessing our nuptials. The wedding breakfast was an important part of the ceremony; the opening act of our grand performance."

'Wow,' thought Julia desperately trying to conceal a snigger, 'what an arse!'

The 'Prince' now positioned himself to the other side of his intended, with one booted leg on the edge of the bed in a fairly classic swash-buckling pose. His left hand steadied the handle of his sword. He used his right hand for gestures and majestic sweeps to bring emphasis to his words. The whole scenario was mind-bogglingly surreal.

"And where are your family? Where are they? Conspicuous by their absence; I shall say no more."

"My mum came," Penny protested weakly, under her 'Prince's' regal onslaught. "it was a bit too much for the others. They're down-to-earth people, they don't understand all this, it's too much for them."

'Now we're getting to the crux of things,' thought Julia, who was conscious that since 'Prince Charming' had burst into the room it was as if she had disappeared. She shuffled slightly as if to get up and leave, but Penny grabbed her trailing hand and with an invisible force prevented Julia from rising any further from the bed. Feeling superfluous Julia plopped back down onto the unmoving, thick and sumptuous duvet without further physical or verbal resistance.

"What do they know? We are in love, no one could foresee it; it was our fate, our destiny, it was kismet," he declared, with dramatic effect.

Beneath the rousing delivery of his words Julia saw the clouds of hurt gather in his blue eyes. His thespian delivery masked a very ordinary insecurity. She made the decision to try and communicate with the man beneath the character he seemed to play.

"Hello," she said, rising an inch or two from the bed and extending her hand. "My name is Julia. I just happened to be passing when I heard Penny crying."

"I see. But for whom did she shed those tears Julia? For me, and what she is doing to me, or for herself?" he asked, ignoring Julia's outstretched hand and looking despondently towards the large window at the end of the room.

Julia looked from the young girl to the pompous man and then surveyed the room they occupied. The whole scenario, the way he spoke, it was, to say the least, bizarre.

For a moment she expected to see a flashing red dot signalling the presence of a video camera, perhaps she had been caught in some weird TV set-up programme. She felt like the butt of some joke she didn't understand, but then again that's how she'd been feeling for months. Why should today be any different?

"I don't know what's going on but I'm sure you two can work it out … "she ventured.

"Work it out?" echoed the 'Prince', as though he were running the notion carefully through his mind. Then his tone assumed its previously haughty and dominant tone, "Work out why the woman, who I was to marry in a few hours, whispered to me at the wedding breakfast table, that she didn't think we were suited and that she couldn't go through with it?"

"I thought you made an excuse about going to the toilet?" said Julia to the girl quizzically.

"That's what I told his mother when I left the table; but I did say the other stuff to Gregory," the young woman confessed a little sheepishly.

"Oh!" said Julia.

"Perhaps she'll tell you, the stranger in our midst, why she has suddenly changed her mind?"

"I don't suppose it's any of my business," Julia stuttered uncertainly, wishing she could just walk out of the room; the room she probably should never have entered. The aching bladder she had temporarily forgotten about began to tingle angrily.

"I really need the loo," she said apologetically.

"It's through that door over there," said Penny, pointing across the room.

By the time Julia emerged from the bathroom the task of interrogating Penny had passed to a higher authority.

"So, Penelope, why won't you marry my son, and why did you leave it until now to embarrass him in front of his family and friends?"

The woman now speaking was an austere looking woman. She was stoutly built with hair that had been sprayed so stiffly that it looked like a whirl of greying candyfloss. Her sturdy figure was swathed in a cloak of heavy fabric that rippled with the outline of her figure from her generous bust down to her swollen ankles. There was something vaguely ancient Egyptian about the outfit, but by now Julia had become hardened to the outlandish style of clothing this event had attracted. She cast Julia a withering look, and a quizzical one to her son, but otherwise ignored her presence in the room.

Gregory stood limply at his mother's side, the arrogance having seeped from him. He looked simply like a little boy lost. Julia was loath to see poor Penny set upon by the large woman but she need not have been worried:

"Leave the poor girl alone," chided another female voice, "she's been roller-coasted into this freak show ever since your precious Gregory decided, that in a world full of eligible and blissfully gormless young women, he preferred a happily married one."

The voice belonged to a handsome woman in her late forties. Dressed simply and smartly, she was tall with fiery auburn hair. She had the deportment of a ballerina and cut an impressive figure emerging from the doorway into the bedroom.

"You would say that," retorted Gregory's mother sharply, "your precious *Penny,*" you could see the visible distaste the large woman felt for the shortening of the girl's name, "didn't seem to take much persuading, and she's done rather well out of the arrangement."

"Young Gregory besieged my daughter with messages and flowers, interfering with her young, impressionable head. It was nothing short of harassment. That is why her father refuses to be a part of this," cried Penny's mother with rising passion. These were undoubtedly words that had been a long time coming. "Your son is no more than a bully and a sex pest who doesn't know how to take 'no' for an answer."

"Penelope knew a good thing when she saw it and jumped at the chance to be with Gregory. That young actor she was with had no future, scraping a living with bit parts in the repertory theatre; that was embarrassing," growled Gregory's mother venomously.

"That boy is a young man who understands the value of hard work, not simply living off the introductions and favours called in by his mother and father."

"We have merely supported our son, his talent has done the rest."

"And he promised Penny the world, and what has been the result? A couple of minor roles in regional theatres and a walk on part as an extra on a soap opera."

Then the penny dropped, not the young 'Cinderella' bride swooning, but the realisation that the theatrical nature of the people around her was no coincidence. Their obvious involvement in the dramatic arts was rapidly dragging even this pretentiously themed wedding into a grotesque pantomime.

"I do have a mind of my own mother," protested Penny, feeling that the argument between the two matriarchs was raging in spite of her, and to a greater extent she was right; this maternal ding-dong had been brewing for some while.

"I made a mistake leaving Christian, that's true. All the more reason to realise my mistake and not want to make another, bigger, mistake today," she screeched at both of the older women. "A mistake in the real world, as far as acting *is* the real world, is one thing, but to make a mistake in this Disneyworld is certifiable," she stormed.

"But when we became intimate during the Little Fenworth production of Rags to Riches, I was your Prince then and I was supposed to be your Prince today, darling. It's what we wanted, it's how we wanted to celebrate our union," whined Gregory.

'So she *is* supposed to be Cinders,' thought Julia, finally rationalising the farce that played out before her.

The mothers stood quieted by the outpourings of Gregory and his girl, instead making do with shooting venomous and accusatory glances at each other.

"Look I'm sure we can sort all this out over a pot of tea. Shall I ring room service?"

The voice belonged to a milder, conciliatory male voice that came from the direction of the bedroom door. There stood a wafer thin man with swept back, dyed hair wearing a simple tweed suit with gaiters, a bright velvet waistcoat and a cravat. Julia couldn't fathom who this character might be, either in the family union or within this macabre fantasy, but at least he seemed keen to inject a little reason into the turbulent proceedings.

"Geoffrey, you cannot solve everything with a pot of tea, it's a hot drink, not a miracle cure!" the sturdy woman scolded him.

"Oh, I'm not so sure. Tea brings sense to a lot of situations," he persisted, pleasantly.

Julia chose the interjection of the man who, in fact, turned out to be Gregory's father, as the appropriate moment to break cover:

"I really should leave this to you. It really sounds like family business to me. After all I was only looking for the loo," she said, smiling at the generally glowering faces of those gathered in the room.

"Oh, don't go," implored Penny, standing up to face Julia as she took a couple of tentative steps in the direction of the door. "I feel like you're the only one I can talk to who will understand me."

"But we've only just met ... by sheer chance," Julia stammered, as the assembled frowns intensified. Only Gregory's father smiled impassively at her.

"Who is this woman?" demanded Gregory's acid-tongued mother.

The assembled cast exchanged cursory glances but no one seemed to know, not even Penny. It was the only consensus there had been in the room for several minutes.

"She's my friend," announced Penny at last. "You can order tea, Geoffrey, but only for two, for me and my friend ..."

"Julia," Julia whispered to the young woman.

" ... Julia," she repeated, as though the name had been on the tip of her tongue.

"Oh, this is outrageous," stormed Gregory's mother, with the force and personality of a typhoon.

Julia's didn't let her sudden promotion to *friend* either go to her head or show in her face, but she couldn't deny that she was a little fazed by it. However, there must have been something in Julia's face that provided a grudging reassurance to the group, because quietly and inexplicably they trooped out of the room. Maybe they were indulging the girl's temporary madness, or maybe they believed the stranger might have a soothing effect on the young woman's troubled breast, nonetheless they left them to it.

"There's a man in a blue boating style anorak in the foyer, he'll be pacing up and down looking annoyed by now; that's my husband. Will you tell him I've been delayed, and to get himself a coffee in the hotel lounge, please?"

She said this to Geoffrey, who had lingered slightly after the others had disappeared into the hall. He smiled kindly at Julia and nodded. He then looked at Penny who returned his gaze and their eyes met briefly. Julia felt sure she had seen the glint of empathy in the man's eyes, before he had turned around and left the room, closing the door behind him softly. After that it was quiet, a still, sterile quiet that is particular to hotel rooms.

Penny broke the silence:

"I'm sorry, I needed someone to talk to, you seem so nice, and who better than someone I've never met before to tell me if I'm mad, bad or both."

"The world you're living in seems mad to me," said Julia a little bluntly, but with no ill intent.

"It's the world of theatre, it's not real. Eventually it becomes difficult to tell what's real and what's make-believe apart. I think that's why I fell for Gregory – it was all part of the *story*. Act two, scene five … of Penny's life, and 'action'. I think I wanted my life to be a fairy tale, what woman doesn't, you know, deep down at heart? I chased a rainbow, but when I got to the end it had just faded away."

"Is that why you were getting married in fancy-dress?"

"A themed wedding," Penny corrected her.

"Yes, that's what I meant, a themed wedding. So it would be part of the magic?"

"An illusion? Yes, I suppose, but eventually I saw through it."

"At the wedding breakfast?"

"No, ages ago really, but at first I wouldn't admit it to myself and then it seemed too late to do anything about it."

"You got dragged along in its wake? That can happen."

"Caught in the slip stream, yes."

Penny recounted the tale of her meeting with Christian at drama school, as two naïve students who shared a passion for the stage and ultimately for each other. At nineteen their love knew no bounds, it heightened with every hard fought success and it brought them closer together with every disappointment, and there were many in the harsh and cruel world of the theatre. They married on the road whilst in a touring play, to the short-lived dismay of their parents. Soon their happiness and contentment was clear for all to see and any teenage selfishness they had applied to their nuptials was soon forgiven.

However as time went on Penny flourished beneath the spotlight whereas Christian struggled to develop his potential. Penny's hunger for greater successes took her to bigger and better productions, which is where she met Gregory. Gregory was cast in the lead of a regional production of Sleeping Beauty, unbeknownst to Penny his casting in the role was a favour to his mother granted by the director, a beneficiary of her generosity to the performing arts, or at least the ones that showcased her son's modest talents. The rest Julia was able to piece together from the earlier revelations that she had witnessed.

"So am I mad or bad?" she concluded, pouring a second cup of tea from the trolley that room service had wheeled in half way through her story.

"You're not mad, but you may have been a little foolish; there but for the grace of God I think. And you are not bad, but you may be guilty of not stopping to think," said Julia, proclaiming her adjudication, but feeling entirely unworthy of the role. "So, what now?"

Penny looked down and shrugged her shoulders.

"Get out of this awful frock!" she said emphatically. Both women laughed.

"I take it you're not going to the ball?"

"And I shan't be kissing any Princes; not today."

With that Penny disappeared into the wardrobe. In a matter of seconds the whole ludicrous outfit flew in fits and starts onto the bed. In a few minutes more Penny emerged in a stylish mini-dress, and low heeled, patent shoes. She dragged a brush across her stiffly lacquered curls and they dropped into fetching ringlets. Penny the princess was transformed into Penny the attractive young woman about town, and looked much the better for it.

"I've made a right mess of things haven't I?" she reflected sadly.

"It would've been a bigger mess in a few hours. Keep moving forward, try not to keep looking over your shoulder," Julia advised, not really knowing why, it wasn't an especially good analogy, but she knew what she meant.

"Speaking of moving forward," said Penny breathlessly.

"Um, what?" said Julia suspiciously.

"Give a girl a lift?"

"Well, I – I, suppose …" Julia stuttered, uncertain what she was letting herself in for.

"Let's get out of here then," said Penny excitedly, beaming as she grabbed her pastel coloured, fitted, modern mac and a soft leather shoulder bag.

In the corridor Julia went ahead as the scout. She called Penny on as she checked each junction to be clear.

Julia peeked into the function room which was situated close to the entrance lobby. There were people sat at tables looking very fed up, and others, mainly the family members she had encountered in the hotel bedroom, pacing up and down looking grim faced. Gregory was sat, appropriately, on the edge of the stage at the far end of the room looking shell-shocked. Julia motioned to Penny, who fled through the reception area and into the pull-in at the front of the hotel with an impressive fleetness of foot.

Knowing Penny was safely out of the building Julia stole into the lobby and searched for Jim. She spotted him flicking through magazines in a seating area near the large tinted windows to the side of the giant entrance doors. She motioned to him urgently. He virtually threw down the magazine he was reading and stomped towards her. She didn't give him time to complain about her protracted absence, she grabbed his shoulders roughly and pointed him towards the sliding doors:

"We need to leave … NOW!"

With Jim safely despatched Julia took one last look around the large open space. A couple of receptionists calmly went about their business ignoring Julia's frantic exertions with practiced ease. Otherwise the foyer was now empty … except.

A thin man stood quietly at the end of the curved reception desk, taking in the activity, his grey eyes catching every movement and every gesture. Julia tried to ignore him, but he caught her eye in his very steady, knowing gaze. It was Geoffrey, Gregory's father. Julia felt like a felon who had been tracked down by a US Marshall, cornered with nowhere to run. Geoffrey saw the defeated look in Julia's eye. He smiled a laconic smile and nodded slowly, knowingly and she understood the unspoken message; 'get out of here, and don't look back.'

Jim was very cross about being abandoned in the lobby in his moment of triumph. He wanted to make that point very clear to his wife but the appearance of the attractive young woman, who accompanied his wife to their car, stifled his opportunity somewhat.

"This is Penny, we're giving her a lift," said Julia to her husband tacitly.

"Oh, er, where to?"

"Wherever she wants to go," she replied imperiously. Jim didn't argue.

In the car Penny sent a text to her mother and arranged to meet her at home. She knew her father would be more than pleased to see her in the circumstances. Whether in the long term the lovelorn Christian, whose wife had betrayed him and obtained a brutal quickie divorce on the back of it, would feel the same, was down to other forces.

Penny's parents' house was a few miles outside town, but the roads were far less crowded and the diversion for Jim and Julia not so painful. At the house Julia hugged Penny on the pavement and they felt an unspoken understanding of each other in that moment, as though they had shared a brief metaphysical connection of some kind. It gave Penny strength and Julia doubt.

"So, when do we get the fridge freezer you won?" asked Julia, as they headed for her mother's house to collect Katie.
"We don't," said Jim irritably.
"What?"
"I spoke to the receptionist and he said he had no idea about any prizes for a raffle, so I asked if I could speak to the duty manager."
"And what did he say?"
"He said he thought I was the victim of a hoax. He said they get all sorts of pranks being played at this time of year. I was livid, well, you can imagine."

Julia could, easily; Jim astride his high horse was an unpleasant sight. How his pompous condescension, in the few situations he had brought it out to play over the years, had never landed him in A&E she would never know.
"So what did you say?" she said, wincing at the thought.
"I told him I had the confirmation on my 'phone, and if they didn't abide by the prize notification, which was in black and

white for him to read, they'd be hearing from my solicitor, and I'd write to the consumer page of the 'Post'."

"And ..."

"I scrolled through my messages five times, and it wasn't there. I couldn't find it. I tried, trash, drafts, folders, not a trace. You saw it though? You read it to me, in the car."

"I did. I read it to you," Julia laboured each word, deep in thought.

"Mad isn't it?" Jim grumbled, "I'll have to check my tickets when I get back to work."

"You'll have to," said Julia, very vaguely.

SATURDAY – Shopping Spree

Saturdays are generally lovely. As a day it has a different feel to all the others. For the Monday to Friday brigade of workers there's no rush to spring out of bed in order to beat the family stampede to the bathroom. There exists the potential for a relaxed breakfast, consumed whilst gazing absently at the TV, or flicking through a newspaper. It is so unlike the weekday ritual of launching breakfast cereal into your mouth as if you're shovelling coal into the engine of a speeding steam train. On a Saturday morning you can indulge thoughts of two whole days of doing 'stuff' which isn't governed by meetings, deadlines and overdue reports. There is no vile commuter journey to face, no roads or trains to resent, no anxious bile rising in your belly during that hated trek. On a Saturday the bed seems warmer, the mattress deeper and the alarm clock less fascist than they were during the week.

Why then was Julia feeling so apprehensive and tense? She lay in a rigid, twisted posture, her arm tucked under the pillow supporting her aching neck. One false move and her bones would have slotted together like the components in a barrel lock, leaving her trapped on the mattress like a deactivated robot. Jim was downstairs happily frying his eggs sunny-side up whilst Julia lay motionless upstairs doubting that she had a sunny side at all.

Then Katie appeared at the bedroom door clutching a shabby but much loved doll in her small arm.

"What are you doing mummy?" asked the little girl sweetly.

"Oh, just having a lie-in," said Julia unconvincingly.

"You still tired mummy?"

"A bit darling."

"Daddy says it's 'cause you were tired when you got in yesterday," said Katie plaintively.

"Yes we had a busy day," she replied, though substituting the word *eventful* would have summarised their day more accurately.

"Are you going out later?" asked Katie.

"Probably, " said Julia despondently, " I didn't finish all the shopping I needed to do for Christmas yesterday."

"So is Santa coming soon?" breathed the little girl excitedly, her eyes widening.

"Only if you're good," came the stock answer.

"Well I'm going to eat all my breakfast and tidy my room," was the girl's earnest reply, as she rolled her eyes skyward to make sure that the *real* Santa was also included in her promise. "Get up now mummy, daddy's doing eggs and bacon."

Julia nodded and Katie trotted off downstairs leaving a trail of innocent happiness in her wake. Julia groaned as she began unravelling her legs and spine from the painful knot she seemed to have got them in.

'When did I become such a bitch?' she wondered reproachfully as she wound her satin dressing gown around her slender frame. 'Why can't I just be satisfied with what I've got?' By now she was seated at her dressing table and she frowned at herself as she tossed her long hair this way and that till it settled into a kind of abandoned wildness. Satisfied with the cave-woman effect she strode into the bathroom where she attacked her teeth with a toothbrush. As whatever inner rage was irking her began to subside she stared at her face in the mirror, lowering her brush so that she could examine the reflection in more detail.

She saw an attractive woman in her early thirties looking back at her. There was a worldliness about her that had replaced the blank, unlined countenance of her youth. There were a couple of irritating crow's feet about the eyes, and maybe a frown line that insisted on making an appearance now and then, but a beautiful, intelligent woman of substance and experience looked back at her.

"Breakfast." Jim's voice wafted up the stairs and through the half open door of the bathroom. "Don't let it go cold."

She remained transfixed by her reflection. His voice bounced into her ears. Everything was so routine in their household. Breakfast, lunch, dinner, supper, what the hell did it all matter? It all melted together, meals, work, school runs, mum, life; it was all passing by and no one was noticing her any more. She was wallpaper, she was carpet, she was furniture; no one took any real notice – it was just *there*.

"Julia? … Did you hear? Breakfast's ready."

Jim's voice focused the frustration like a piece of glass focuses a light ray, and Julia felt a burning sensation, a flame of resent that licked angrily deep inside her.

"Come on," he repeated, "it'll get cold."

'It already has,' she thought, rinsing her mouth and spitting out the water like venom.

Before taking the short trek down the stairs to the breakfast table Julia diverted back into the bedroom. There she retrieved her 'phone from her bag, and looking furtively about her, poked it into life willing there to be a steamy little text from Andy, waiting on the screen, to captivate her senses. She was disappointed.

Andy would doubtless be tucked up with his lightly tanned, dark haired, stick insect of a girlfriend, planning a bohemian day of loafing around his smart flat drinking cappuccino and listening to Radio 2. She could just see this giggling, pouting female skipping around the flat with naïve girlish abandon, wearing nothing but an over-sized pyjama top and a tiny pair of knickers. She would have long, slender legs which were tanned and faultless that stretched endlessly from her tiny, perfect feet. ' What a bitch,' she growled, under her breath as she tossed the 'useless' 'phone back into her bag. One way and another she was 'losing it' with her state-of-the-art mobile handset.

Only the magic aroma of fried bacon turned her frown into a passable smile as she emerged into the kitchen. "Morning," she chirped, the false smile cracking her lips.

Katie sat at the table feeding her doll, with real egg. She was quiet, but things were getting very messy.

"Hi mommy. I'm feeding Emily," she announced proudly.

"Lovely."

"Do you want me to pop your breakfast under the grill? It'll be almost cold by now," said Jim by way of greeting, and with a little irritation in his voice.

"It'll be fine," said Julia without conviction, pulling out a chair and plopping herself listlessly at the table.

Jim just looked over towards Julia and shrugged. He rarely wasted words, and this morning was no exception, he simply brought her food over to the table and placed it in front of her.

"Not getting dressed?" he asked, as he returned to the stove.

"Dunno. Not yet," was all she said in reply. She pulled her dressing gown a little tighter around her shoulders as a kind of protest. It went unnoticed. 'Why should I?' she thought bitterly, slicing viciously at an egg with her knife, 'it's not like he'd notice what I wore anyway.'

Jim carried on about his business, oblivious to his wife's simmering discontent. Jim liked his routine; it felt safe and secure – to him. He had served his marital apprenticeship. He'd spent the early years complimenting her when they went out, saying nice things to her at dinner, remembering birthdays and anniversaries, spontaneously buying her things for no particular reason. If he now considered himself time-served and a marital master-craftsman, then it was about time he got his tools sharpened. Julia, on the other hand, found herself increasingly in need of attention. Time and age weren't making her more confident and self-assured with each passing year, quite the opposite in fact. She needed to be nurtured and cherished and in this regard she found her husband to be increasingly lacking.

She scooped a piece of the bacon into her mouth. It tasted good; it was a Saturday morning taste, a little weekend luxury. It was hard for her to sustain her grumpiness whilst she was relishing the salty, savouriness of the rasher with every chew. A little light conversation even crept into proceedings as Jim joined her with the last portion of food from the pan.

"Are you going out today?" asked Julia tentatively.

Jim sensed that the winning answer for first prize was 'no', the answer for the booby prize and the road to purgatory was inevitably 'yes'. Unsurprisingly he chose the former.

"No, I've got a few things to do in the house," he replied airily.

"Ok, that's good. We didn't get everything we intended to yesterday, so I thought I'd brave the traffic and go and finish up – without Katie trailing behind me."

"Yeah, fine. She can stay here with me, she won't want to be dragged round the shops today."

Katie was already kneeling on the floor at the far end of the room organising some sort of event with an array of assorted dolls and teddies.

"I'll get dressed and go then."

"Good luck, try and get back for the 'big day'," quipped Jim heading back to the sink with the dirty plates.

Luck? Luck didn't come into it for Julia. She was an inveterate shopper, a skilled and fearless spender of money, a woman capable of turning a quick trip to get milk into an epic adventure. She was the Lara Croft of window displays and card terminals; surfing the perils of the clothes shops, vanquishing the lure of the jewellery counters, defying the surprise attacks of heavily made-up demonstrators brandishing perfume samples. She used no hunting knife to face these tasks; Julia Carter went out armed only with a mighty purse and the magic power of a Platinum credit card. No ordinary furniture display, bathroom accessory or shoe shop stood in her path. In the world of retail commerce Julia Carter was feared by all and feared no one.

"Right, I'm off to town then."

The journey into town was every bit the vehicular hell she had envisaged. Stuck in long queues of traffic at every traffic light and island her attention was forced to endure the true tackiness of the season. Houses on the way competed for the title of gaudiest outdoor display, most vulgar house decoration or greatest disservice to Christmas and humiliation for the street. It was a tough competition but this year's winner had to be the house with a life-size plastic Santa crawling into an upstairs window bearing his plump and rounded posterior to the viewing public. The tired strings of council erected decorations swaying between lamp standards weren't much better, and in any case they had been on display since late October, but they weren't lit due to new council regulations on street lighting. It was a relief, therefore, when she finally parked the car after a quick circle or two of the uppermost level of the multi-storey car park, which at other times of the year was invariably empty. As the engine faded and she put on the handbrake her phone pinged.

'*Meet me in Lotsa at 12 – panties optional x,*' read the cheeky message.

'He *is* a tosser,' thought Julia, shamelessly plagiarising her daughter's terminology, but nonetheless flushing like a teenage girl.

She deleted the text having read it a couple of times, as was her habit this far into this dangerous flirtation. The secrecy and deception was a drug, and she was hopelessly addicted. For a second she wondered how Andy knew she was in town before realising that she had fallen victim to her own predictability. It was 11.30 am on a perfectly good weekend shopping day, where the hell else was she going to be?

The sprint to the lift and the race through town were indeed comparable to a Lara Croft pursuit. Deftly she power-walked between the shambling, brain dead shoppers, clipped their festoons of bags with but a fleeting contact and stumbled breathless across the threshold of Lotsa Coffee.

"Hello gorgeous," breathed a voice from behind her.

The coffee shop was busy to bursting and as she swivelled round in surprise she almost uprooted a baby from its pushchair. It was just as well that the child's mother was far too engrossed in a conversation about her latest encounter on Internet dating to notice. The child made a little yelping noise, but the mom zoned it out as she often did. The little girl persisted and her mom, without breaking sentence, shoved a biscuit at the child and order was resumed.

Andy guided Julia to a seat in the window, his hand gently grasping her waist as he did so. She sat down, puzzled by his choice of table. Was he just brazen? Did he want her husband or his scrawny, baggy jumper wearing airhead to see them? She had no idea why she instinctively hated Andy's girlfriend, she'd never met her and the poor girl had done nothing to her, but she couldn't fight instinct, or whatever it was. All she could visualise was a posh, giggly bag of bones that could throw on any random assortment of rags she found lying on the floor in the morning and end up looking like Keira Knightley. The image was borne of spite, but uncannily was not inaccurate.

"I got you a latte, I hope it's still hot."

He smiled, raising one eyebrow as he did, he was nothing if not smooth.

Julia took a brief sip from the voluminous mug of froth that took two hands to lift to her mouth, and just one hand to wipe the milky foam that settled on her nose.

"It's fine thanks," she said, taking a breath and starting to relax.

"Still got to get a few things then?"

"A couple of stocking fillers, nothing much. Shouldn't take long."

She didn't say that they were for Jim and Katie. She was loath to use their names in front of Andy. It made it easier somehow to temporarily airbrush them from her life, just while they were stealing their precious moments together. Maybe she was subconsciously hiding them from the deceit?

"Well I hope you get something nice," said Andy breezily. "I had to get Sophie a set of books she wanted; something to do with the research she's doing for her dissertation next year, so I got first edition hard backs. They really look the business."

He had no such reservations about introducing his significant other into his conversation; it didn't faze him at all. Could it be that that was part of the thrill?

"That sounds really thoughtful," said Julia dryly, raising the huge cup to her mouth, to cover the look of irritation that played on her lips.

"What's she studying?" she asked sweetly, lowering the cup.

"Her Master's in Victorian literature," he said, with a degree more pride in his reply than Julia liked.

"How interesting," she lied, coldly. 'Should help her get that dream job on the counter in WH Smiths,' she thought, less charitably.

"She hoping to work in publishing," said Andy, unconsciously shooting her down.

"I see," said Julia, already long fed up with this topic of conversation.

"Smile Julia, it's Christmas," cooed Andy, finally picking up on Julia's irritation, "You never know we may be spending the next one together?"

It was more what Julia wanted to hear, but it was hardly said with any real conviction. It came across like one of those half-promises made to fob off sulky children. Julia could be many things, but she was neither sulky nor childish and really didn't deserve to be treated that way. She thought briefly about a tear strewn Sophie packing her precious first editions into a bundle, her eyes puffy, mascara streaming onto her cheeks as Andy broke the news that there was someone new in his life. She wanted to imagine that for once Sophie wouldn't retain her shabby chic perfection, but she guessed that even in the depths of despair she would cut a wistfully romantic figure; 'the scrawny cow!'

It was Andy's quizzical stare that broke her reverie. Suddenly the inconsequential chatter all around her, the smell of coffee pervading the air, the constant ballet performed by the staff behind the counter all returned to her consciousness.

"Do you think we might get together before Christmas day, it would be nice to see you nearer the day?" ventured Julia nervously.

Andy turned towards her and for the first time that day looked serious.

"Not sure, I'll try," he said unconvincingly, "I've got a bit on …" and the words petered out feebly.

"Sophie's parents due over?" she asked, waspishly. 'Coming over to watch the silly cow open her presents under the tree, like they've done since she was two,' she thought sneeringly.

Then she shook her head as if to dispel her unkind thought, because in a couple of days that's exactly what she would be doing with Katie; watching her tear the paper from a pile of presents with the unfettered joy of a doting mother. With a shudder she wondered if that would still be the case a year from now.

"You ok?" asked Andy, seeing Julia's involuntary head movement.

"Oh, sorry, yes, I'm fine. Just thinking about everything I still have to do for Christmas day," she replied distractedly.

"I really have to be going," said Andy, glancing at his watch, then slurping the last vestiges of tepid coffee from the bottom of his cup.

This was always the frustrating part of their meets, the clock watching, the sudden restlessness, the time that had ruthlessly sped past and was now lost. Often she wondered why modern marriage couldn't be more like enlisting in the services, signing up for a few years after basic training with the option to resign or walk away afterwards. No, as a wife, the vows imposed a whole life contract with the Royal Matrimonial Logistics and Catering Corps. 'As you were Private Carter, wait for it, wait for it.'

"Yes, ok," she conceded, sadly, "I've still got things to get in town anyway … but you won't forget to give me a ring about meeting up before Christmas day?"

"Of course, if I get the chance. I'd love to see you, I'd like to see a lot more of you," the raunchy inference at the end of his sentence was designed to mask the noncommittal beginning of the sentence, but it would take more than that to hoodwink Julia.

"Try," she persisted.

He smiled, a glassy, evasive smile and stood aside holding the door of the coffee shop open so that she could re-enter the commercial maelstrom that flowed in the packed aisles of the busily throbbing shopping centre. They walked a few short paces together. As they passed a passageway that led to the car parks Andy gently guided her inside. He grabbed her shoulders and spun her round to face him. She looked surprised and flushed and suddenly felt a little breathless. He planted his warm, moist lips on hers as her eyes darted from side to side, desperate to make sure that she wasn't seen by someone who might know her, or her husband. The kiss lasted just a second or two, but her stomach tingled in response and her knees weakened, just a little. It was like a tiny but pleasant electric shock that ran through every major organ at once.

"See you kiddo," he said coolly, as he detached his face from hers.

Julia said nothing; she just stood looking disoriented as he strode off towards the fire doors covered in dirty handprints that led to the car park. Talk about leaving the audience wanting more!

In a slight daze, or was it swoon, Julia resumed the original, or at least purported, reason for her trip into town, the last minute shopping. It wasn't easy because her mind was elsewhere. Thank goodness that the shopping force was strong with her that afternoon, by some act of will she began to amass a sizeable collection of carrier bags all emblazoned with a seasonally adapted logo for each store she favoured with her custom. She could only hope that the goods she bought would be what was needed and moreover what would be appreciated, but that was really down to the power of the subconscious shopper within.

In the very last shop she intended to grace that afternoon a man's cashmere cardigan caught her eye. She hovered next to the display rack, touching it and enjoying its soft sheen on her fingers. She put her bags on the floor and took it from its hanger. She held it up and cast her eye on it, examining it back and front. She liked it. It was neat, slim fit and contemporary. She could see Andy wearing it with a plain cotton shirt and a narrow wool tie. It would suit his smart-casual, catalogue model looks perfectly. She stood there frozen with indecision.

Ding ding, 'seconds out!' Conscience took a defensive stance as infidelity danced arrogantly out of its corner. The referee circled the ring; he wanted a good clean fight. Infidelity was having none of it he teased and ducked and weaved. Conscience stood upright and resolute. A camera flashed from the unfeeling ranks of the hacks at the ringside, they wanted blood; they wanted it soon! Conscience was momentarily blinded by the flash of light and blinked just as Infidelity threw a hard right hand and knocked conscience clean out. The referee counted, looking concerned for the fallen combatant, the crowd roared. 'Eight, nine, ten … out!' The seconds raced into the ring to tend the fallen conscience, whilst the referee held infidelity's arm aloft. ' Infidelity wins by a knockout.'

Julia pulled the cardigan towards her, folding it in a small bundle, as if to conceal it from onlookers. She scooped up all her bags, at least she thought she had, and furtively wandered off to the nearest till. She would work out how to smuggle it into the house later.

SATURDAY - Jean and Ken

Her secretive purchase had been her last of the day. She left the shopping mall with the clandestine aspect of an escaped prisoner. Bags in hand she threw herself into her car, her face and neck clammy with the sweat of a guilty person desperately evading capture. She launched the clutch of shopping bags onto the back seat, and with the car park exit ticket clamped firmly in her teeth she departed the town centre, flinging her car round the labyrinth of downward ramps in a muted parody of 'The Italian Job'.

Such unrestraint on the main roads was not so forthcoming. The traffic had been moving with the pace of a slightly asthmatic fat kid all day and as the fleeting daylight clocked off from another short-hours shift, late afternoon proved to be no exception. As she sat patiently in the line of traffic waiting for the lofty favours of the traffic light system to be bestowed upon them, she dabbed a little extra lipstick on her mouth to replace that which now adorned the car park ticket she had surrendered to the exit barrier moments earlier.

'Not bad,' she thought, examining the reflection that looked back at her from the rear view mirror.

Each time the lights changed two minutes of madness ensued, handbrakes were wrenched off, gears engaged (the brains of many of the vacant motorists took a little longer) and slowly, so slowly, the line moved forward. Occasionally a lane changer would impose his vehicle upon the advancing traffic and cause a ripple effect of indignation behind him, and everyone would grind a few paltry spaces forward, stomachs churning with inner angst.

The red light seemed redder today. It seemed more compassionless and contemptuous than usual. Today the lights were inhabited by the restless soul of a deceased parking warden, displaying the sneering disdain that only a person in an ill-fitting uniform, clumpy shoes, peaked cap and a ticket pad can carry off. The lights were very Jobs-Worth today; a red, amber, green Grinch stealing Christmas from the motoring public.

Eventually she made it through as the lights 'played chicken' with her, seeming to speed up the progression between green and red as she took her turn at the junction. She hesitated for the briefest of seconds during their game, which meant the large SUV behind her was left stranded at the broad white line. A fat man behind the wheel slammed his palm on the horn and his pudgy, sweaty face contorted in anger. The sudden blare caused Julia's hackles to rise and she raised two beautifully manicured fingers in a salute to his unmusical blast.

Aside from the rat-run of 'safety' cameras the journey home was now a relatively straightforward affair.

Those cameras which in no way gathered additional revenue from the soft target of honest motorists who teetered a few mph above the speed limit of a horse and cart. The honest motorists who actually registered their cars to an address at which the DVLA could mercilessly hunt them down like dogs – *those* cameras!

It would be a matter of minutes before she slung her car onto the tarmac drive of her home, where every room would be lit up brightly, whether occupied or not. This was good news for the poor directors and shareholders of the energy firms who toiled selflessly to eek a meagre living from the power that is so greedily consumed by the rich and fat consumers, but not such a boon for Julia's beleaguered household budget.

'The house is lit up like Blackpool Illuminations,' she heard the ghostly voice of her father echo from beyond the grave.

It spooked her, therefore, when the screen of her 'phone lit up as his words evaporated from her recollection. A message icon appeared on the screen, and after a second or two it too evaporated into inky greyness as the image faded back into stand-by mode. Since things had begun to hot up with Andy Julia had found it harder and harder to ignore the text alert. The impulse to deal with it after completing the task in hand had been long abandoned in favour of 'drop everything, check the text!' The compulsion was strong within her and seeing a pull in opportunity just ahead she steered the car to the side of the road and pulled up.

'U left 1 of ur bags in shop. Its @ 23 Herbert Street. Be in all nite'

The number meant nothing to Julia, but then again why would it? Julia pawed through the collection of bags flung across the back seat and sure enough she was one short. She went over her purchases in her mind as she peered into each bag. 'Oh no,' she thought, closing her eyes in exasperation, 'it was the Wii game that Katie had been going on about for weeks. The one all her friend's had.' This was the 'Killer Stocking Filler'; she had to get it back straight away. She cursed herself; 'this wouldn't have happened if I hadn't been fretting over the cardigan for Andy.'

She picked up the 'phone and pressed the number on the call log so that it redialled. The line opened and the number displayed on the screen but as she pressed it close to her ear there was no sound, no dialling tone, and no ringing tone. She cleared the call and tried again. The same thing happened. Once more for luck … nothing. It was so frustrating, all those satellites spinning in the weightless vacuum above the stratosphere and not one of them was picking up the call. 'They must be in a black spot,' she reasoned to herself, tossing her 'phone back onto the passenger seat. On the plus side Julia knew where Herbert Street was. A short detour and all would be well. She looked at the time displayed on the dashboard – almost four-thirty. The last of the light had drifted away and the street lamps had taken on the mantle of providing illumination, though a watery moon was lending a hand.

Julia turned the car round and headed back towards town. Herbert Street sat on the other edge of the retail district. A long stretch of road with a variety of styles of houses dotted along it, nothing more recent than the early sixties and nothing further back than between the wars. There were tall fluorescent lamps at regular intervals and the road was patrolled by single decker buses that busily ploughed a furrow on their way into and out of town, despite a sparsity of passengers for their service. They were like empty-bellied monsters roaming the streets for food.

The street was intersected at intervals by side streets, and between two of these intersections there was a group of local shops, nothing fancy, but always doing a brisk business. Cars came and went from the kerbside outside the shop fronts like worker bees flying to and from the hive.

As Julia drove slowly past the shops, craning her neck to spot a house with a number on it at all let alone a discernable number '23', a bus chugged up behind her, unhurried but steadfast on its route. She pulled into a pub car park so it could rumble past, its single passenger, starkly illuminated by fluorescent lighting, staring absently through the partly steamed up window. The pub was open but only a subdued light escaped the heavy velour curtains that were pulled tightly across its windows. There were a couple of tatty looking cars on the pot-holed car park, but otherwise little evidence of activity, unlike its heyday in the fifties and sixties. The loud voices yawping 'goodnight' 'all the best' at each other, or loudly singing maudlin ditties at chucking out time were just echoes embedded deep in the faded brickwork these days.

A rickety looking smoking shelter stood near to the main building. A lone man stood in it lit only by the orange glow as he sucked on his filter tip. Julia pressed the button, which wound down the passenger window:

"Excuse me," she called to him.

The man turned to her, dipping so that he could see beneath the rough wooden frame of the shelter. He screwed his eyes up so that he could see better in the dark:

"I'm looking for 23 Herbert Street."

"You're looking in the right place then," he replied, pointing directly across the street, "I'd leave your motor in the pub car park, the road's a busy one."

"Will that be ok do you think?"

"It'll be fine love, it'll make the place look busier," he laughed, stubbing his cigarette underfoot.

"Thank you."

"Merry Christmas," he called cheerily, sloping back into the pub, looking frozen to the bone.

Light was fading fast now and the streetlights glowed a harsh, yellow hue. The homage to Christmas in this no-nonsense hard brick and rendered part of town was more subdued than the newer 'rabbit warren' estates elsewhere in the conurbation. It had a stoic 'don't panic, carry on' feel to it, the brick facades contained an air of fading pride, from an era disappearing into vague memory. Behind the plastic doors and windows, that had long ousted the peeling wood and single-pane glass, TVs linked to satellite dishes flickered endlessly whilst the younger generation dabbed the screens and keyboards of tablets and iPhones, oblivious to any external stimulus.

It was no different at number 23. The doors there were often closed all day, with no visitor to enter or exit. Inside the TV was insanely loud and the gas fires blared in spite of the terror tactics of the energy companies. The people who lived here carried the memory of the time when this street was vibrant and proud. Admittedly the sense of excitement for the '66 World Cup victory and the moon landing had faded and tarnished with the passage of years, and the bitter creeping cynicism of old age. The house was riddled with the early onset of decay and its residents along with it.

Julia squinted in the inky darkness, the hazy glow of the street lighting only compounding the reduced visibility. She could barely make out the tiny plastic numbers screwed to the porch door. The heavy curtains were roughly drawn across the windows, though there was a faint glow, which suggested there might be a light source behind them. She wandered up to the porch door. It was frail from damp and there were patches of wood you could probably poke into a hole with a determined push of a fingertip. Each of the two doors had a pane of grimy frosted glass, which was impossible to keep clean because of the constant spew of emissions from the traffic – even if you'd wanted to, which the occupants didn't. Suddenly a security light activated, blazing down on Julia so she was caught in its glare, like a searchlight that had swept across an escaping prisoner. She strained her ears and faint, scrambled noise hummed through the secondary glazing.

Julia poked a long, agile finger at the bell push. It made no noise, but inside the house the occupants were alerted to an outside presence. As they always did, they looked quizzically at each other as though it was a sound that was new to their ears. Then the glance extended to determine who was going to respond. The battle of wills was invariably short, but it was a time-tested routine. Inevitably the old lady heaved herself awkwardly out of her armchair, and the old man's attention returned to the telly, hoping that whoever it was would quickly go away.

A light illuminated through the frosted glass and the shadow of a heavier door opening swung across the backlight. A short, round figure stood in silhouette on the other side of the porch door to Julia.

"Who is it?" the voice called tentatively.

"My name's Julia, you texted to say you've got my shopping bag," Julia called back.

It was far too much information at once and the obviously elderly female voice simply shouted back: "Who?"

"Ju – li – a … you left a message on my 'phone," she replied slowly and loudly.

"Is it our Jim?"

"No …. my name's Ju – li - a, you 'phoned me," Julia persisted, more in hope than expectation.

She saw the old lady hesitate through the frosted glass. Julia's shoulders dropped, this had the potential to descend into farce, and she was cold, fed up and wracked with guilt about the cardigan.

Luckily and perversely the uncertainty about the identity of her visitor simply caused the old woman to open the door anyway. A door chain rattled, bolts, top and bottom, slid across and finally a latch clicked before one of the rickety wooden porch doors opened inwards. Julia looked down; a very short but equally stout elderly woman stood in front of her, like a troll guarding a bridge. Her hair was thin and wispy and held traces of a recent perm, which was fast surrendering any semblance of hold. Her bottom lip pouted beyond the top lip, giving the woman an austere, even challenging expression. She scanned Julia top to bottom with a disapproving glare.

"Hello," she said sweetly, " I got a message to say that someone here had found a bag belonging to me?"

"Ken," she hollered down the hallway, to no response. "Ken?"

There was a brief pause then the volume of the TV dipped noticeably.

"What?" a hoarse sounding male voice shouted back.

"Have we got a bag of shopping? There's a woman at the door says we've got her shopping."

"Joanie dropped some shopping off this morning on her way to work. Is that it? I thought that was for us. Ring Joanie, she'll know what it's about."

With that the TV volume resumed its ear-splitting setting.

"Come in," said the woman, ushering Julia into the chilly hallway.

Julia had no real option but to follow her, closing the porch door gently behind her. She had the sinking feeling that this was going to get very complicated, but she couldn't leave Katie's present here until she could speak to whoever it was that had left her the message in the first place. The hall was brightly lit by a fluorescent light that hummed constantly. There was a strange aroma in the cluttered hallway, which seemed to be a combination of mothballs and bleach. The old woman disappeared from sight, but only momentarily.

"Don't stand there, come in the front room," she said in a tone that sounded cross, but wasn't intended that way.

Julia stepped into the front room. It was cluttered with mismatched ageing furniture. The carpets needed hoovering and almost every flat surface played host to some sort of discarded item: magazines, half eaten packets of biscuits, knitting, empty, stained cups. Most of all there was an overpowering heat. The gas fire, set in an old fashioned tiled hearth, radiated like a small sun. The filaments were scorched and some had simply burnt away.

Ken sat in a large armchair, his legs tucked under a roll-along TV table. The headrest of the chair was shiny with age and use, Ken could boast both age and use but was not so 'shiny' these days. He occupied himself by folding bits of paper and sliding them into polythene bags with automatic efficiency, the piece work he'd done from home for many years for the pocket money the big company, which profited from his efforts, and thousands like him, paid him. He seemed to give Julia scant attention, but through the corner of his wily old eye he had clocked that she was a slim and pretty young woman. He thought that he might just have to turn on the old charm, but like the valve in an old TV set he needed time to 'warm up'.

The elderly woman shuffled back into the room, barely keeping her feet in the over-sized and well-worn fluffy slippers that she dragged along the carpet. She flopped onto an armchair in the centre of the room, the cushion supported by a plank of MDF where the springs in the seat had given up the ghost.

"Sit down," she said to Julia, having abandoned the finer etiquette of conversation some years ago.

Julia gently pushed a couple of magazines to one side and perched uncertainly on the sofa.

"Get her a cup of tea Jean," directed Ken, suddenly coming to life. His armchair was clearly the command pod from which he ran the household.

"Ah, ok, tea or coffee?"

Julia sensed that the invitation was more of a direction than a question and not wishing to offend she acquiesced hesitantly.

"Erm, tea please, no sugar for me, thank you."

With that Jean hauled her small frame out of the armchair she'd literally sunk into a few seconds before and disappeared from the room once again. Ken scrutinised Julia a little more intently. She seemed like a nice young woman. She didn't seem to be after anything and, as far as he could tell, she wasn't trying to sell anything.

"What brings you here, love?" he asked in his croaky, ageing voice.

"A bag of shopping. I left one of my bags in a shop in town and I got a message to say it was here."

The old man looked puzzled:

"Well we haven't been out. I never go out, not these days, not with my blood pressure and these legs." Julia wondered briefly what other legs he had access to, but wisely decided not to pursue the matter. "And Jean, well she hasn't been out today either. Our Joanie gets the shopping, we give her a list, but she dropped it off this morning on her way to work. Got me the wrong butter," he added testily, "she gets the cheaper rubbish and keeps the difference," he muttered reprovingly.

At that point Jean reappeared. She tottered in with three cups of tea on a metal tray. It all looked very precarious and Julia noticed a small tide of tea, which lapped between the cups. Jean placed the tray on the TV table in front of her chair. There were two mugs with tea bags still floating on the surface, like miniature whales about to blow a tiny tea spout, and a mismatched china cup and saucer, which nonetheless sported the same arrangement. The milk had already been added, so the mixture had a treacle-like colouration. Julia's mouth smiled gratefully, but her lovely blue eyes told a different story.

"Thank you," said Julia sweetly, extracting the teabag with a tarnished spoon.

Jean handed one of the mugs to Ken, a little of the fluid spilling from the overfull cup as it came to rest. She then plopped down on her own chair with a sigh.

"Have a biscuit if you want one," she said, as she regained her breath from the exertion. She thrust a half open packet of value brand digestives at Julia and held it steadily aloft until Julia was forced to wiggle a biscuit from the packet. The process dislodged a tiny cascade of crumbs onto the carpet, where they found themselves to be in good company.

"She says she's come to get a bag she left at one of the shops in town," Ken told Jean, as though Julia wasn't even in the room.

"I haven't been to town today, Joanie got the shopping yesterday and dropped it off this morning," Jean protested, likewise omitting Julia from the conversation.

'I am sick of hearing about their shopping arrangements with Joanie, whoever she is,' thought Julia crabbily, balancing a cup and saucer in one hand and grasping a biscuit with the other.

"She got the wrong butter. She knows I like the one where you can't tell the difference," moaned Ken, prolonging their exclusionary chat.

"I'm sick of hearing about the butter. It all tastes the same. It all comes out the same!" Jean said, clearly baiting her husband.

"That's crude," he chastised, his eyes flashing angrily in the direction of their visitor, "You're showing us up."

Julia winced but at least she was 'back in the room'. Ken's hands proved quite dextrous for a man of his age as he stepped up the pace at which he stuffed the polythene envelopes with the paper he had folded.

"We do a bit of outwork for a firm. It keeps us busy and gives us a bit of money on top of our pension," Jean explained, as she saw Julia staring at Ken's surprising manual dexterity.

It was repetitive, mind-numbing work that they had done for as many years as they cared, or in fact didn't care, to remember. It gave them something to do during the endless hours they spent in front of the TV, drinking strong tea, and ignoring each other or bickering. It kept their old hands busy and, helpfully, off each other. It was a poorly paid, workhouse style labour but it had sustained them during an increasingly sedentary old age; an old age that had been going on for a very long time.

"So, are you saying there's been a mistake? You don't have my shopping bag?" asked Julia, a hint of desperation emerging in her voice.

She balanced the biscuit precariously on the saucer, now she was left with the task of extricating the teabag from the cup. It floated like a half submerged lifejacket in a muddy coloured sea. She managed to scoop the teaspoon under it and she flopped it onto the saucer, on the opposite side to the biscuit. It was all very intricate and difficult, but neither Jean nor Ken seemed to notice.

"What was in it?" asked Jean, after some consideration.

"A game for my daughter."

"Aah. How old is she?"

"Seven, nearly eight."

"No, we haven't got your bag, or your game. Why do you think it's here?" asked Jean, abruptly ending any further enquiry into Julia's offspring.

"Because I had a message on my 'phone to say it was here," said Julia, her even tone cracking with the first indications of exasperation.

There was a pause while they all stared at each other. Ken even stopped stuffing paper into packets for a few seconds. Then Jean resumed her deliberations:

"Our son, Jim, rang just before you arrived, he said he was on his way round."

Ken shot his wife a look of angry contempt from the safety of his armchair:

"What's that got to do with it?" he demanded irritably.

"I don't know, it might be something to do with her bag," retorted Jean irascibly.

Jean and Ken were clearly comfortable with such grumpy verbal skirmishes. In their claustrophobic environment these flashpoints were a daily occurrence, hourly sometimes. Their routine was set, their pattern of existence engraved into the stale, overheated air of the small living room they occupied side-by-side, day after repetitive day. To them the venting of their frustration at each other was normal, healthy in its own way. To an outsider, such as Julia, it appeared childlike and felt very uncomfortable. External venting was less frequent and often limited to their grown up children, whose visits became less frequent and shorter in duration as time passed.

Julia looked from one to the other trying to imagine them as nervous, young lovers, drunk with amour, unable to find enough time simply to be together. How many years had it been since that love eroded to reveal something grittier and earthier beneath? Love became the joint labour of raising a family, of worries about the children, about money about how the world was overtaking them at an ever-increasing speed. When did even those last vestiges of unity of spirit transform into a bonded companionship, which would see them through old age to infirmity and then to the grave? Two souls tethered together, breaking rocks until eternity granted them a pardon. She shuddered. Was she looking at her own future? Was this where it would all lead? She needed to break her reverie before it became unbearable and she began to tremble:

"What time will your son be here?"

"Oh he just suits himself, always has," Jean replied huffily.

" Sometimes comes to watch the football results," Ken offered, more to annoy Jean than to assist Julia.

"Oh, ok," said Julia finally, putting the cup and its overloaded saucer on the hearth.

"Don't you want your biscuit? Our Jim never eats a biscuit here. Our food's never good enough for him, or his snooty wife … not that she ever graces us with her high and mighty presence. Too busy tarting up the 'mansion' they live in." Jean ranted.

"It's not that, I'm trying to diet before Christmas," was Julia's rather transparent excuse.

"Diet?" gasped Jean incredulously, "There's nothing to you as it is. She's like a twig Ken, and she's frightened of putting on weight!"

Julia smiled coyly and opened her mouth to make her excuses to leave, but as often is the case in such circumstances something suddenly intervenes: in this case it was the doorbell. It rang loudly, twice. Jean and Ken looked intently at each other from their respective armchairs, an unspoken exchange commencing. Was this the 'phone or the doorbell ringing, and who would answer? Though this well-rehearsed ritual routinely lasted several seconds it would inevitably end with Ken gesturing to Jean to respond, which she invariably did. Having decided it was the doorbell she heaved herself from the armchair and shuffled away, tripping over her slippers as she went.

Julia smiled weakly at Ken who grinned back at her with his yellow-brown tobacco stained teeth. He sat there, dressed in an old woollen jumper and a loosely fitting pair of workmen's dungarees, worn for comfort not style, wiry stubble on his face like a recently harvested field of grey corn. It was a small kingdom, but in this crumbling castle Ken was indisputably the King. They sat in silence as Jean slowly and mechanically raised 'the fort's' defences to allow the caller inside.

Eventually the sitting room door opened and a man in his early forties stepped through it. He had a pleasant smile and seemed pleased to see another younger face sat in the room. He said his 'hellos' and held out his arm. In it was the carrier bag Julia had left behind in the clothes shop.

"Yours I imagine?" he said warmly.

Julia reached over eagerly and took the bag. She peered inside and saw the game nestling within.

"Oh, thank you. I don't know what to say. It's a present for my daughter. I would never have heard the last of it if it wasn't under the tree for Christmas morning."

"I guessed as much when I saw it. I assumed you were going to come back for it when you'd paid for the cardigan you were struggling with, but you didn't. I was trying on a pair of shoes. I did try to run after you but I hadn't laced my shoes up properly and I slipped. By the time I got to the exit you'd gone. You must have been in quite a rush."

"I think I was just getting a bit flustered and I wanted to get home," she replied, flushing slightly. "How did you get my number?"

"I didn't, there was a lady who saw me running after you and when I explained what had happened she told me she knew you. She gave me your address and I was going to drop it off later, after I'd visited mum and dad."

Julia looked puzzled:

"But I had a text message to say my bag would be here."

"Not from me I'm afraid, perhaps your friend texted you to let you know. I gave her mum's address in case I couldn't get hold of you. I would have left the bag here if you hadn't been in when I called, because mum and dad never go out. All's well that ends well, eh?"

Julia suddenly felt a little nervous. If someone that knew her was in the shop they would have seen her performance buying the cardigan, a cardigan that was not destined for Jim Carter's Christmas stocking, a cardigan that was a whole size too small for her husband.

"What did the woman you spoke to look like?" she asked anxiously.

"An older lady, short, grey hair … I can't really remember much about her. She was really nice. She said she would have taken the bag but she didn't know when she'd be able to drop it off. Well, I guessed it was a kiddie's present so I said I'd do it, to make sure it got to you for Christmas. I've got two of my own, I know how they'd be."

"Well we wouldn't," grumbled Jean, out of the blue, "they hardly come and see their Nan and Granddad these days."

"Mum … not now. I haven't got time …"

"I see, rushing off as usual. Carol got you running round doing jobs as usual while she has a bottle of wine with her friends?"

"She's got a lot to do, as you well know, with Christmas in a couple of days."

"Well sit down and have a cup of tea."

"This woman, she didn't say her name?" interrupted Julia, frantically wondering who might have seen her; fretting that the same woman might have seen her passionate embrace in the corridor leading to the car park, or her intimate tete-a-tete in the coffee shop.

"No, sorry. If she did I've forgotten it. It didn't seem important."

"No, probably not," sighed Julia resignedly, knowing that it might in reality be critically relevant to her immediate future.

"Do you want another drink, love?" asked Ken, still folding paper, but not missing a word of the conversation.

"No. No, thank you. I should go, I'm very late for tea as it is and I haven't rung home to let them know I'm running late."

"They'll be worried," said Jean flatly.

"It'll be fine," Julia reassured Jean, though not feeling greatly reassured herself, "thank you, er, Jim, for getting this back to me."

"No problem, I hope you have a happy Christmas," he said kindly.

"You too, and the same to you Jean and Ken. Thank you for the tea, you've been very kind."

"You didn't drink much of it. Neither does he," grumbled Jean, nodding accusingly towards her son.

She got up from the settee clutching the shopping bag, with which she had just been reunited, tightly. She furrowed her brow, so much so there was a danger of permanent creasing there. Jean led her from the fiery heat of the sitting room into the sudden chill of the bland, characterless hallway.

"Sorry to disturb your evening," said Julia as Jean went through the unbolting and unlocking process once again to let her out.

"That's alright, any break from Ken's moaning is welcome," she smiled, slyly, "Happy Christmas, love."

Julia shivered as the cold outside air wrapped around her like an icy blanket. The door locks clunked in sequence before the hall light was extinguished and the house became a stranger in the night once more. She pulled her 'phone from her coat pocket and tapped the screen to bring up the message that had taken her for a brief glimpse into the insular life of the elderly occupants of this unassuming house. It opened in a flash of tiny light, but before the words had formed the screen went black again. Impatiently she prodded the device once more, but the message was gone: 'I've gone and deleted the darned message now,' she groaned, poking her way to the 'waste-bin'. She needn't have bothered, the message was gone altogether. 'Bloody 'phone,' she cursed. They do say that it is a bad workman who blames their tools.

SUNDAY: Bloody Sunday

Christmas Eve. Christmas bloody Eve; and not a snowflake in sight. No carollers in snug mufflers heralding the advent of The Lord's birth in song in the street outside. There was little evidence of red-cheeked urchins running excitedly between market stalls, dodging happy faced couples in frock coats and fur stoles. It was, as most December days are, a grey, nondescript kind of day. It was Sunday to boot and the whole short, inconsequential span of daylight hours wreaked of boredom from breakfast till teatime. At least that's how Julia felt as she sloped around the house avoiding Jim and painting on a smile only when Katie bounced across the horizon full of gleeful, childish excitement. 'Charles Dickens has a lot to answer for' she thought crossly as she moped around.

Julia felt low, but it was more than that, she felt annoyed and frustrated. Christmas should be so much more, but it seemed the more she strived to find the unbridled thrill of Christmases past the more it evaded her. This was a time of year, more than any other, which induced sombre reflection. It should be a time of joyous anticipation and consuming happiness, but like life itself it often, if not inevitably, failed to live up to the hype.

The tree was up, decorated and lit with a twinkling cascade of lights. Underneath there were a pile of brightly wrapped presents, those intended for grown ups, the ones Santa wasn't delivering personally. Santa would break and enter silent households across the country, in the dead of night, to bring enticing gifts for young children whilst their parents slept. Thank goodness the armed response units of the world would be drinking tea and eating mince pies, back at the nick, on double time.

Julia plonked herself on the sofa in front of the TV. Images danced and cavorted in front of her but hardly registered, they could have been a Disney classic or they could have been a Bond film, it was all the same to her jaded senses. She flicked absently through a magazine in which seasonally attired celebs smiled brightly, exposing their bleached white teeth, from tastefully embellished rooms in holly-strewn mansions. Her 'phone sat beside her like a faithful pet. She glanced at the screen, but it remained blank and lifeless, as it had done all day.

"Mummy, is Santa coming tonight?" came a small voice, as Katie entered the living room.

"Yes, but you have to be good and go to sleep at bed time."

"Can I stay up a bit later so I get really tired then?" asked Katie, showing remarkable skills of negotiation for a seven year old.

"A little bit I suppose, but not too late," sighed Julia, hoping that such a concession might mitigate any pre-Christmas bedtime delirium.

"I'm excited," the girl replied simply, which implied that a full night's sleep was a hopeful ambition at best.

Julia watched her daughter settle on the rug near to the hearth and begin playing with a box full of dolls she had carried in with her. She watched as the little girl brought them to life, presiding over their interactions and putting each carefully chosen word into their mouth. She moved their arms and legs, made them friends or enemies, made them happy or sad, at will. As the game progressed each doll was given its place in the pecking order, its role in the game. For a moment she wondered if she was the marionette of some ethereal little girl playing a celestial game in front of the fire, her fate the child's plaything ... until she got bored.

"Tea love?" called Jim, as he put his head round the door. He'd been looking for Julia upstairs; it felt almost as if she was avoiding him.

"Oh, no thanks," she replied distractedly.

"There's a rom-com on later set at Christmas, we could all watch it together," he said good-naturedly, leaning against the doorframe, not quite sure if he wanted to go into the room or go back to the kitchen.

"We've probably seen it ten times haven't we?" came the unenthusiastic reply.

"I'll take that as a 'no' then," said Jim, pushing back against the architrave and springing back into the hall.

He seemed unaffected by his wife's melancholy response to him, but inwardly he fretted. Julia had been 'off her game' for a few weeks now, morose and quick to find fault. There had been no major rows, no domestic worries, and no reason for her malaise. He pulled the lid off the kettle and put it under the tap. Jim pondered as he watched the clear stream of water clatter into its belly.

'It's ever since that idiot from her work 'popped in' with those brochures' he mused sourly, 'and didn't he really think he was something?' Jim snapped the lid back onto the kettle and dropped it heavily back onto its base, 'I'm probably wrong, but he *was* an arse.'

For the rest of the afternoon the three members of the family co-existed in splendid isolation from one another. Katie abandoned her dolls in favour of some crayoning which she did upstairs in her room to the flickering accompaniment of a full-length fairy-tale cartoon on her DVD player. Jim aimlessly meandered around the Internet using the desktop computer, they kept in a small sitting room at the front of the house. Julia flicked through the TV channels, her knees tucked underneath her bottom, on the sofa in the lounge – nothing on the myriad channels at her command caught her interest.

Eventually the light from the TV alone was insufficient to illuminate the large front room, which alerted Julia to the fact that it was probably teatime. Reluctantly she dragged herself from the warm comfort of the sofa and took her place peering into the kitchen cupboards trying to decide what she could rustle up for tea. Julia's mother had let herself into the house through the back door as she had been invited for tea, much as she was most weeks. She watched her daughter peer half-heartedly into the cupboards.

"The cupboards are bursting with food," she commented tersely, "and still you can't decide what to have for tea."

"I can't decide what I fancy," said Julia distractedly.

"You should have come to my house, like I asked. Tea would have been on the table by now."

"I didn't want to take Katie out, you know, with it being Christmas Eve. I was hoping to get her in bed at a reasonable time."

"She's seven, she'll be excited. Honestly Julia I think you've forgotten what it's like to be a little girl at Christmas. You were quite hyper by this time of day when you were Katie's age."

"Yes, she's very good. Shall we have tinned salmon on rolls?"

"Did you get that from the Nigella cook book?"

"I just want something quick and easy tonight, I can't be bothered with anything fancy."

"Julia, it seems to me that you can't be bothered with very much just lately. Is there anything the matter? Has Jim been upsetting you?"

The assumption that Jim was the cause of his wife's melancholy was unfair but Julia's mother struggled to see anything beyond marital disharmony as the reason for her daughter's languor.

"No, everything's fine," Julia retorted, but lacking the conviction to satisfy her mother.

"You don't sound fine."

"Mum stop it, I'm just tired. I've had a long and unusual week. Would you cut and butter the rolls while I open the salmon and put it in a dish?"

Grudgingly mum agreed and they carried out their tasks in an uneasy silence, both women brooding on the source of Julia's disaffection.

They all sat and had tea but the atmosphere between the adults was strained. Luckily an effervescent Katie was oblivious to any disquiet between the grown-ups. Julia's mum watched as Julia nibbled at her roll with no real enthusiasm and pushed a few crisps around her plate. Jim watched Julia's mother watching Julia. Julia's mother scowled a little when she saw Jim looking at her, he looked down at the table. There was conversation but it was stilted and awkward. Luckily they had Katie to chivvy them along, so they focused on her and not on each other. At the end of the light supper Julia smiled at Katie:

"You know what tomorrow is?"

"I can't wait," said the little girl in a trembling voice.

"You need to be asleep for Santa to come."

"I know, but what about his beer and his mince pie?"

"Daddy will sort that out."

"Can I help him?"

"Quickly then. Jim?"

Jim nodded and he and Katie went about setting a bottle of beer and a glass and a plate with a mince pie on it by the French doors, which led to the garden. Their modern house had no chimney down which jolly old Santa could descend. Luckily modern Santa's are accomplished housebreakers and can get past most multi-barrel Euro standard dead bolts. French doors - no bother!

"You hardly spoke a word to each other over tea. It was embarrassing," hissed Julia's mother as soon as Jim and Katie were out of earshot.

"It's fine mum. I've got a lot on my mind and Jim's ... well Jim's not the most conversational man at the best of times."

"I'm used to him not having much to say to me," said the older woman snidely, "but you two are far too young to be ignoring each other."

"We're not," Julia protested limply.

Her mother pursed her lips and shook her head in frustration.

"Will you take Katie to bed and read her a story please?" asked Julia sweetly.

Julia's mother nodded sternly, she knew that in some way her daughter was fobbing her off.

"Nanny's taking you to bed to read you a story," Julia called brightly to Katie.

Katie beamed. She threw her arms round Jim and planted a massive kiss on his holiday stubble.

"Yuk. You need a shave daddy," the little girl complained.

"Off you go with Nanny," he laughed," you don't mind *Santa* having a beard though do you?"

"Well he's old and I don't have to kiss him," replied Katie with the rapier logic of a child.

"That told you," said Julia, more in response to Katie's retort than to engage her husband in family banter.

Jim smiled, but it was a faded smile. He might not have established a solid rapport with his mother-in-law but they were sharing the same concern about Julia's distracted demeanour.

"I've got a couple of things I need to do while Nanny reads Katie a story," announced Julia, "what are you going to do Jim?"

"There's a Top Gear Christmas Special on I wanted to see," he said, a little meekly, as if he was fearful of Julia's reaction. He needn't have worried:

"That's fine. You can have a beer while you're watching it. Get into the Christmas spirit."

"Was that a joke?" he asked tentatively.

"I'm not big on jokes. Anyway beer's not a spirit."

"Oh, ok."

Jim fished a bottle from inside the fridge and sloped off to watch his programme. Katie led her grandma by the hand up the stairs jabbering away to her excitedly. Grandma glared at her daughter, willing her to tell her what the matter was, careful that Katie should not pick up any subliminal message. Julia ignored her mother's penetrating stare and made a show of tidying up the plates and cups from the tea table.

In the bedroom she took the carrier bag containing the cardigan from its hiding place, under a pile of shoes in the wardrobe. She glanced furtively towards the door in case Jim was suddenly lurking there in the shadows of the landing. She held the cardigan in her hand. It was soft to the touch and had the sheen of newness about it. She held it under her nose and smelt the fibres, they smelt fresh and new. It had been a spontaneous act, a purchase borne of a moment of irrational, irresistible impulse. In many ways it represented the stolen moments she'd had these last few weeks with Andy. It was instinctive, exciting, another moment of a racing pulse and unstifled desire. This simple knitted garment represented all those furtive, quivering meetings and the lingering, uncertain goodbyes that followed. Above it all it now symbolised *that* coffee flavoured kiss in the walkway. This was a secret, special gift for Andy, which she had chosen with love and hope and expectation.

The problem was that Andy hadn't rewarded the expectation with the call she had suggested, that last snatched opportunity to be together, before Christmas Day demanded them both to do their duty by their current partner. Hurriedly she engulfed the cardigan in a sheath of coloured paper, the label attached but left blank. She would fill that in somewhere on route to whatever rendezvous they eventually managed to contrive. Reluctantly and with disappointment etched on her pretty face Julia stashed the clandestine gift back into the uncharted depths of her wardrobe.

She picked up her phone from where it lay on the bed. She routinely muted the devices alerts when she was in the house; it was less intrusive that way. She lived like a spy, checking for coded messages and wiping the memory clean once the details had been read and committed to memory. She lived on the bursts of adrenalin that a contact would initiate; she was a double agent, devoted to one side by day, dallying with the other under the cover of dark. Looking left and right to make sure she was not being watched she scrolled desperately through the days' messages, but the one she sought was not there.

'Bastard,' she thought, but didn't mean it for a single second.

She grabbed the bag, containing the game for Katie that she'd almost abandoned in her pursuit of a little something for her would-be lover. She held it and imagined Katie's face in the morning, the happiness of a child's innocent beam of excitement, and it almost distracted her. She wrapped the present thoughtfully and popped it back under the bed, out of sight. She'd send Jim to put it under the tree once he had settled himself in bed. He would grumble about having to get out of his warm bed but a quick trip in the bracing air of the sleeping household would be certain to cool any Christmas ardour he might have entertained. Only Santa was due to come this Christmas Eve.

"Julia, you coming down? We're going to watch 'It's a Wonderful Life'?" called Jim from the bottom of the stairs.

"Ok, in a minute," she replied listlessly.

She sensed Jim spin around and go back to the lounge after a short, silent pause. It was in that moment of quiet the 'phone vibrated sending out the tiniest buzzing noise. Julia's hand was a quick as a frog's tongue lassoing a passing fly, she snatched the 'phone from the duvet and stabbed at the screen.

'Meet me at the flat. I want you to see me. A x'.

It was a strange little message. It was clearly from Andy but the number was unfamiliar and it hadn't come up with 'Sandy', the none-too-discreet androgynous handle Julia had allocated to his number should Jim see it flash up on her screen. It lacked the cheeky spark of his usual messages. On the other hand it might be that the sultry stick insect was giving him a hard time, and he needed Julia's counsel. Could it be that Christmas had finally made him reflective, as the season often did, and he finally realised how much he needed to be close to Julia at this special time of year? Perhaps he was using a 'back up' 'phone for some reason. Reason? Julia didn't want to reason, she wanted this moment, she wanted to leap at this romantic opportunity for all it was worth. After a whole day submerged in the doldrums there was a spark of light.

"Are you alright up there?" came Jim's voice, once more stationed at the bottom of the stairs. "I'm getting us all a drink, what would you like?"

"A white wine with someone dynamic and sexy," she muttered to herself.

"What did you say?"

"NOTHING," Julia shouted, more angrily than she had intended.

She heard her husband's footsteps stomp heavily towards the kitchen. Then the fridge door thudded shut a little harder than usual.

Julia contemplated her options. It had taken all day for Andy to send even a simple text. Now he wanted her to go to his flat. It was 730 at night on Christmas Eve. No doubt Saint Sophie had been more attention seeking than usual and had consumed every waking second of his time, but where was sexy Sophie now? Perhaps she did some sort of charity work with the poor and needy on a Christmas Eve, Julia could picture her giving food parcels to the homeless, the sanctimonious cow! Or perhaps there was an annual family carol service conducted by their good friend the local reverend.

It didn't matter how many permutations Julia could conjure, or how much her common sense told her to stay put, she was besieged by confusing, conflicting emotions. Her longing to be with Andy shackled her judgement like a helpless slave. Every fibre of her being told her again and again that her place tonight was at home, however unfulfilling that might seem. But weeks of repressed and growing passion surged wildly through her blood. She slipped on a pair of heels and ran her fingers through her hair to give it extra volume. She quickly sprayed a little scent behind each ear. That was all she had the time or inclination to do; she had to act before the impulse faded. Clutching a carrier bag with the wrapped up cardigan inside it, she tripped lightly down the stairs. As she passed the front room she grabbed her coat from the stand in the hallway. She could see the faces of Jim and her mum watching the film as it began.

"I have to pop out. I shouldn't be long," she called, grasping her car keys tightly and fleeing hastily through the front door.

She didn't hear anyone reply, but then again she wasn't listening. Jim made it to the front door to watch the brake lights of his wife's car flare, then die off as her car left the drive.

"Where's she gone?" called Julia's mother.

"She's had to pop out for something," said Jim in a low voice, his words grinding out from between gritted teeth.

"Do you think she'll be long? The film's started."

"I really don't know," he replied, pulling the front door to, feeling the cold draft of air he swept in from outside, "she might be a while," he added under his breath.

SUNDAY - The Nightmare Before Christmas

The apartment block where Andy lived, with his girlfriend Sophie, was in the trendiest part of town. The block itself had once been one of six large, square warehouses. In their day they had been busy, bustling buildings, an integral feature of the industrial heritage of the town. They had unceasingly fed the factories and transport companies at each end of the production process until they had fallen derelict in the 1970s as industry in the area declined. They had become damp and squalid husks until the 'yuppie' movement of the late 1990s had breathed new life into the neglected and unloved brick and concrete structures.

As Julia turned into the visitor's car park at the rear of the apartment block she couldn't fail to notice the large glass frontage in the centre of the building, which marked the main entrance to the complex. She caught a glance of the seated figure of the concierge in his blazer and tie; it really was quite an impressive set up. As his outline registered in her mind she suddenly realised that she had no recollection of her journey there. It was as if she had just awoken from a brief trance. Inside her tummy gambolled as she panicked about the stop signs, traffic lights and roundabouts she had blanked out during her journey. She hadn't travelled a great distance, but her mind had been elsewhere the whole way. She hoped that her inner autopilot had not let her down. She parked her car neatly in an end space and when she got out she peered at the front of the car. There didn't appear to be any body parts attached to the grille and that, at least, brought some momentary reassurance.

'Trust Andy to have a flat in the swankiest part of town,' she thought, immediately regretting the use of the term 'flat'; Andy would be mortified – he was quite insistent that it was an apartment. He could be a little pretentious, but did that make him a bad person? Surely not, pretension is just ambition with a swagger after all.

She felt nervous though she wasn't sure why. She had no idea why Andy would want to see her late on Christmas Eve. Where was Sophie? Had they argued? Was he alone, waiting for her? A person possessed of their right senses would have stayed away, but Julia wasn't *that* person, a wilder, more impulsive Julia had delivered herself into this unfolding and unpredictable situation.

She walked to the front of the building, following the subtle security lighting from the rear car park to the main entrance with its mood-lit vestibule within. She tentatively pressed the buzzer, peering across at the man behind the wood panelled reception desk. He peered up from the book he was reading by the light of a desk lamp on the counter. He screwed his eyes up slightly so that he could quickly scrutinise the person calling his attention. She passed the test and she heard a subdued buzz as the concierge released the electronic lock on the entrance door.

"Good evening madam," he cooed, as she approached the desk.

"I'm here to see Mr Braxton, flat … apartment eight," she replied, a little shrewishly.

"Is Mr Braxton expecting you?" asked the man politely, rising to his feet and meeting Julia's slightly furtive gaze, eye to eye.

"He messaged me about half an hour ago."

"I see," said the receptionist, as though the whole thing had become crystal clear in his mind.

In fact he used the time to examine the young woman who stood nervously before him. He detected no obvious mischief in her presence and she seemed nice enough.

"Go on up, madam, I'll buzz Mr Braxton and let him know that you're on your way," he smiled a kindly smile and jabbed a button that was concealed underneath the shiny surface of the desk.

"Thank you," said Julia quietly, and shuffled away to the glass-panelled door, which led to the luxury dwellings beyond.

Each floor of the development was accessed by a plushly carpeted stairway. Lifts for residents were situated at the egress from the underground parking area and at a loading bay for the use of removal men and heavy deliveries, a function martialled by the ever-watchful attendant at reception. For everyone else there was the genteel climb through the pristine magnolia stairwell, its walls adorned with pastel coloured paintings mounted in tasteful tarnished-gold coloured frames. Julia wondered what Andy would be doing, now that the doorman had announced her arrival. She imagined him checking the chilled chardonnay in the integrated wine cooler, or maybe he was in the bathroom putting the finishing touches to his carefully gelled hair and inflated ego. It didn't bother her that Andy might be a little too slick and confident, at least he was making an effort, something she felt was all too rare in her own staid existence.

Finally she reached *his* floor. She pushed open a heavy door consisting principally of frosted glass. It made a swooshing sound across the landing carpet as it glided over the twisted pile fibres. Either side of the half-lit hallway were the impressive wooden outer doors of each apartment sharing that floor. There seemed to be three - one on each side and one at the end. How the design of the apartments worked, where they intersected or adjoined she had no notion, but it all felt quiet and opulent. Andy's apartment was one of the dwellings on the side of the hallway, the one at the back of the block rather than facing the road where the trendy bistros and exotic, foreign eateries had established themselves. It was distant from the steady flow of people that milled around the modern night-time community that the redevelopment had heralded for the smart side of town. How the estate agents ached for a call to price up another lucrative sale in this wealthy enclave.

She reached out to ring the heavy, white doorbell, illuminated by the steady glow of a tiny yellow light. There was a speaker beneath the bell, though it was largely redundant most callers having been identified well before entrance to the inner sanctum had been sanctioned. As her finger reached forward she felt nervous, her stomach fluttered, it felt as if the simple act of pressing a doorbell might be highly symbolic. Was she about to 'ring in the new'? In fact it was another ring that rudely broke her reverie. This time it was her 'phone. The word '*Jim*' flashed accusingly at her from the screen. She stiffened with irritation, but she paused to consider whether she should answer his call. Almost instinctively she used the finger that she had been about to ring Andy's doorbell to stab the 'cancel' command on the screen of her 'phone and the ring tone ceased, suddenly and dramatically. She had shocked herself at how angrily and dismissively she had cut Jim off. Would it be easier the next time?

She tossed the handset back into her bag and once more reached towards the bell push. She heard a noise. It was muffled and sounded distant, but she heard it nonetheless. It wasn't a nice noise, like music, it had a strident, discordant tone. She leaned in towards the sturdy and highly glossed door with its gleaming silver number eight disguising a carefully placed spyhole. There was no doubt that the noise was coming from within. Though muted by the thickness of the door and the layers of insulation that had turned these lofts into desirable homesteads, the noise persisted. Julia's heart pounded as she pressed her ear against the smooth, cool paintwork of the door.

The source of the noise was undoubtedly human. 'Television' she thought. But the noise moved location as though it was shifting from room to room. Sometimes it was a little louder than others, but it was voices, of that there could be no doubt.

Julia was in turmoil. Why would Andy invite her over to see him if he had company? Moreover why would he invite her into the middle of some kind of row? Had Sophie returned unexpectedly from her parents and interrupted his plans? Had his hand been forced and he was in the process of telling her:

"It really isn't anything to do with you. It's me, it's my fault. I'm so sorry, I'm just in a different place. I need space to find out exactly who I am?"

Even Julia knew that such a speech was crass, but sadly she didn't expect much more of the man she currently fantasised about. Was that not a warning sign in itself? Julia had removed the battery on her emotional smoke alarm when she had succumbed to Andy's initial advances and this was no time to rush to the shop to get a replacement 9 volt cell.

She felt like turning and leaving, but her ear remained fixed to the paintwork of the door as if someone had super-glued it in place as a trick. The voices continued but another sound was now interspersed with the vocal exchanges. Punctuating the ascending volume level of the dialogue was a more inanimate racket. Clattering, a thud maybe, something breaking?

As she strained her ears to focus on the furore within she discerned that there was a male voice, loud and thunderous and a female voice, more screechy and tremorous. It seemed that the magic of Christmas was visiting this flat ... apartment early. The ferocity of the tirade was unmistakeable and seemed to be escalating. At one point it flowed along the hall and got so close that Julia feared that one of the parties was about to burst into the hallway itself. She recoiled away from the door and stepping backwards, her eyes fixed on the entrance to the apartment, she bumped clumsily into another figure, digging her heel into his moccasin slipper-shod foot. She squealed in shock and surprise and he jumped back and yelped in discomfort.

There was a brief hiatus whilst the pair composed themselves. The man limped painfully back towards her: "You heard it too?"

His voice was stern. He frowned, not at Julia but in the direction of number 8.

"It's not the first time," he commented, shaking his head resignedly, "two nice people, but every so often it's like World War Three in there."

"Shall I ring the Police?" asked a timid little voice from a crack in the doorway opposite.

"Not just now Simone, I'm going to knock the door; see what's going on."

"Be careful Edward," she warned, her voice little more than a whisper.

All six feet one and fifteen muscly stones of Edward silently promised to be careful.

Edward strode forward edging Julia aside. Now the voices were clearer, both the volume and tempo had increased. There was a loud thump as something struck the door of number 8 from the inside. Julia and Edward jumped and Simone, frightened by the sudden noise, shoved the front door of her apartment shut, shielding her inside and isolating Edward and Julia in the hallway.

Edward knocked the door with the side of his fist, producing a dull beating sound. It prompted no reply. He repeated the action, this time using his knuckles to make a determined rapping noise. The door remained fast, only a loud scream breaching the barrier between the occupants of the apartment and the worried duo in the hall. The scream was that of a woman and fear resounded in its piercing echo. Then another loud thump filled the air as the scream died away. The door opposite cracked open a few inches once more and Simone's frightened face looked out.

"You might want to ring the Police now," Julia suggested, urgency tingeing her voice.

Edward decided not to test the response times of the local constabulary and leaned his tall, proportionate frame against the door. Under gentle persuasion he felt the door yield very slightly.

"They're good doors," he muttered, almost conversationally, "but I reckon I can take it."

With that he stood back and braced himself. He dipped his shoulder and took a short run up, meeting the door as if it were the back row of a rugby scrum. The door groaned under the attack but stayed firm. A second determined assault brought splinters and door furniture crashing into the hallway of the apartment, the door itself flew open and Edward stumbled in after it under the force of his not inconsiderable momentum.

The flat was indeed a war zone, there was broken pottery scattered everywhere. Pictures lay shattered on the floor and torn photographs had fluttered onto flat surfaces in almost every room. Edward steadied himself and Julia went up to him, making sure that he was alright.

"I'm fine," he said, shaking himself down, " nothing compared to what they dish out on a Saturday afternoon."

They stood and listened, the argument had abated, probably because of the unexpected disturbance, but the sobbing of a woman still permeated the hallway. It came from in front of Edward and Julia, from the direction of the living room ahead of them. Together they walked forward, each taking strength from the other.

The door to the lounge was only partially closed and Edward pushed it open forcefully. A surprised and angry male glared at his uninvited guests, his nostrils flaring, and his eyes wild and full of rage. He took a step forward, almost by instinct, but paused almost straight away. Whether it was the size of Edward or simply the sight of Julia that caused him to stall was hard to tell, either way he froze to the spot.

A slight and pretty female was perched on the settee, her back heaved with effort of sobbing, the air coming from deep within her lungs and stuttering upwards painfully. She wore a baggy jumper and slim fitting jeans but had nothing on her feet. Her eyes were etched with sadness and fear, and in addition to the streaks of mascara, which ran down her cheeks, there was a trickle of fresh blood in the corner of her mouth. She clasped her arms around her knees and trembled amidst the wreckage that had once been treasured keepsakes.

"I think you need to take it easy mate," said Edward evenly.

Andy ignored the serious expression of the hefty man, looking straight past him to Julia.

"It's not how it looks. You don't understand," he said feebly, before collapsing into an armchair, head in hands.

The violence in the air evaporated, like a storm cloud driven away by a summer breeze. Edward towered silently in front of the defeated Andy staunchly fulfilling the role of peacekeeper. Julia looked at Sophie, her tiny frame hunched inconsolably on the settee, knowing not who to look at, not knowing who was friend and who was foe. Silence fell like a heavy blanket in the room, no one daring to speak, no one having the right words to break the quiet.

Simone had ventured from the safety of the apartment she shared with the steadfast Edward. She stood at the threshold of Andy and Sophie's flat, next to the splintered doorframe, looking along the line of debris into the lounge, where she could see Edward standing silently and resolutely. There was an unearthly quiet in the apartment and though she was glad that the shouting had stopped, she still felt a sense of unease.

"Are you OK, Edward?" she called timorously.

"Everyone's fine," he called back sternly, his gaze never lifting from Andy's bowed head.

"The police are on their way."

It hardly seemed possible for Andy to shrink further, but as the word 'police' clattered into his ear the very life drooped out of his rounded shoulders and his head sank completely into his shoulders as if they were made of quicksand. It was over.

It was all over.

Even with their contemporary walkie-talkies the electronic cackle of police radio was undecipherable to the casual listener, just a crackle of muffled and indistinct chatter. To Julia the noise resembled modern day Punch and Judy, which was ironic considering the grotesque scenario she had just encountered. Nonetheless this specific brand of muted electro-babble still seemed to add tension to the air wherever it played its perplexing rhapsody in blue.

Andy was led away by two weary looking men in high visibility blousons. Neither wore a hat, but then they rarely seemed to do so these days. Gone were the shirt and tie, in had come the collarless, nylon polo shirt and fleece. Gone was the concealed twelve inch truncheon, so long part of the British Police iconography along with the tall helmet, in had come the utility belt with their multiple pouches, speed-cuffs, incapicitant spray and baton. Tall, short, fat and thin the *Constabulary* had seamlessly given way to a gaudily clad county militia, masquerading as a *Service* Industry, when the people longed for the resolute protection of the old-time copper. No wonder TV sets flickered longingly to the past when nice, incorruptible coppers on mopeds patrolled the dales, or tough, no-nonsense thief takers put the fear of God into the unruly of urban society; when opera fanatics nailed the intellegentsia of crime and female Inspectors took rural beat stations by the scruff of their initially unwilling necks.

Julia and Edward stood silently by as Andy was steered out of the room, no handcuffs applied, just the guiding, gloved hand of one of the grim-faced cops on his elbow. Simone catapulted nervously from the doorway at their approach, but Andy never even saw her. His eyes were fixed downwards, glassy and defeated, disoriented and ashamed. His head felt heavy as if it had assumed the density of concrete, his shoulders barely capable of the task of supporting it.

Another cop with a digital camera took snapshots of the debris and disarray in the littered apartment. They didn't always remember to bring the camera, provided by donations from women's aid charities, but luckily this time a female officer had conscientiously packed it in her bulging briefcase and wasted no time in capturing the scene for her report. It whirred and flashed at the smashed pictures and mirrors and the holes punched into plasterboard, at the remnants of broken china and the shreds of torn photographs. Finally she turned it on the pale, trembling girl who sat in stunned helplessness on the settee. Sophie blinked and shrank back each time the light blazed in her aching, tear stained eye, but the female officer captured the fresh cut to the young woman's lip and the darkening under her eye as damning evidence of the sickening furore that had preceded their arrival.

The woman constable's partner took out his notebook and began scribbling down Edward's account. As the officer with the camera turned her attention away from Sophie with a wordless smile, Julia sat down next to the shivering young woman and put her arm around her.

"Perhaps you could make Miss Watson a cup of tea?" said the officer who was talking to Edward.

Tea: a drink so long in the British psyche, which held remedial properties for so many types of shock, distress and upheaval. How the hard-pressed GPs and crumbling A&E Departments could have reduced their intake of patients had there been the proper and timely administration of tea by first-aiders and paramedics. Julia felt no inclination to dispute the magical quality of this mysterious Eastern beverage.

"Yes, ok. Anyone else want a cup?"

A few minutes later Julia had managed to corral sufficient unbroken cups to provide drinks for both remaining officers, poor Sophie, herself and Edward. She extended the offer in a call along the hallway to the nervous looking Simone, but she declined with a vigorous shake of the head, maintaining her safe vantage point at the threshold of the apartment.

By now the policewoman had switched off the camera and placed it on the coffee table, which her colleague had righted from its previously upturned position on a rug by the hearth. The officer knelt on the rug speaking to Sophie and trying to make sense of the words that bubbled out the young woman's tearful, injured mouth. She looked up at Julia as she handed out the mismatched collection of mugs and cups.

"Good job you were here. Are you a friend of theirs?"

"Just visiting," said Julia noncommittally.

The officer nodded, taking her cup gratefully. "We'll need a statement from you," she continued.

Julia looked perturbed and coloured slightly. She had made enough of a mess of the evening without becoming a material witness in a case of domestic abuse. Andy was bound to reveal their relationship, such as it was. For all she knew that could well have been the catalyst for the ugly row in the apartment that evening.

"Really? Aren't the photos and Miss Watson's account enough?"

Julia carefully used Sophie's surname, revealed earlier by the male officer, to introduce a façade of formality and detachment. It didn't work.

"Well you're a witness whether you like it or not," said the officer, firmly but tactfully, "your evidence would corroborate

Miss Watson's evidence and I'm sure you want to support your friend?"

"But ..."

Julia paused right there. She was going to say that it was Andy that was her friend, not Sophie, and despite the truthfulness of the thought it seemed neither appropriate nor helpful. Feebly and with a feigned smile Julia nodded, "Of course."

Sophie was curled in a tiny, fragile bundle on the settee clutching her cup but not drinking from it. Everything seemed to be going on around her. She heard the voices, saw the people but felt detached from it all, as if she was having some kind of disturbing out of body experience. "Would you like us to call a doctor?" asked the male PC in a slow and loud voice, as though he were talking to an imbecile.

Sophie flashed a worried look at Julia as though looking for some kind of guidance on the matter. Julia stared back blankly and Sophie shook her head emphatically. "I don't think it's anything too serious," he continued with the same slightly condescending delivery, "but if you change your mind let us know, or you could go to your GP in the morning."

"We'll probably ask the police surgeon to take a look at her at the station," the female officer interjected.

"The station?" said Julia in surprise, " I don't think she's in a fit state."

"We need a statement as soon as possible really. Mr Braxton is in custody and we'll need to interview him as soon as we can. We have a few more things to do first though, perhaps you can bring Miss Watson to the station later, when she's composed herself," said the officer in a kind and compassionate voice.

"We'll take your statement while you're there," added her colleague.

With that both officers placed their cups on the coffee table and gathered their things together. The male officer spoke conspiratorially into the mouthpiece of his radio, from what Julia could gather it was a coded message for 'we're getting the heck out of here.' The policewoman handed a card to Julia:

"I'm on all night. When you come to the station, just ask for me."

With that they swept out of the apartment and past the dithering figure of Simone in a few strides of clumsy, luminous yellow.

Julia looked at Edward and he looked back haplessly. "There's not much more I can really do," he said awkwardly.

Julia knew that this signalled his imminent exit back to the wavering arms of his skittish wife.

"No, I suppose not," she conceded reluctantly.

"Will you be alright with …" and for some reason he mouthed his neighbour's name as if it was a forbidden word:

" … Sophie?"

The inevitable moment had arrived where Julia was saddled with picking up the pieces of Andy's mess, of providing support and comfort to the woman who had, until a short time ago, been her rival for his affections. She wanted to go, to flee this horrible, uncomfortable scene, to dash home to busy herself with some domestic damage control. It wasn't going to happen. Destiny had wickedly shouted 'tick, you're it,' and run, giggling, far out of arm's reach.

"Yes. That's fine. I'll see to Sophie. You go home."

With no further persuasion necessary Edward ran, ran like the wind, leaving Julia cradling the slight, bony frame of her 'rival'. In return the young girl snuggled up against Julia like a child who'd had a bad dream … a nightmare before Christmas.

SUNDAY – Making a Statement

Julia stood in the reception area of the police station. It was never going to be a nice place to be, but the early hours of Christmas morning put an altogether more unpleasant pallor on the grubby, sick-coloured walls of the lobby in which she stood, more or less supporting Sophie, whose facial colour was disturbingly in tune with her surroundings. A couple of tattooed women sat on a metal bench looking defiantly at anyone in their field of view. A young male in a baseball cap which was partially covered by the hood of his sweatshirt lolled on a wooden chair on the other side of the counter. His eyes were open but there wasn't much in the way of stimulus going either in or out of them. Above his head was a colourful poster, advising people to say 'no' to drugs.

Julia sidled up to the glass hatch, which separated the public from the tired staff who tapped on computer consoles in the small office beyond. A middle-aged woman in the vestiges of a uniform slowly desisted her typing, albeit that her industrious inputting actually related to her Facebook page, and wandered over to the hatch. She breathed in slowly, a cynical look of disdain etched on her weary features:

"Good evening madam, how can I help you?" she asked politely enough.

"I've come to see WPC Bates, she gave me her card earlier this evening," said Julia in a tiny voice, nervously looking at the two women who continued to glare at everyone malevolently.

"*PC* Bates, we dropped the 'W' a few years back, all officers are PCs now," corrected the counter clerk mildly, taking the card and glancing at it with a certain amount of disinterest. "I'll give her a call on the air to see if she's in. What name is it?"

"Mrs Carter and Miss Watson," said Julia with her face pressed up against the screen, not wanting the scary looking women to take note of their names. The act was in vain.

"They got your blokes locked up as well? Pigs!" said one of the women with a sneer.

"Pigs," said the other loudly, just to make the point that she harboured no love of the Constabulary.

"All he was doing was defending himself, then the copper grabs him and throws him in the van," continued the first woman, clearly outraged by the blatant miscarriage of justice. "I mean the copper only had himself to blame when my Keenon kicked him, he hadn't done nothin'."

"He hit that geezer with a bottle …" said the second woman blankly.

"Well he asked for it," said the first woman, indignantly, "he wouldn't give him a light."

"I dunno how he managed to get it across his head, he'd had fifteen pints, he must have slipped."

"That's right. My lovely Keenon, goes out for a quiet drink and the filth lock him up … for nothing. Pigs!"

"Pigs."

"You can come through now," said the counter clerk wearily.

The electronic buzzer rasped like a trapped wasp and Julia bundled Sophie through the heavy door, which led inside the station.

"Don't tell 'em nothin' love," came the sage advice of the second woman.

"Just tell 'em all to f…"

With a reassuring thud the door slammed to behind Julia and Sophie, insulating them from the cold, indifferent world outside.

"Thank you for bringing Miss Watson in," said PC Bates warmly, "I'll take you to an interview room and we'll get you some tea."

Julia and Sophie followed the officer to a room that had been adapted as a 'soft interview' suite. In other words a place where victims and witnesses could give their accounts away from the harsh, grey sterility of the rest of the station. Julia sat on a sofa which had once boasted a sprung interior, but that had evidently been a long time ago. There was an ancient looking coffee table ringed with the legacy of a thousand mugs of coffee and an asthmatic looking pot plant balanced on a dented filing cabinet. It was like a room in a well-meaning hostel for vagrants, but the nearest thing to humanity that the cops could offer to the innocent victims of crime. Sophie looked around her, wide-eyed and frightened.

"You'll be fine," whispered Julia, holding the girl's hand gently.

"Thank you, I'm so grateful," said Sophie quietly, tears welling in the corners of her eyes.

It was a testament to her sweet, trusting nature that Sophie had not thought to ask what had brought Julia to her apartment during that horrible fight a few hours before. It was almost child-like the way she had accepted Edward and Julia's sudden intervention. She needed nothing more than kindness and support, even if it was from people who were largely strangers to her.

There was a thump as PC Bates applied her boot to the bottom of the door to the interview suite before struggling into the room balancing a tray containing mugs of tea on a box full of forms.

"Sorry about that, the door sticks sometimes," she announced airily.

"How's Andy?" said Sophie tearfully.

"He's fine, don't you worry about that, we'll look after him, but this is about you. I'm here to make sure you're alright. You've done nothing wrong, you don't deserve to be treated the way Andy treated you tonight. We need to make sure it doesn't happen again. You do understand that don't you Miss Watson ... shall I call you Sophie? It's much less formal. I'm Cathy."

Both women nodded at the officer who busied herself sorting out the tea and generally making Sophie and Julia feel at ease, even in the downtrodden, bleakness of the interview room. Amidst the tatty array of wall posters and thrown together furnishings Sophie provided her account of the evening, not always completely coherently, but buoyed by the care of the officer and Julia she told her story. Here is the statement compiled by PC Bates through an hour of whispers and tears.

"We had been at home all day on Sunday, Christmas Eve. We got up late; Andy wanted to spend the morning in bed. I wanted to get things ready for Christmas Day, my parents are coming over for the day, they're due to arrive around breakfast time so we can exchange presents round the tree. I've done it since I was a girl."

Julia couldn't help rolling her eyes at this point, she hoped that neither Sophie nor PC Bates had seen her do this, but the power of 'I told you so' is very strong, especially when you're saying it to yourself.

"Trouble is that Andy insisted on sex more than I insisted on sorting out the table setting. It was probably around lunchtime when I finally got out of bed. I made Andy some tea and toast and took it in to him. He was watching a film on the portable television. I hate having the TV in the bedroom, but Andy loves it. Anyway relationships are about compromise so I put up with it. I asked him if he would help wrapping a few presents and doing a bit of tidying round, but he got a little cross and said he wanted to see the end of the film. I could see that he was on his 'phone and I told him that I hoped he wasn't going out because we had a lot to do.

"I got on with a few jobs and eventually Andy got up. He helped with a couple of things then his 'phone beeped. He'd had a message and said he needed to pop out. I wasn't very happy about it because I had a few errands to run myself, but he said I was being a 'Grinch' and spoiling his Christmas, so I said it was fine to go and meet his friends but that he wasn't to be too long. He said 'fine', grabbed his coat and went out.

"It got to about four o'clock and Andy hadn't got back. I had three or four presents I had to deliver to my aunty, a cousin and some friends. I went out in my car to take the presents but when I got to my friends' house they were out. I texted them and they said they were at the pub, so I arranged to meet them there.

"I'd been in the pub about twenty minutes, I wasn't going to stay at all but Johnny insisted. He's a lovely chap, engaged to my friend Maggie, and he's very hard to say 'no' to, he's a real social animal. Maggie was there but had gone to speak to some work friends on the other side of the bar. I had an orange juice and chatted to Johnny and his friend Keith. Then Andy walked in. I noticed a young blonde woman walk in at the same time but she disappeared off somewhere so I'm sure they weren't together. I didn't recognise her anyway. Then Andy saw me with Johnny. He came over and said hello, but I noticed that his breath smelled of drink and he looked a bit flushed. He knows Johnny and Maggie but not very well. He let Johnny buy him a pint but he drank it really quickly and said he wanted to go. I whispered that he was being a little rude and that I'd only been there a few minutes myself. That seemed to annoy him and when Johnny and Keith turned to speak to Maggie, who had come back from talking to her friends, he pinched me really hard on the soft skin on the underside of my left arm (2cm bruise to skin exhibit CB1). He whispered to me, 'I want to go, now,' he sounded really angry. I started to feel embarrassed so I lied to Johnny and Maggie that I'd left something in the oven and that I had to go. They all gave me a kiss and wished me 'happy Christmas' and I got a bit tearful, I don't know why.

"Andy didn't speak at all when I drove him back to the apartment. He just sat there with his arms folded and staring in front of him. I could smell drink coming off him really strongly, but I didn't say anything. I thought he might 'go mad'.

"We went in through the main entrance. Andy was quite pleasant with Charlie, the man on the reception desk, he even wished him a very happy Christmas. I thought he might be coming out of his sulk, though to be honest I didn't know why he was in one in the first place.

"Then we got to the front door of the flat. Andy couldn't find his key, I think he was a bit too tipsy to know which pocket it was in, so I got my key out, but it was in the bottom of my bag and I had to rummage around to find it. He was getting really impatient, he said: 'I need the toilet, get a move on you silly cow.' I got a bit flustered then. It's not the first time he's spoken to me that way and it frightens me. I try to stay out of his way when he gets that grumpy. I managed to open the door but it took me longer than usual because I was trembling a little. When I opened the door he pushed me really hard in the back with his palm so I stumbled into the flat. He said 'about time,' and stormed off to the toilet. (Reddening and scratches to small of back, exhibit CB2).

"I thought about going out for an hour until he had calmed down, but I thought that might make him more angry. Instead I put the kettle on to make us both some coffee. I thought a nice strong cup of coffee might be what he needed.

"Then Andy came into the kitchen. He seemed really wound up. He said: 'I turn my back for an hour and where do I find you? In the pub wrapping yourself around that idiot Johnny.' I said: 'I was just delivering their present. If you'd been here we'd have gone to their house together.' He said: 'any excuse, you slag.' I said: 'I'm not a slag, don't be silly. They're our friends. Maggie was there she was just talking to some friends from work. Keith was there too.' It was no good, he just said: 'lining yourself up for a threesome then were you? You slut.'

"The next thing I knew he picked up the coffee cup and threw it across the kitchen, not at me, but it smashed against the tiles. I could see in his eyes that he was losing it. I switched off the kettle and ran into the lounge, but by then he'd gone mad. He was picking up pictures and ornaments and throwing them across the room. I tried to go to other rooms out of the way, but he just followed me, pulling things over and throwing things. He was shouting horrible insults at me, getting louder and louder. Nothing I said, no matter how nice I was, nothing would make him stop. Whatever I said to him he just got more angry.

"Eventually I made a dash for the front door. I just wanted to get out of there. I didn't know what the matter was. I had no answers and I was really terrified by now. I shouted for help at one point and that's when he hit me with the back of his hand. That's how my lip got cut, just in the corner. It's still very sore. (3cm cut to lip and bruising, exhibit CB3).

"He chased me back into the front room. He was screaming at me, 'you don't deserve me, you slag. You think you're something special, but look at you – you're just really ordinary. You should be glad to have me, but instead I catch you with your hand inside Johnny's trousers. An idiot and a tart, you make a great couple.' Then I heard the door crash open and a man I recognise as a neighbour came in, and a woman I hadn't met before called Julia. I was surprised and relieved. If they hadn't come in I think Andy would have hit me again. The flat was a wreck by now; Andy had smashed most of the things in it. (Photographs of damage, exhibit CB4).

"I am devastated by what happened today. It has made me feel ashamed and helpless. I do not want to be treated this way by any man, and although I think I still love Andy I want the police to prosecute him for what he did." (Signed Sophie Watson, Witnessed by PC 87 Catherine Bates.)

"Just one more question for now Sophie," said PC Bates quietly and gently, "is this the first time this has happened?"

Her reply was made in the tiniest voice imaginable, but in the silence of the tatty room it almost echoed with its power:

"No."

PC Bates looked at Julia as much as to say 'you wouldn't believe how often this happens'. Both women, irrespective of the walks of life they came from, were disgusted, shocked and saddened.

"How do you know Miss Watson?" asked PC Bates as an afterthought.

"I know Andy through work, I was just popping round with a last minute Christmas card," Julia lied, her expertise in this area growing by the day. Truth was she was ashamed to be associated with Andy and felt, justifiably, that she had already, in some way, added to Sophie's burden.

"That's kind of you," said Sophie innocently, smiling at Julia through a fresh veil of tears. The forlorn young woman might just as well have dragged her perfectly manicured fingernails across Julia's exposed heart.

"What do you want to do now Sophie?' asked PC Bates kindly, gathering her papers, checking that she had signatures on every sheet where it was required.

"I want to go to my mum's, but I need to get some clothes from the flat."

"Ok, we can arrange that."

Sophie flashed a pleading look across at Julia, one that suggested that as kind as they had been that she had had enough of the law for one night.

"It's ok," said Julia, glancing resignedly at her watch, "I'll take Sophie back to the flat and then to her mum's."

PC Cathy Bates nodded understandingly at both women.

"Well, if you need anything else you just need to call. Otherwise I'll be in touch tomorrow, I've got your mobile number haven't I? We can talk about what happens next, bail conditions and so on, then. Don't worry we won't be sending him back to your apartment Sophie. Remember, you've done nothing wrong; you're the victim here. I'm not saying that Andy's all bad, but he needs help, and that starts with him facing up to what he did tonight."

Julia nodded and Sophie looked blankly at the officer. Sophie's mind and body had frozen over with shock and she found herself unable to feel anything, other than the reassuring gentle grip of Julia's arm around her shoulder. 'Santa would be on the home straight by now', thought Julia as she supported Sophie on the short journey through the door into the reception area of the police station.

The young man in the hoodie and baseball cap was now fast asleep on the hard tiled floor, snoring loudly and smelling badly. The tattooed girls were gone, their forlorn hopes of taking their combative boyfriend with them abandoned. The black bags under the counter clerk's tired, watery eyes had grown visibly darker, and her fingers had slowed to a crawl on the computer keyboard. A small special constable wearing a large stab-proof vest led a dog on a piece of string into the lobby, no doubt an unwanted Christmas present from last year.

"Do we still take strays?" he shouted at the clerk.

"All shapes and sizes, all times of day and night … dogs too," replied the tired woman cynically.

CHRISTMAS DAY – Opening the Present

Julia watched Sophie as she walked to the front door. The short trek from Julia's car began as a melancholy trudge but quickly turned into a moving sprint, as the door flung open and a tall, elegant woman in her fifties stood on the threshold, backlit by the hall light. Arms were thrown asunder and the two female forms melded into each other in a deep, emotional embrace. It was time for Julia to move on and face her own dramatic reunion. What she would say to Jim, and how she would say it evaded her entirely. All she knew was that she felt foolish, but most of all she felt as if she had been robbed. Deep down she knew that she was both the victim and perpetrator of that particular crime.

In her car she turned the heater on fully and zipped her jacket up as far as it would go. There was nothing on the roads and on the one occasion she wouldn't have minded her journey being impeded all the traffic lights remained courteously and obligingly on green.

The sky was clear and a pale three-quarter moon shone benignly amongst an array of twinkling stars. When she pulled onto the drive of her home the wheels of the car crunched on the frosty tarmac. She watched the car lights dim and listened intently as the engine noise faded. She took a very deep breath before walking nervously into the darkened house, shooting her key ring from the hip producing a clunking noise followed by a double beep. At least that had a reassuring familiarity about it. It was such a routine thing to do at the end of such an irregular evening.

The house was silent, almost eerily quiet. The lights were off and there was a pall of emptiness about the downstairs. The central heating boiler hummed quietly and the clocks ticked methodically, but nothing else stirred. She poked her head round the kitchen door, expecting to see Jim drumming his fingers angrily on the table, waiting in the dark to demand explanations from his errant wife. She was surprised and not a little relieved to see that this was not the case. The unlit Christmas tree stood resolutely in the corner, looking a little drab in the dark. Jim and Katie must have been in bed.

The awkwardness was therefore to come. Would there be no sleep until Katie burst excitedly into the bedroom? Would the rest of the night be spent in urgent, anxious whispers of hurt and recrimination, half felt apologies and temporary promises? Would they be able to feign normality for Katie's sake, the adults playing out Christmas Day in some kind of tragic farce, desperate that a seven-year old girl would not sense the over-riding feeling of heartbreak amongst the tinsel and glitter?

With guilt almost overwhelming her Julia silently took off her shoes and tiptoed into Katie's room. She stooped over the bed just to look at her daughter's sleeping form, but it was absent. For a moment Julia's stomach churned, but then she calmed herself, telling herself: 'she must have snuggled in with Jim, too excited to sleep.'

Taking another deep breath and closing her eyes just for a second she then turned and made the short journey across the carpet of the landing, which tickled her feet as she trod. The bedroom was in darkness and was every bit as still as the rest of the house. She picked up the pace, dropping her shoes in the doorway as she rushed towards the bed. There were no obvious bumps where two sleeping bodies lay, the bedding was flat and neatly made, as if no one had been in the bed tonight at all. Julia tore back the duvet, as if the pair might have wriggled down to the bottom of the bed, sinking into the mattress as they did so. It was a desperate act and like most desperate acts it went unrewarded. These birds had flown.

In a fit of sudden panic Julia turned and ran out of the room. Jim must have left a note to say where he had taken Katie. He had probably gone to his mother's house in the next county. Goodness knows what he had told her, but given Julia's tenuous relationship with her mother-in-law it would surely mean confrontation and outpourings of deeply suppressed resentment. Jim's mother had always considered Julia to be 'flighty' and had waited ten years to tell her son 'I told you so.' She could see the smug, judgmental expression on that woman's face, and in fact it was the last image she saw before she tripped clumsily over her own discarded shoes and flew headlong into the wall opposite her bedroom.

Julia found herself in a waiting room. It could have been a doctor's or dentist's surgery, it was hard to tell. There were the usual colourful posters and flyers on the wall, and the glossy, high quality magazines on the low wooden table in the centre of the room. It seemed to Julia that it was bad enough being in a doctor's surgery without being force fed a literary diet of life-styles that were patently beyond most people during the awkward, lengthy wait for your name to be called. Let's face it, those rich enough to aspire to the country houses, hand-crafted furniture and bespoke extravagant fittings adorning the expensively glossy pages would not be sat in the waiting room of an NHS local surgery. Moreover, they wouldn't be *waiting*.

She wriggled on the uncomfortable dining chair that had been drafted in, amongst the other mismatched items of furniture, as seating in the plain, slightly sterile room. Her head spun and ached at the same time, she even felt a little queasy. They were never very pleasant places. If you were lucky there would be a radio station playing at very low pitch by way of distraction from the coughs, sneezes and rattling throat clearances, which tended to be the only other sounds in the room. Speech and eye contact were not traditionally great features of a doctors or dentists waiting room. Julia wondered if God had the same set up for Purgatory. Were there gaudy posters pinned to the noticeboards warning of the perils of Hell and the preventative measures to avoid its onset, and glossy magazines, on tired looking low tables, showing elite clouds specially designed for the well-to-do reformed sinner?

Julia wondered how she had got there. She had a vague recollection of tripping over in the house, but after that everything was a blank. She seemed to be in one piece, apart from the annoying headache. There was no one else in the room, and she glanced across to the counter but there was no receptionist in view. She wasn't too surprised, other than the fact that a GP was even open on Christmas Day. It must be an emergency service; morning surgery only. If only she could remember how she got there, or come to that why she was there at all.

She flicked through one of the magazines, but more as something to do with her hands, as she gave each page only a cursory glance. After a few more mind-numbing minutes had passed she peered over the pages of the booklet, discreetly surveying her surroundings. An elderly woman sat opposite her on the other side of the room separated from her by the shabby coffee table and its untidy pile of periodicals. It caused Julia to double take and she wondered why she hadn't seen her before.

Without meaning to Julia broke the unwritten etiquette of the waiting room and caught the woman's eye.

"Hello," she ventured apprehensively.

"Good morning," said the old lady civilly.

Julia's gaze remained on the elderly lady for a few seconds. A clock ticked laboriously over the enduring stillness of the room. Little flecks of dust played in the weak daylight that managed to pierce the grubby net curtains covering the old sash window next to where the woman sat. There was nothing distinctive about the old lady. She appeared to be short but stoutly built, she wore a quilted jacket over a crimplene dress, and her grey hair, cut in a neat bob, shone where the shafts of light strayed into the room over her shoulder. She clutched a large, well-used leather handbag, which appeared to be as aged as the old lady herself.

"Have you been waiting long?" asked Julia, aware that she had been staring at the woman for longer than was courteous.

"Not long," she replied pleasantly, at normal speaking volume, clearly either deaf or oblivious to the British protocols of waiting room speech levels, which are based on those of lending libraries. "I don't think they'll keep us too long, they're generally quite quick here."

Julia nodded politely and glanced behind her to the counter. Still there was no sign of a receptionist. Above the counter a dusty single speaker was fixed to the wall, but it remained silent.

"Are you alright?" asked the older woman kindly, watching as Julia looked anxiously around the room, "you look a little perplexed."

"No, I'm fine. I think I banged my head at home. Thing is I don't know how I got here."

"Oh dear, perhaps you have a concussion. That can be serious; someone should be watching you. You would have thought that someone would have stayed with you."

"Hmm, you would have thought so," Julia remarked distractedly, "if someone cared enough," she added under her breath.

She rubbed her head as if it might soothe the throbbing sensation from inside her skull, but it didn't. The elderly lady watched her intently. Her eyes were bright and kindly and her tranquil manner was oddly reassuring.

"I've had a really peculiar week," Julia began, "everywhere I've gone in the last few days I've seem to have been drawn into other people's lives."

"Oh, I've had weeks like that dear," said the old woman, "you're going about your own business, and suddenly life seems to open up right in front of you."

"It sucks you in and spits you out the other end," Julia commented pithily.

"That's one way of putting it I suppose," said the woman with a twinkle in her eye and a curl of her lip.

Julia felt strangely drawn to the old lady, she seemed to understand Julia's plight better than any counsellor the doctor might recommend, when he or she finally got round to seeing her. Concussion could be serious; the old lady had said as much, she should be a priority then, surely? Julia got up from her chair and went to the reception area. The small office behind the counter was empty. She supposed the receptionist was in with the doctor helping him or her to set up for the day. On the other hand there was no obvious sign that the little office had been occupied at all that day. There were no teacups in evidence, there were no pens or pads lying around and the handset of the old style telephone had a shimmering layer of dust on it. It hadn't been used today, she thought.

Julia returned to her seat to find the old woman sat on the chair next to where she had been sitting.

"Saves me shouting across the room," she said, smiling kindly.

"Yes, I suppose. Taking their time though, aren't they?"

"Oh, they'll take as long as they need. They always do."

It seemed like a strange thing to say, but perhaps a senior citizen had more reason to routinely visit the doctor's, so maybe she was more familiar with the routine of this particular surgery. It was certainly a lot more old-fashioned than the smart, whitewashed, teak furnished health centre where she was registered as a patient.

"So, how did you hurt your head, dear?"

"I tripped in the house, that's all I remember."

"It's no good rushing around, that's the trouble at your age, always rushing around like there's no tomorrow," said the elderly female sagely.

"It wasn't really like that ..." said Julia, tailing off mid-sentence, unsure how much she wanted to reveal to her aged, unofficial confidante.

"I was in a bit of a state. I panicked ... well, it doesn't matter, I'll just have to sort it out later," she continued, trying desperately to grasp why she didn't just tear out of the door there and then.

"There's always later. Gather yourself, think it through and then do what you need to do," said the woman evenly.

"Oh, I don't know. I've made a mess of things lately," groaned Julia, sighing and sitting fully back on the dining chair, so that her eyes were fixed on the uneven brush strokes that were evident on the cheaply painted ceiling.

"You're not the first nor the last to feel that way, dear."

"Maybe not, but if you knew the full story you'd know I had royally 'dropped the ball'. I just wanted a little bit more from life. It had become so stale and boring, I just needed something else. Something for me, something that showed I was still important, still special ... to someone."

"Sometimes even if you have everything, it can still seem as if it's not enough."

"I think that's it. That's how I felt. I had everything I'd dreamed of really, but somehow it became a drudge. School runs, work, bills, getting the dinner ready, there was no spark. I needed a spark. Perhaps I was being greedy?"

"Needy, greedy, it can all be very destructive if we're not careful."

"Huh! Destructive, that's about right!" said Julia, scornfully.

"Oh, don't be hard on yourself. Life is about deciding what you want, recognising what makes you happy, not what you *think* you want or what you *think* makes you happy."

"That's an obvious thing to say," retorted Julia defensively.

"Oh yes," agreed the old lady pleasantly, "just a far less obvious thing to actually do, otherwise we would all live in a state of blissful harmony, and without wishing to be rude, I don't think that has been your experience recently, has it?"

Julia hung her head slightly, like a naughty schoolgirl who had been reproached for sullen behaviour:

"No. Sorry," she muttered sulkily.

The woman looked Julia in the eye, her stare penetrating far beyond the blue of the younger woman's iris.

"With a lovely young woman like you it usually comes down to love. Am I right?"

"It's more complicated than that really ..."

The older woman shook her head knowingly.

"Is it?"

"Yes. I think so. It's about being wanted, appreciated, and not being taken for granted. I want to be desired, cherished …"

"Loved. Loved in every true sense of the word," the old woman interjected without malice. "You're a beautiful young woman, with so much to offer, who feels trapped in a mundane life-style. A vibrant, intelligent woman who is simply questioning where she is in life, and whether it's truly where she wants to be."

"How can you possibly know all that about me, we only met a few minutes ago, strangers in a doctor's surgery. I don't even know your name."

"I just see what's in front of me," the old lady replied simply and inoffensively, holding Julia's fiery gaze.

Julia yielded, her eyes dropping slightly, her defiant glare softening immediately.

"So, are you saying that I'm being selfish then?"

"Not at all," said the woman gently, "you just want to be noticed. You think you've become invisible, part of the background. You think the spotlight has swept across the stage and left you in the shadows, unnoticed, starved of the applause from those in the audience of your life. You want to be centre-stage again …"

"And what's wrong with that?"

"That depends on the script, and the part you're cast in."

"I don't understand," Julia mumbled, confused by the analogy.

"I think you understand more than you're admitting," chided the woman by way of a friendly challenge.

Julia knew what she meant, and admitted to herself, if not the older lady, that she was being mischievously obtuse.

"Won't be long now, dear," said the old lady matter-of-factly.

"You keep saying that, but there seems to be precious little going on here."

"More than you'd think, dear."

"I wish I had your faith in the system," Julia muttered.

"Faith is so important," agreed the old lady mysteriously.

The clock ticked rhythmically as the seconds passed by in the musty old room. A gloom seemed to settle over the two women as it began to go a little grey beyond the netted portal to the outside world.

"Thank you for chatting to me," Julia said, breaking the heavy silence that had formed between the two women, "it's helped a lot. After the week I've had, the things I've seen, the people I've come across, I needed someone to talk to."

"These things seem to happen for a reason," she said simply.

"Not the stuff that happened to me. No way?" said Julia emphatically.

"I don't know as much. All sorts of things go on around us that we normally wouldn't see. Maybe you just had your eyes opened this week?"

It was another odd remark from the old lady, but Julia couldn't help feeling that there was an astuteness about the woman, she had an aura about her; she seemed so worldly-wise. She watched the old lady fumble in her huge handbag, her arm disappearing almost to the elbow in the process. When her hand re-emerged from the cavernous bag she was holding a very out-dated mobile 'phone.

"I know it's ancient, like me," laughed the old woman as she caught the look of distaste in Julia's eye, "but it's done me proud for many a year, and it hasn't let me down yet. I just need to send a quick message, excuse me a moment, won't you?"

The old lady tapped laboriously on the keypad of the brick shaped device, which seemed to Julia to be larger than some modern notepad devices.

"That's better," she said, concluding the lengthy operation of sending her message, "it was so important that I got a message to someone. I wouldn't want them to go the wrong place at the wrong time."

Without warning the dusty old speaker burst into life. "Julia Carter to room five," came the tinny announcement.

"Oh, that's me," she said, springing to her feet. "I'd better go. Nice to meet you, …"

The old woman didn't offer her name but replied:

"And it was lovely to meet you at last."

"At last?"

"Take no notice dear, slip of the tongue, I'm just a silly old woman. Ask anyone, they all know me here, I'm a regular."

'I would if there was anyone around,' thought Julia, taking a last look around the waiting room.

"Which way do I go?" she asked, realising that she was totally unfamiliar with the lay out of the dowdy little surgery.

"Down the corridor, dear. Safe journey."

The old lady smiled enigmatically and pointed to a gloomily lit corridor just past the reception desk. 'She really is a dotty old bat,' thought Julia uncharitably as she followed the direction the old woman indicated with a pudgy finger. As she reached the passageway leading to the examination rooms she turned to wave a final goodbye to her companion in that dull, dreary waiting room, but she was nowhere to be seen.

'Quick on her feet for an old 'un,' she thought, 'must've needed the loo."

She started down the corridor, which was very poorly lit and a lot longer than she had anticipated. Much longer than seemed necessary for such a small, unextraordinary practice. Room five evaded her as she squinted at the various doors that disappeared into the dark passageway, which seemed to darken more the further she stepped along it. The pathetic little bulb, which provided the only inadequate light source for the corridor, flickered, and then faded. The passageway went as dark as a starless night, as dark as a dreamless sleep.

BOXING DAY: Stepping into the Future

Julia's eyes fluttered, then opened briefly. It was dark, and it was chilly. Her head felt heavy and her cheeks ached and she was sure she had dried drool in the corners of her mouth. There was a noise, a low droning noise, but clearly audible. As her senses slowly returned she knew that she was lying on her back in the darkness, the only light coming from the radio/alarm clock at her side. The noise transpired to be voices, voices joined in conversation that also originated in the speakers of the same audio device. Julia scrunched up her eyes so that she could focus on the time shown on the display: 03:00.

Her head still ached, but it was a dull congested sensation that felt as if someone had emptied a bag of porridge into her skull. 3am! But what day was it? She pressed back with her arms and shoulders and they dissolved into the soft layers below her. At least she now knew that she was lying on a bed, which felt like her own bed, so that was good – wasn't it? She arched her back, pushing harder so that she sat up. She felt stiff and sore; she had definitely been lying in that cold room for some time. The voices continued to babble in turn, back and forth in relentless, sober discussion. She drew her legs up so that she could draw them close to her chest, linking her arms around her knees. She was so cold. Surely she hadn't been there a whole day?

The radio droned on quietly. At first the words were meaningless but in the absence of any other noise they began to form coherent sentences in Julia's still tired mind. "And this is your tenth novel? Some critics are saying that it covers some very familiar ground to your previous books?" said a honey-toned, serious sounding female.

"Well I do tend to write about what I know. I focus on the human condition, the desires and emotions which drive us to do what we do, and to be what we are," responded a second female, who was clearly being interviewed.

Julia was no great fan of these intellectual programmes in which journalists explored the thoughts and motivations of artists and thinkers. Jim, on the other hand was a deep thinker, a reflective man, and he thrived on such material. She assumed that the radio had turned itself on by some means, probably a minor power cut or something. Whatever the reason it had woken her up and had now caught her attention.

"Your latest character has been described as complex and possibly a little self-centred?" continued the earnest woman. "I think that's a little harsh," countered the interviewee, in a mature sounding voice, "she's simply a little confused about where she thinks life is taking her, and where she wants to be."

"I see."

"I wanted my main character to go on a voyage of discovery, to see life and relationships for what they are, so that she could reach her own conclusions about her situation."

"She undoubtedly went through the emotional wringer in the days leading up to the climax of the book. Without spoiling the ending for listeners who have yet to read it, would you say she learned enough to save her from disaster?" asked the interviewer profoundly.

"I hope so, but you never know. She always had the capacity to be what she wanted to be, but I deliberately left the ending open, the conclusion is left to the reader."

"Some readers may argue that that is a cop-out," challenged the host.

"That was never the intention, dear, I want the reader to believe there is always hope, but ultimately her destiny was always in her own hands," said the interviewee serenely.

"Well, that's all we have time for in this edition of *ChitChat*. My thanks to my special guest author and psychologist, Brenda Bickerstaff ..."

The presenter continued with her raft of closing credits and acknowledgements while Julia rolled her eyes and shook her head.

'What a load of highbrow twaddle. Still, what else are they going to put on at three o'clock in the morning?' she thought irritably.

She reached over to slam her hand on the 'off' button of the radio as the continuity announcer said:

"That was an interview with the renowned author Brenda Bickerstaff recorded ten years ago, just a week before her unexpected death from a heart attack during a routine visit to her doctor. A wonderful and regular contributor to the popular radio programme on the arts, *ChitChat.*"

Julia silenced the radio and swung her legs off the bed. She felt so confused. How had she got there? Who had brought her back from the doctor's? Everything was so fuzzy. Nothing made sense.

Downstairs she paid scant attention to the Christmas tree, which had been inactive since Christmas Eve. She barely noticed that the pile of presents had diminished to the tune of all of Katie's gifts. Outside it was pitch black. Not even the light of the moon breached the thick, dark clouds. It was cold in the house, the central heating barely ticking over at this time of day, but outside it looked positively Siberian. Julia grabbed a remote control and the TV flickered into life, she jabbed the mute button, unable to contemplate listening to any more inane media jabber. As she pressed the text button the screen confirmed that it was December 26th. Somehow a whole day had evaporated from her consciousness. She slumped into a dining chair staring out of the window at the barren, wilted winter garden outside.

There was a hard frost, but a white Christmas had once again passed the nation by.

Where was everyone, she wondered. Jim, Katie, her mother – anyone who cared about her. Anything could have happened to her since she'd fled the house on Christmas Eve. She made herself a cup of tea and paced up and down the kitchen while she drank it. She still wore the same clothes she been wearing on that fateful night, and they clung to her, smelling of violence, sadness and police stations. She felt a sudden need to shower.

She felt the hot water in the en suite cubicle beat down on her flesh and hair like a hundred thousand lashes of shame, then she tried to soap away the uncertainty and confusion. When she threw on clean jeans and a cotton jumper she felt fresh and clean but inside she felt no less mucky than when she'd walked back into the house twenty-four hours earlier. It was now 5am and she could wait no longer. She sat on the edge of the bed and nervously picked up the 'phone. She dialled, the line rang out and then someone picked up.

"Mum?"

"Julia, where on earth have you been? I've been going out of my head with worry," screeched Julia's mother with an inevitable mixture of worry and anger.

"I came back in the early hours of Christmas morning," cried Julia, equally as emotional.

"Well, why didn't you ring? Jim said you'd gone to meet another man. He said something had been going on for a while."

"It's more complicated than that ..."

"Not when you have a child it isn't. What about Katie? How selfish can you be, Julia?"

Julia heard her mother start to cry.

"Is Katie with you?"

"Of course she is, I couldn't leave her there on her own could I?"

"On her own? What about Jim?"

Julia's voice was rising in both decibels and pitch with each desperate word.

"We talked for a while and then he just dashed out of the house saying he would find you and bring you back if it was the last thing he did. I hadn't heard from either of you until now. Julia how could you do this? To Katie and to me?"

"So Jim's not there?"

"No."

The doorbell rang, twice.

"Someone's at the door, mum," said Julia quietly, with trepidation and terror in equal measures.

Almost before the second ring had faded it was followed by a loud, determined knock. Julia threw the 'phone back on its rest and sprinted to the door.

"Julia Carter?"

There were two men in fluorescent jackets standing in the porch. They had sheepish expressions on their pale, tired faces. Muted chatter crackled from the radios on their coats.

"It's about your husband. Jim Carter? Do you mind if we come inside please?"

Julia felt the colour drain from her cheeks and the world began to spin in front of her. She thought about the things she had seen and experienced during that turbulent week, she saw the kindly face of the woman in the surgery and heard her reassuring voice. She thought about her life, and what she wanted it to be. One thing was now for certain – it would never be the same again.

Printed in Germany
by Amazon Distribution
GmbH, Leipzig